Snacks & Jockstraps

The Men of Haven Grove

A.D. Ellis

Quotes of Inspiration

"And then I met you, and slowly but all at once, my whole world began to change."
~R.M. Broderick

"Love is when he gives you a piece of your soul that you never knew was missing."
~Torquato Tasso

"When your eyes met mine, my soul pointed at you and whispered to my heart, 'Him...'"
~LR

Chapter 1
Casey Joe Riggs

"I COULD HAVE DIED, *AND* MY HOUSE BURNED down. Pour me a damn shot, it's my birthday." I tapped the shot glass on the bar at the Riggs Family Roadhouse. My oldest son, Henry, ran the place. He was damn good at what he did too. One of the best bartenders around— could mix up pretty much any drink a person asked for. He came up with great menus, was a pretty dang good cook, and kept the place running smoothly. For someone who didn't really like a lot of people, Henry could small talk with the best of them. Pretty much everyone loved Henry.

"Dad," Henry started, but he stopped when someone sat down beside me. Based on the schmoopy grin filling Henry's face, I had no doubt the new arrival was my future son-in-law, Jack.

"Better save room for your birthday cake and cocktail," Jack said as he elbowed me. The kid was adorable, and he'd somehow wormed his way into my heart. While I pretty much felt like I'd failed miserably with my own boys, Henry and Hudson, Jack coming to Haven Grove had breathed a bit of new life into me. He was younger than Henry by about ten years, but the two of them had clicked from the first moment Jack walked into the Roadhouse.

Jack hadn't had the best childhood or teen years—he really missed out on having positive male role models in his life—so he'd taken to me showing him things like a father figure should have. It was a win-win situation because Jack learned things he needed to know, and I kinda got a second chance.

But Jack also took on the role of a third son, and the last thing I needed was *three* sons and my best friend nagging me about my health and the dangers of drinking.

"It's a second shot," I said, tapping the glass on the bar again. "I didn't ask for the entire bottle." I was well aware I needed to be taking better care of myself, but sometimes my past—and a sad excuse of a future if I stuck to the path I was on—caught me off guard and sent me spiraling a bit. Turning another year older wasn't helping things.

Henry drew in a deep breath as his eyes traveled from me to Jack. I felt the shrug of Jack's shoulder next to me. Henry poured the shot. They'd been working together for a bit now—Henry manning the Roadhouse and Jack running Cake & Cocktails in the attached expansion—and they made a really good team, even when they were communicating secretly about me while I sat right there.

I wasn't a damn child, and I didn't need them treating me like one.

I downed the shot, cursing the burn as my youngest, Hudson, took a seat on the other side of Jack. Hudson was the golden boy of Haven Grove—although, Jack might have been set up to give him a run for his money. Whereas Henry was good with small talk and making folks feel welcome even as a self-described grumpy introvert, Hudson was the more outgoing of the two. He could talk to a brick wall, was constantly doing odd jobs around town, and had single-handedly saved the Riggs family peach orchard over the past eighteen months. The town of Haven Grove thought Hudson walked on water.

I caught a glimpse of the grim look Hudson shared with Henry and sighed. My boys looked like me in a lot of ways. Henry was broader than me, thicker, and had his mother's darker hair. Hudson wasn't built as broadly as Henry or me, but he was just as tall, and he'd gotten my lighter hair color. I'd learned a lot about body type labels over the years since my boys came out to me—both queer, Henry bi and demisexual, Hudson gay—and I knew Henry would be described as a *bear* and Hudson was more of a jockish *otter*. Where that put me, I had no clue. Not that I needed a body type label.

I didn't.

I wasn't as hairy as Henry, and the hair I did have was lighter. I was broader than Hudson, but not as thick as his brother. I needed to put back on some of the weight I'd lost since my heart attack—hell, who was I kidding, I'd lost a lot of it before that—and get back some muscle mass. I was looking scrawny and feeling it too. Nothing some time at the gym wouldn't remedy, but dragging myself on runs or to lift weights was a monumental feat as of late.

"Happy birthday, Dad," Hudson said as he put Jack in a headlock and ruffled his pretty blond hair. Hudson had pretty much adopted Jack as his little brother from the first time they'd met, and Jack soaked up every single bit of being part of a real family—even when he had to deal with some of our Riggs family bullshit.

I grunted a thank you. "Not like fifty-four is some milestone birthday. Just another day closer to kickin' the bucket."

"I see the birthday boy is chipper today," Hudson teased.

"Where's your Daddy?" I shot back.

Henry huffed out a sigh. Jack bit the corner of his lip. And Hudson grinned. "He's over there talking to that absolute snack." He nodded his head toward the opposite end of the bar.

I craned my head and saw the back of my former best friend's head. "What the fuck you mean he's talkin' to a snack? Like chips or a Twinkie? He done lost his mind or somethin'?" I motioned to Henry. "Gimme a beer."

"Dad—"

"It can be that light shit." I cut him off with a rap of my knuckles on the bar. "It's my birthday. It's been a shitty year. Hell, it's been a shitty life."

Henry stuck his damn finger in my face. "*You* aren't supposed to be drinking. The stress from the fire added to your recovery isn't good for you."

"Shut up and give me a damn beer. I'll exercise it off tomorrow."

"Did you see the doctor yet?" Jack asked as Henry gave me the weakest looking, most pathetic excuse for a beer I'd ever seen.

"Not yet. Supposed to go in for a few tests and a follow up. But I'm feeling good."

I wasn't.

I mean, I was, but I knew I could be following the doctor's orders better. But hell, who wanted to eat rabbit food all the time? And running was a bunch of shit. "Be better once I get back into my house." I leaned around Jack and cleared my throat to get Hudson's attention. "My stress will be a lot less once I'm not listenin' to my ex-best friend plow my baby boy nightly."

Jack broke out into giggles, and Hudson had the good manners to at least blush and dip his head. Even Henry chuckled behind his beard. I'd been staying with Hudson and Lance ever since my house was set on fire, and I was beyond ready to move out.

"Now, tell me what talkin' to a snack means," I said. "I thought we were havin' cake later. If Lance gets to have snacks before cake, I should too. He'll be turnin' fifty-four next year."

Hudson grinned as Jack buried his face in my son's shoulder and continued to giggle.

"Damn, who's been drinkin' here, you or me?" I elbowed him and couldn't help the smile on my face as he dissolved into another round of giggles. This kid was sunshine personified, and he deserved every single good thing that came his way.

"A snack, Dad. Not food like chips and sweets. A hot guy—or girl." Hudson nodded again toward the other end of the bar. "In this case, a guy. Lance saw he had on a sweatshirt from some restaurant out on the west coast, so he asked him about it. Must be a nice guy, they've been talking for a bit."

Lance had been my best friend growing up. If I was being honest, he was still—and would forever be—my best friend. He'd seen me through a toxic relationship with the boys' mother, been there for me when she cheated on me with my brother, Billy, before she left town, and stood beside me when Billy drank himself to death while almost destroying our family business.

When Lance left town, he took a piece of me with him. He'd been a constant support for the boys and me, and I damn near lost myself to all the shit when Billy died. I should have been there for the boys, helping to take over the peach orchard and general store—the Juicy Peach— both of which had been in the Riggs family my entire life. Instead, I buried my head and ignored pretty much everything—including my family, my health, and our livelihood.

But Lance came back to Haven Grove just over a year ago, and his being home was part of what pulled my head out of my ass. Lance was a lifesaver for me, but he also ended up striking up something more than just friendship with Hudson. The two of them had always been close— and as much as I liked to give Lance shit, there wasn't a single ounce of my soul that thought there was anything inappropriate way back then—but something had clicked between them when they met up as adults. They'd kept it from me while it was still new, but I'd very unfortunately discovered their relationship when I walked in on them. Probably would have kicked Lance's ass had I not ended up having a heart attack. As it was, I ended up getting in a pretty good fist to his jaw. Figure I still owe him a couple good rounds.

Don't get me wrong, I've figured out Lance and Hudson are good together. Like, really good. I didn't get it at first, but the heart attack scared me pretty damn good, and I was forced to calm my ass down and really give their relationship some thought. They love each other like I'm not even sure I knew was possible. Just like Henry and Jack. Hell, maybe I'm just jealous of what my boys found. But damn, give a guy a little warning before he walks in on his best friend bonin' his son.

Speaking of my asshole ex best friend, Lance sauntered over and grabbed me by my shoulders, jostling me roughly. "Happy birthday, old man."

"Fuck off," I grumbled.

Lance laughed. "My best friend, ladies and gentlemen. Such a way with words; so welcoming."

I flipped him off.

"Who's that?" Hudson asked Lance.

"New gym owner. I was telling him about the fall fest, told him to get in touch with town hall to get himself a booth." Lance squeezed my shoulders. "Seems like a nice guy." He slapped me on the back before moving off to brush a kiss to Hudson's cheek.

Damn.

A wave of longing washed over me.

I wanted that.

Wanted it so bad I was pretty sure the blood ran green through my veins.

But fuck that. I didn't *want* to want that. I didn't *want* to feel the longing for a close connection to someone.

I used to think I would never get over Missy, but several shitty years—and a lot of recent therapy—had shown me that Missy and me were a disaster waiting to happen from the get-go. We weren't meant to be. We weren't the perfect match. We were oil and water, and the only thing better than her leaving me would have been me never getting involved with her in the first place.

But I couldn't completely regret the years Missy and I were together since I got the two most important people in my world from it.

And I was honestly so damn happy for both my boys.

They'd each found their person and looked to be journeying toward their own happily ever afters. And what was I doing? Recovering from a heart attack by drinking too much. Homeless while insurance fucked around on getting my house renovated. And wishing like hell I had what my boys had found.

But exactly what was it I was wishing for?

My person.

Girl? Guy?

Hell, I didn't know. And wasn't that just icing on the cake of my fucked-up life? Since when was I unsure about who I was attracted to? Back when I was a teen, that thought would have sent me into a panic for sure. Hell, it *did* send me into a panic back then if I was being honest.

Fuck.

Where had that thought come from? I hadn't let myself revisit those feelings in years.

That was in the past, right?

Right.

But now, in my present? Honestly, I didn't even think I cared anymore.

Therapy had helped me a lot, and I knew I needed to open myself up to building relationships—not even romantic or sexual ones, just relationships period.

But then I'd spiral through a chunk of time and convince myself no one in their right mind would ever be able to put up with me. Who wanted to spend their time with a cranky, foul-mouthed, middle-aged man battling a defective heart?

Damn. Depression and getting older was for the fuckin' birds.

Just as I was about to say fuck it and call it a night, Jack strummed his fingers on the bar. "Who's ready for cake?"

That boy and his cake.

Jack was truly talented both in baking and decorating cakes, but his truest skill came into play when he matched his cakes with Henry's meals and cocktails. The kid had a real flair for pairing cake flavors with just the right mixed drinks, and it showed in how successful the Let Them Eat Cake portion of the Roadhouse menu had become. Henry and Jack hadn't been running the addition for long, but I was damn proud of how well it was going.

And I wasn't one to brag, but it felt fuckin' fantastic to be a part of it. Something my boys hadn't known until recently was I'd spent some time getting a certification in graphics and design, so I'd been able to help Jack with quite a bit when it came to setting up the business and putting our best foot forward on social media.

Getting that certification and working on the projects

throughout the course had been one of the only things that kept me sane a couple summers ago. Maybe I needed another project to keep me busy—keep my mind occupied and productive—so I could get myself out of the funk I'd fallen back into.

Hudson stood and stretched before yanking Jack off the stool. "Let's goooo," Hudson crowed. "Cake, cake, cake, cake," he chanted with his hands on Jack's shoulders like they were in a conga line.

I glanced between Lance and Henry, noticing my son's eye roll for his brother before a softening for Jack. Lance's face held the same gentle affection as he watched Jack and Hudson make their way to the little addition. I knew damn well Lance's eyes were on Hudson's ass, but I couldn't even muster the energy to give a fuck.

"He's really excited about the cake he made you," Henry said softly, the underlying threat of *don't you dare hurt him* very much present in his words. He nodded toward our little group. "Go ahead. I'll finish this up and be there in a minute."

Taking a deep breath, savoring the tiny bit of peace that washed over me when I allowed the air to fully expand my lungs and flood my body, I took a last swig of the shitty light beer and turned to join my friends.

Just as I shifted, the guy from the end of the bar stood. He tossed a couple bills on the bar, gave a quick nod to Henry, and moved toward the door. As he made his way across the Roadhouse, his eyes traveled to the little addition where Jack baked, decorated, and sold his cakes. A lift of his chin made me think he'd maybe made eye contact with Lance. Right as he reached for the door, the guy's eyes landed on me.

Damn, he had pretty eyes.

Nice smile.

Fuckin' hell.

Never should have mixed liquor with beer.

I averted my gaze and made my way toward the birthday cake.

I was lonely, getting older every damn day, possibly one day closer to another heart attack—and my old ticker might just do me in with one more chance—but the least I could do was enjoy some cake.

To hell with the doctors saying I needed to cut back on snacks and sweets. I wasn't dead yet, and a little bit of cake wasn't going to kill me. At least not right then.

I'd do better.

After cake.

Chapter 2
Bryce Daniel Armstrong

I RAN A HAND OVER MY FACE AS I HEADED OUT the door after a long day at the gym. Eventually, it would be Armstrong Health & Fitness, but I faced a shit ton of work before it was ready for that. Buying and renovating the old place was very likely going to be the death of me.

Hell, just moving back to the Midwest would probably give me a run for my money in that department.

I'd come back to visit family often, and I'd been home a few times over the last year, but now I was here to stay.

My sister, Cassie, and I had grown up amongst the corn fields and pig farms of the Midwest. Throw in the amber waves of some wheat and soybean fields, beef and dairy cows, sheep and goats, and some horses, and I was a small-town farming community boy through and through.

Cassie had never once thought about leaving. She'd married her high school sweetheart, Rex, moved a few counties over, and now divided her time between raising kids, being a kickass nurse, and doting on a new grandbaby while Rex continued to farm and raise a small herd of dairy cattle.

Me, on the other hand, I'd been champing at the bit to escape small-town life from the first moment I ever realized there was something else out there. I turned eighteen, graduated high school, headed out west, and never looked back.

I didn't necessarily *hate* small town living. I just wanted to see more. I longed for bigger and better.

I definitely wasn't trying to get away from my family. I loved my sister, my parents, and my aunt. For a small-town family in the Midwest, they were about as progressive and open-minded as you could get. Many of my extended family were as well.

Which made it easier on me than most when I came out as gay during Christmas break my senior year of college. There were no fights, no drama, no harsh words. My sister hugged me, my parents apologized if I'd felt I couldn't tell them sooner, and my aunt asked me if I'd been to any good drag shows out in California before launching into a story about an old boyfriend who'd done amazing drag performances back in the day.

And that was it.

I continued living my life out in sunny Los Angeles upon graduating from college with a degree in Exercise Science and a minor in Marketing. I made it home to see my family about three times a year, upgraded from renting a tiny room when I landed a killer job training some of Hollywood's biggest and brightest up-and-coming stars after working at a franchise gym for about ten years, and dipped my toe into the gay dating scene from time to time.

After about ten more years of living in an apartment the size of a shoebox, my clientele list finally exploded when one of my regulars made it big, and I was suddenly *the* trainer to work with in L.A.

The money poured in, and I soaked it all up.

I moved to a bigger, better apartment.

Fell in with what would turn out to be a toxic group of people—big names, big personalities, big spenders, big problems, and small…like non-existently small…souls.

Became obsessed with my on-line presence—constantly chasing the next high from likes, follows, and comments.

Fought imposter syndrome and a bad case of comparison-itis.

And continued toying around with the gay dating scene.

It wasn't that I didn't date. I just never stayed with anyone for long. The guys I met ended up being a way to scratch an itch, but there was never a connection. I wasn't ever sad to see them walk out of my life.

Then one day, pretty near my forty-sixth birthday, it all hit me. I didn't like who I'd become. I no longer even remotely resembled the man I used to be. I felt like shit inside and out if I wasn't scrolling—each little like or follow or comment giving me the dopamine rush I craved. Hell, I was a physical trainer, and I'd started allowing myself to skip workouts just to scroll my social media or sit at my laptop repeatedly refreshing my platforms while I looked for that next hit.

I didn't recognize myself in the mirror.

I hated the way I felt—physically and deep in my brain, like I was constantly in a zoned-out state, only feeling that high if I got a certain number of likes or new follows or comments from fans.

The money was still coming in.

I was still sought after by high-profile clients.

Still had an amazing apartment.

Great car.

But an itch at the base of my brain had started, and I couldn't escape it.

This isn't who you are.

Is this the way you want to live the rest of your life?

Do you have one single person you'd consider an actual friend?

If social media disappeared tomorrow, what would you be left with?

This isn't what you dreamed of doing.

You've let this become a problem; it's taken over your life.

After about two years of that constant buzz of doubt and self-contempt eating at me—while still chasing that dopamine high—I finally had enough.

I gave my clients a month's notice that I was leaving L.A.

I packed up about half of my clothes, sold some pieces I doubted I'd ever need to wear again, and donated the rest, sold my car and most of my furniture, sold my apartment in under a week, and rented a U-Haul.

By the end of the one month notice period, I'd packed up my entire life and hit the road toward home.

Was I really longing to return to my roots? Pining away

for the Midwest like some homesick small-town boy? Did I miss a simpler life?

Yes?

No?

I really couldn't tell you.

All I knew was I wasn't going to break free of the drain on my mental health and the brain fog I'd acquired if I didn't separate from all of it in one fell swoop. Like ripping off a bandage, I deleted my social media accounts, left L.A., and never looked back.

For a bit, I lived with my parents and aunt. It wasn't the perfect set up, but it put me close to my sister and her kids. Hell, not only was I a proud uncle, I was even a great-uncle. I loved my nieces and nephews, and it blew my mind my sister was a grandma, so I soaked up kid and baby time while I detoxed from social media.

My parents lived in a nice house in a tiny town best described as the suburbs of a very small city, and they let my aunt rent the in-law quarters of their home. That left me living in their basement, but it was a nice break from the ritz, glamour, and fast pace. I let myself wallow in self-pity and disgust for about twenty-four hours, then I pulled up my jockstrap, reminded myself it was only temporary, and set to work on a plan.

The fact I was already sleeping better, focusing better, and feeling better overall after such a short time being away from my old life was all the proof I needed I'd made the right decision.

When I saw a local news channel feature a story about the Haven Grove gym being in desperate need of a renovation, I couldn't quite believe my ears. Haven Grove was one tiny town over from my parents. It was known for its peach orchard and general store called the Juicy Peach.

And it supposedly had a gym located in a great building at a great location. It was a fixer-upper looking for just the right person to bring it back to its old glory.

Had I really left behind my entire life in L.A. at age forty-eight only to return to the Midwest and give even a minute's worth of thought to buying a gym in Podunk, USA?

Within a week, as I stood in front of the rundown gym with a key in hand, I realized I had my answer.

As the weeks passed, I also realized I was a physical trainer with some knowledge of marketing. I was *not* a general contractor, a construction worker, or a handyman.

The gym renovation was good for my body and mind, but it was going to take me five years at the rate I was going. I needed help, and I wasn't too proud to admit it.

Haven Grove was a great little town, very similar to the one I'd grown up in. The people were all up in your business, but they'd give you the shirt off their back if you needed something. As much as the small-town annoyances had gotten to me way back then, the quirks of small-town living brought a comfort I hadn't really known I needed.

I did a few stretches on the sidewalk outside the gym as I studied the giant glass windows I'd opted to have installed. I loved how they let in so much natural light, and they looked fantastic from the outside. Eventually, I'd have Armstrong Health & Fitness painted on the windows —with the Armstrong logo of two bent arms showing off muscular biceps and a heart alongside a dumbbell—but until then, I'd just fret over whether folks in the small town would want to be on display while they worked out.

My hope was that the healthy natural light would have people feeling good, so they wouldn't be concerned about anyone walking past seeing them. Plus, a lot of folks liked to either show off their hard work or let others know they were doing something healthy.

Hell, some of the regulars at my gym back in L.A. really only worked out there so they could be seen at an elite gym. It was a way of letting others know they had money and prestige.

Seriously, I needed to stop thinking about the damn windows.

What I needed was a run. For the physical exercise, but also because I desperately needed to clear my head. A run first, and then maybe I'd stop in at the Roadhouse again for dinner. Eating out wasn't usually the healthiest option, but I'd taken a look at the menu on my first visit, and I could get chicken, fish, and veggies in various dishes which was rare at a bar and grill type restaurant. Whoever they had cooking the food was talented; I'd really enjoyed my meal that first night. I was a good cook, and actually enjoyed healthy cooking, but sometimes it was just nice to have dinner prepared for you.

Plus, the people at the Riggs Family Roadhouse had been friendly.

I'd been slowly meeting some of the local folks and settling back into small town life nicely. Well, as nicely as can be expected after spending over half my life among millions of people in a city with shopping malls larger than the postage-stamp-sized town I now called home.

After a few more stretches, I took off at a slow jog. I wasn't out to beat any personal records on this run, just enjoying the warm sunshine, the hint of a bite on the breeze, and the beauty around me. Haven Grove was a gorgeous little town, and it was putting on a spectacular display as it held tightly to summer with all its might and tried to stave off the fall for a few more days.

Behind me and down the street a ways was an auto shop, an empty store front that used to house a video store, and The Sweet & Creamy Dairy Palace which I'd been told had the best ice cream in the state. I avoided dairy most of the time, but for a really good bowl of ice cream, I'd been known to break that rule. I had no doubt I'd be stopping in the cute little ice cream parlor one of these days. We'd see how long I could hold out.

My place—I was living in the apartment above the gym for the time being—was on the main street that ran through town. It was at a great little corner location across from the only gas station in town on one side and Glazed Buns on the other. The irony of a health and fitness business being so close to a bakery and coffee shop wasn't lost on me. I had no problem with snacks and sweets in moderation. Hopefully people who indulged at Glazed Buns would be motivated to work off the calories at my place, and maybe the folks who worked out at Armstrong Health & Fitness would treat themselves at Glazed Buns.

Pretty sure sweets first and a workout later was better for a person's health than rewarding a workout with a treat, but if the bakery and I could work together to bring people in, I was all for it.

As I left the main drag, I took in the school on my left

and the church on my right. The preacher had already introduced himself to me. I wasn't impressed with the red-faced, heavily jowled man who spoke of "his flock of sinners," but I figured I'd withhold my judgement for the time being. I wasn't a church goer, much to my parents' dismay, but I didn't hold it against anyone who opted to participate. It wasn't that I didn't believe in a higher power of some sort, I'd just seen too many people hate and discriminate in the name of their god, and that wasn't something I wanted any part of.

The school looked like pretty much any small-town school in the Midwest. If it was like the school I'd gone to, it likely housed grades Kindergarten through eighth, and the kids were bussed up the road for high school.

The road curved and descended a slight hill, and the Juicy Peach—the local general store—came into view. I knew most folks in town did their best to shop local as much as possible, buying what they could at the Juicy Peach and only heading up the road to the larger discount store for big stock ups and items they couldn't get in town. Partly this was because everyone wanted to work together to support local businesses, and partly it was because a lot of folks in town had no desire to head up the road to the big box stores.

The Juicy Peach was absolutely adorable. It looked like it came straight from an old-time movie. I'd taken a quick stroll through one day on a break from renovations, just to see what types of products they carried, and I'd loved the wooden floors and rustic charm of the peach and rooster décor. I was all for supporting local, and I pledged right then and there I'd shop the Juicy Peach as often as feasibly possible.

As I passed the general store, I took in the marvelous expanse of trees in the orchard behind it. The Riggs family owned the Roadhouse, the general store, and the orchard. My understanding was all of it had been in the family for multiple generations. I'd heard a bit of rumblings about some family drama—not surprising since small towns always had big drama—but it appeared the Riggs family was doing well for itself based on the reverence and respect attached to their name as well as the prominence of their businesses.

The peach orchard was at least an acre, a bit longer than it was wide, and it spread out between the base of the two Haven Grove hills. The Juicy Peach bordered the orchard on one side, and the two Riggs family homes sat at the top of the hill on the other side.

Upon moving to town, I'd discovered what had quickly become my favorite running path through town. Depending on if I took the long way around the orchard or veered off to make the distance a bit shorter, I could get a good one- or two-miles in. The shorter distance allowed for a slightly steeper hill on the last leg of the run and brought me out on the side of one of the Riggs houses closest to the road that would take me back to town.

The longer distance provided a slightly less steep hill, but it brought me out on the far side of the other Riggs house and required a longer homestretch run to get back to town. I enjoyed both circuits, and I knew without a doubt I'd be making the most of the outdoor runs for as long as the weather held off. Hell, even in the winter, if we weren't covered in snow—something I was kinda looking forward to and kinda dreading—I had a feeling I'd bundle up and run outside just for the benefits of the fresh air.

One thing I'd definitely missed while living in L.A. was the beauty of nature. Sure, I could find it out there, and it was nice to be close to gorgeous beaches, but there was just something about quaint little mostly undisturbed towns glistening in their natural glory.

The thought floated through my head as my feet pounded the ground, and I took in the diminishing green of the peach trees. After several runs around both sides of the orchard, I'd surmised the majority of the peaches had been harvested. Now, the waning heat of the summer warmed the late season grass and trampled peaches to mix on the air in a heavy, sweet scent. The leaves, not yet losing their green completely, fluttered in the breeze. A hint of crisp coolness in the air battled the afternoon sun alternating between chilling my skin and making me break out in a sweat. I had no doubt the orchard would be breathtaking when the leaves changed.

Hell, for that matter, the whole town of Haven Grove would be. There was nothing like fall in the Midwest and a low-key excitement for all things autumn purred in my belly.

My legs burned as I headed up the hill on the backside of the orchard. I'd emerge next to a Riggs house before finishing my run back at my place. I wasn't positive, but I had a feeling running behind the house put me right on the border of Riggs property and public property. Hell, maybe the tree line behind the house separating the yard from the rolling hill that led down to the orchard actually belonged to the Riggs family.

I truly had no idea, but I was already emerging from the sparse trees, and the thought of running back down the hill only to have to run up another one was *not* something my burning lungs and screaming muscles wanted to do.

Opting to act first and ask for forgiveness later—later as in *if* I got caught—I continued on the path.

The song floating on the air caught my attention first, but I quickly recognized the man sitting in a camping chair in the yard as the patriarch of the Riggs family. While I hadn't yet met the guy in person, his name was well-known around Haven Grove.

Casey Joe Riggs sat in his yard, beer in hand, crooning along with Eminem and Jelly Roll about needing somebody to save him from himself.

Shit.

Maybe the rumors I'd heard around town were true.

But I didn't like to pass judgement on a person before getting to know them, so I pushed aside everything I'd heard about Casey Joe. I'd met Lance at the Roadhouse. I wasn't exactly sure how he fit in with the Riggs family, but he joined them for a birthday party after talking to me, so he was at least a friend.

Just like my first evening at the Roadhouse, my eyes caught on Casey Joe, and I couldn't look away.

He had that look of a big guy who used to be in his prime—and still could be with a little work—but he'd let himself go. Either by choice or because of a health condition. But it was clear Casey Joe could easily bulk back up and turn what was already a very attractive dad-bod into something smoking hot.

He had what I'd describe as dark blond hair, just dark enough for the grays I could see patching his scruff to show through on his head as well. But he wore it well. He was broad. It was hard to estimate his height since he was sitting, but I'd seen him stand up the other night, and he was at least as tall as my six-feet two-inch frame.

And just like the other night, Casey Joe's eyes snagged on mine and stuck. Damn, he had pretty eyes. Almost a cornflower blue, but the enhanced color could have been because of the redness rimming his eyes.

Just as I thought I'd give a friendly wave and be on my way, Casey Joe stood, squinted his eyes, took a long sip of beer, and shouted, "Who the fuck are you, and why the fuck you on my property?"

Shit.

Chapter 3
Casey Joe

FUCK.

My head pounded and every damn bad thing I'd thought about myself over the years raced through my mind with each heartbeat.

It had been a while since I'd spiraled this badly.

Damn birthdays.

Fifty-four wasn't even some milestone.

Maybe it was a big deal I'd survived to see my birthday.

Between all the shit with Missy, being a shitty father to my boys, losing my brother, having a heart attack, and my house being set on fire, I guessed I should have just counted myself lucky.

Should have celebrated being alive and having my boys in my life.

Instead, I drank too much the other night—treated everyone like shit if I was being honest—and I hadn't been able to pull myself out of my own ass ever since. As I sat in my yard, wallowing in self-pity, the words of "Somebody Save Me" echoed in my head.

Lifestyle…bad for my health…don't waste your time on me… shattered hopes and dreams.

More than anything, the song reminded me I wasn't the best dad I could have been for Henry and Hudson. I was so damn proud of my boys. They'd done some fuckin' amazing things. Kept the family businesses going, supported my damn ass when I couldn't focus on anything but the pain of betrayal, and helped me recover from Billy's death. Then I had to go and have a damn heart attack, and both boys were right there taking care of me.

Hell, Hudson and Lance were letting me live with them while my house was unlivable.

And how did I pay the whole crew back? I got drunk and lost myself in my damn head.

Fuck.

All those therapy sessions seemed like they were helping, but one lousy birthday and I found myself drinking too much and croaking out a depressing song like a fuckin' hound dog howling at the moon.

Lost cause…somebody save me…

Hell, that was for damn sure.

A flash of red and yellow from the corner of my eye caught my attention.

What the fuck?

I stood up, knocking the camping chair over. "Who the fuck are you, and why the fuck you on my property?" I knew exactly who it was, but that didn't stop the words shooting from my mouth.

Okay, that wasn't exactly accurate.

I knew who the man was in that I was aware he was the new owner of the run-down gym in town—the *snack*, as Hudson had referred to him. However, I hadn't caught his name the other night after Lance talked to him at the Roadhouse.

And he was running on my property, so I had every right to ask him.

Running in a very form-fitting yellow t-shirt and red shorts that weren't exactly what I'd describe as booty shorts—the kind Jack would probably wear—but they weren't as long as basketball shorts. The man was in great shape. Which made sense if he was the new gym owner. No one wanted to go to a gym if the guy in charge was some out of shape blob who clearly didn't take care of himself.

He'd stopped when I yelled at him. After making his way over to me, the guy pulled up his shirt to wipe sweat from his face.

Must have gotten some damn bad beer again because my stomach flip-flopped. Probably out of jealousy if I was being honest—and I was just buzzed enough to be honest. The guy had an amazing set of abs. Not completely flat and toned like Jack's—that kid was too young and pretty for his own good—but definitely more in shape than my own.

Hell, I hadn't been in good shape since just after high school. I remembered back to when Hudson was first born. There was a picture of me shirtless holding him to my chest with Henry on my shoulders. That was probably the last time I'd taken care with the way I looked.

Ended up busy with being a new dad, way too caught

up in all the toxic shit with Missy. Once she and Billy fucked around, and she left, keeping myself in shape was the last thing on my mind.

And now?

I knew I looked like roadkill run over twice for good measure. Any muscles I used to have had taken a hike long ago, and I was too skinny for my frame. Definitely not a looker like this guy probably liked.

The fuck?

First of all, Riggs, why the hell are you assuming he's even into guys?

Second, why the fuckin' hell would it matter if you weren't the type to catch his eye?

Damn skunk-ass beer.

Messing with my head and my stomach.

When he dropped the shirt and held out his hand, I studied him for a moment. I clocked him as younger than me but not by much. He was attractive—no way around that—and even if I hadn't been getting a bit more comfortable with *whatever* my sexuality might have been, there was no way to ignore the fact this guy was very good looking.

Not that I was saying I'd be into him or anything like that.

I mean, if I *was* into guys, I'd definitely be into him.

If that was what I was into…he'd be my type…I think.

If I had a type…when it came to guys.

Did I?

Have a type, I mean. In guys.

Or girls.

Probably both.

Could you have a type in one or both?

Not that I was saying this guy was my type.

But I wasn't *not* saying that either.

Holy fuckin' hell.

Fuck.

Double fuck.

Get it the fuck together, Riggs.

The guy cleared his throat, and I realized he was still waiting to shake my hand.

When I took his hand in mine, I gave serious thought to suing my damn cardiologist because I was pretty damn sure he'd put some sort of faulty pacemaker in my chest based on the jolt of electricity zinging through me.

Just like being electrocuted, I found myself holding tighter to the man's hand, unable to let go as I stared into eyes the most fascinating shade of hazel I'd ever seen. His hair was a bit lighter than mine, and it didn't have the same amount of gray filling in around his temples or in his scruff. But he wore the tiny bit of gray very well.

Damn it all to hell. I needed to stop staring at him.

Even if I was gay or bi or whatever—and I wasn't saying I was—I was being a damn perv with all the staring.

The guy smirked and cocked his head. "Hi. I'm Bryce Armstrong. I just moved to town."

I dropped his hand with a grunt. "The gym guy."

"Ah, my reputation precedes me." When I didn't say anything, he huffed out a laugh. "And you are?"

"The owner of the land you're runnin' on without permission." I crossed my arms over my chest. Bryce was thick and fit, but my shoulders were just as wide, even if I wasn't in tip-top shape.

"I see the rumors of you being prickly as a cactus are true." Bryce's pretty hazel eyes twinkled.

"I ain't...wait just a fuckin' minute, who said that?"

Bryce just laughed. "No worries, I'm good with pricks."

"Fuck off," I growled, not liking the way it seemed like he was laughing at me, but kinda loving the fact he pushed back a little. And was the comment meant to relay something he wanted me to know about him?

Did it matter?

Why would I care if he was good with pricks?

What the hell did that even mean?

Did he mean pricks like...

Hell. No.

I wasn't letting my head go there.

Bryce grinned and used his shirt to wipe his face again. "All joking aside—and I was, you know? Just joking? It's nice to meet you, Mr.?" When I didn't answer with anything more than a scowl, his grin grew bigger. "I'm going with Mr. Riggs because I've gathered enough around town to know you're a Riggs."

I sighed. "Fuckin' dumbass small towns." I finally held my hand back out. "Casey Joe Riggs." I only shook his hand a second time out of politeness. It had nothing to do with wanting to see if I'd been planted with some sort of janky pacemaker.

But there it was, that low-level thrum of electricity through my veins when our bodies connected. His hand was big and warm, slightly damp from perspiration, and a sudden flash of *something* triggered in my brain. It wasn't even a full-on thought or image, just a vague recollection of a...dream? Maybe?—and then it was gone.

Definitely needed to talk to my damn cardiologist. Whatever they did to me in the hospital was affecting my damn head too. Probably have to sue for malpractice or some shit like that.

"Nice to meet you, Casey Joe," Bryce said. His tone sounded like he might be teasing, but those eyes locked on mine came across as serious as could be.

"I've been known to go by Casey, Case, and CJ at times too, so you can pretty much call me whatever and I'll come." The moment the words were out of my mouth, I wanted to grab them and yank them back.

But then Bryce cocked a brow, and I kinda loved the way his nostrils flared.

No.

No, no, no, no, no.

I was *not* going there.

Look, I'd been working with a therapist. We'd maybe talked a bit about sexuality—I had two queer sons, so that made sense. We'd maybe talked a bit about *my* sexuality and how it had been something I *maybe* questioned a long time ago. And we'd possibly talked about the fact sexuality and sexual attraction was fluid, so it would be perfectly fine if my location on the sexuality spectrum had moved either one way or another over the years.

We might have even talked about the fact labels weren't something everyone needed—while others found labels helpful and a way to feel like they had a bit of control—and the fact some people chose one perfect label, some opted for multiple labels that worked for them, some didn't want a label, and some found no one label fit them.

Maybe we talked about all of that.

But none of that talk meant anything.

It didn't mean I was attracted to men.

And so what if it did? What if I was?

Attracted to men, I mean.

It didn't mean I wanted a label.

Or *needed* a label.

And if I did, none of it meant I'd found a good one.

It definitely didn't mean I felt the need to come out about anything regarding my sexuality.

But if and when I *did* feel that need, it would be okay.

Look, I hadn't been completely celibate since Missy left me.

It wasn't like I was hooking up left and right, but I hadn't been in a thirty-some-year dry spell.

Had any of those trysts spawned into something more? No.

Had I found myself set on fire for any of the women I'd spent a night or two with here and there over the years?

Again, no.

Had I even dared to allow myself to think about the possibility of something sexual with a man?

Hell to the no.

Okay, that wasn't exactly true.

I'd allowed myself to *think* about it. I hadn't allowed myself to act on those thoughts.

I forced my attention back to the man in front of me.

The man who was still holding my hand.

Who was still grinning at me.

"Fuck off," I said. "You know what I mean. You can call me whatever. I answer to pretty much anything."

"Good to know," Bryce answered as he let go of my hand and nodded toward my phone as it repeated "Somebody Save Me." "You good? That's kinda a depressing song."

"Don't I fuckin' know it," I said before I could stop myself. "I'm sure you've heard stories around town about what a shit-fuck dad I've been to my boys."

Bryce looked genuinely surprised. "No, not at all."

I snorted and patted my shirt pocket for a cigarette.

Fuck.

The down times were when I hated the fact I'd quit smoking.

Reaching into my front jeans pocket, I grabbed a damn Dum Dum sucker and tore the wrapper off.

"Quit smoking?" Bryce asked.

The sugary candy gave just enough of a rush, and having something to do with my mouth and hand eased the nicotine craving.

Not by much, but enough I could grit my way through the desire for a long drag.

"Yeah, bunch of fuckin' shit if you ask me, but my doctor was all blah, blah, blah you gotta get healthier or you might not survive the next heart attack." I spoke around the tiny globe of sugar. "What the fuck ever." Honestly, I truly was worried about not surviving another heart attack, but talking logically about my health wasn't something I did well in the midst of a nicotine craving.

Holding the sucker stick just like I would have a

cigarette, I took it from between my lips and flicked at the end of the cardboard. "What *did* you hear about me?"

I refused to beg the guy to tell me good shit, but the words of the song rang so true in my head—so full of regret and hating myself for all I missed out on—I couldn't help but wonder just what he'd been told about fuckin' Casey Joe Riggs.

Chapter 4
Bryce

I GESTURED TOWARD THE TIPPED OVER CHAIR. "Care if I sit for a bit?" What I should have done was offer a quick apology and finish my run. My muscles were going to get stiff, and getting back to my apartment was going to be a total drag.

Casey Joe glanced back and forth between me and the chair with a scowl, but he finally shoved the sucker in his mouth and shrugged. "Fine by me. Grab that other one over by the tree."

Why I found myself drawn to this man, I had no clue. I'd seen him the other night at the Roadhouse, and I'd heard bits and pieces about him around Haven Grove. He looked a lot like his boys—both Henry and Hudson got a pretty decent chunk of their dad's good looks.

He was as crabby and cranky as I'd been led to believe, and there really wasn't one single reason I should want to stop and talk to him.

But there I was, setting up a second camping chair and

taking a seat next to him. "Maybe you can turn off that sad shit." I nodded toward his phone.

"Maybe you can keep your damn opinions to yourself," Casey snapped.

The moment the words were out of his mouth, he chomped on the sucker, crunched the candy between his teeth, and yanked another one from his pocket.

I cocked a brow. Why was this guy so intriguing? Since when was I drawn to cranky-ass, foul-mouthed men?

"Sorry, sometimes the nicotine withdrawal really gets to me." He held the sucker between his fingers the way I imagined he'd do a cigarette. "But I'm sick of the sugar, too. I like sweets and snacks, but these damn suckers make me feel like my fuckin' teeth are rottin' out."

I nodded. "Never tried to quit smoking, but I've had some other addictions," I said, thinking about the dopamine high I'd get from my socials getting likes, views, comments, and shares. "You ever try going for a run when you feel the need for a cigarette? Or lifting weights?"

"Yeah, I fuckin' tried it. Feels like I fuckin' tried it all. Sometimes it works better than others."

"I hear that. I've put a rubber band on my wrist and snapped it every time I wanted to do something I needed to stop doing."

Casey Joe wrinkled his nose. "That work?"

"Some days better than others."

He nodded and rolled the sucker on his tongue. "Real talk, though. What did folks around town say about me?" He held up a hand. "Not tryin' to fish for compliments. I know damn well I don't have the best reputation."

I shook my head. "Hundred percent truth, this town

loves you. Probably loves your boys a bit more, but the Riggs name lines right up with honesty, integrity, and respect in Haven Grove."

Casey Joe narrowed his eyes. "And?"

I huffed and rolled my eyes. "Fine. A few folks mentioned you were maybe a bit hard to handle."

He chuckled, and after a few beats of silence, he said, "Where's the lie?"

Unable to catch the snort before it escaped, I joined him in laughing. "It's all good. I don't mind a handful."

His eyes caught on mine, and I swore there was some sort of *something* in that gaze. Interest, maybe? It definitely didn't seem like disgust or anger.

Damn. I had no reason to think the guy was interested in me. Hadn't heard he was gay or bi or anything else along the spectrum. Just because I'd caught tidbits about his sons being queer didn't mean their father was.

Doesn't mean he's not either.

For fuck's sake.

I needed to stop.

Was Casey Joe looking at me like I was a snack he wanted to gobble up?

Yes. Yes, he was.

But I didn't know the man that way. Maybe he looked at everyone like that.

I needed a date with my right hand—a hookup with an actual man would be even better—and then I needed to get my damn head focused on getting my business up and running.

The folks in Haven Grove seemed nice for the most part. I'd met and talked to Lance, I'd seen his group of friends, I'd picked up on a few names here and there, and now I'd met Casey Joe.

I'd never had a close friend group once I graduated college. Honestly, the lack of friends—oh, I'd had acquaintances, just no one I felt drawn to or close to—was one thing I thought had led me to getting way too wrapped up in my social media and falling in with a toxic crowd.

Moving back to the Midwest was going to be good for me in more ways than one, and I was determined to take hold of my redo when it came to picking better friends this time around.

"So, why you sitting here drinking and singing depressing songs?" I asked, shaking off how much I'd liked the way his eyes roamed over me.

Casey Joe sighed, a hand automatically moving to cover his eyes. "Guess you might as well hear it from me." He ran his hand over his face and then took a deep breath. "The Riggs family may be held in high regard in this town, but we're also known for a lot of the drama."

I clapped my hands together, rubbing them like I was preparing for a delicious meal. "Let's hear it."

Casey frowned.

"What?" I asked, a chuckle bubbling from me. "I grew up in the Midwest, I know how small-town drama works. Plus, I moved here from L.A. The drama out there might be flashier and pricier, but big city drama got nothing on the petty drama of Podunk, USA."

For a split second, I thought I'd maybe pissed Casey Joe off—well, pissed him off more than he already seemed to be just naturally—but then he grinned and threw his head back in a booming laugh.

Fuck.

What a laugh.

I wanted to hear it again and again.

And damn, the way his smile lit up his face did funny things to my insides. This man was gorgeous. Yeah, he could stand to beef up a bit—not because I didn't like men with thin builds, but because it was evident from his frame he was built to carry a more filled-out body—but that didn't detract from the fact he was something *fine* to look at.

"Well, you asked for it." Casey took a look at the house which I'd noticed had a huge section that looked like it had been burned, before he glanced toward the tree line. "I've lived in Haven Grove my whole life. Thought for sure I'd fallen for my forever girl back in high school." He paused as if thinking about something, but he shook his head and continued. "I was just as young and dumb as so many teenagers, and I went and fucked things up gettin' Missy pregnant." He turned the most genuine look my way. "Don't for one second think I regret those boys of mine because I don't. They're the best things that ever happened to me." Casey shifted in his chair, and I did the same, leaning in for his story. "Missy convinced me we should get married. I didn't want to. Thought we were way too young and would ruin our lives. I wasn't too upset with knowing we had a baby on the way, but the idea of marriage wasn't something I could wrap my head around. I was just a kid, so maybe the thought of havin' a kid didn't scare me since I didn't really grasp the heaviness of it all. But my gut sure did twist at vowing to love Missy forever." He shook his head and sighed. "Lookin' back, it was just one more mistake in a series of bad choices. I thought I loved her, but I didn't want to commit to spending the rest of my life with her. That was red flag number whatever after all the petty, shitty stuff she pulled even before we got pregnant. I wish to hell I'd been smart enough back then to say no. I would have taken care of my boys no matter what, but Missy and I had no right being together—even if, at the time, I couldn't see it. But we got married—wedding day is supposed to be something special. We fought all day long. I ended up taking Henry over to Lance's place. We spent our wedding night sleeping in separate beds. That was the beginning of the end." He blew out a breath. "Missy wanted her boys to be close together, so we had Hudson when Henry was barely two. Being a dad was a lot of work, but I loved those boys with every ounce of my soul from the moment they took their first breaths.

"Being married was a lot harder. I hated my life married to Missy as much as I'd feared I'd hate it if we broke up instead of getting married. We fought like some people breathe. Oil and water, that's what we were. Hell, we were more like gasoline on an open fire. Young, stupid, not ready for anything real life would throw at us. Definitely not ready to be parents." Casey Joe leaned forward on his knees, rolling the sucker between his fingers. "But damn, them boys kept me going. They were like little pieces of my heart walking around outside my body."

My chest squeezed. Casey Joe Riggs may have been a

cranky, crabby handful, but the love he had for his sons was one of the most sincere and beautiful things I'd ever seen. It flowed from him, and I knew without a doubt his love for Henry and Hudson was one hundred percent genuine.

Casey continued. "I worked the orchard, the store, and the restaurant with my brother Billy from the time we were old enough to help with the businesses, and that's what I kept doing once me and Missy got married. Henry and Hudson were with me pretty much from sun up to sun down. The boys learned everything there was to learn about runnin' things around here. Missy's parents had moved down to Florida by that point—wanted nothing to do with their daughter or grandkids...thought I'd gone and ruined her life and stolen her from the church." Casey snorted and shook his head. "My own parents pretty much disowned me when they found out I'd gotten Missy pregnant. Mom was mortified what her church ladies might think. They retired from the family business, let me and Billy run things, and traveled across the country while me and Billy kept things afloat here..." Casey Joe trailed off like he was lost in a memory. Standing abruptly, he popped his neck. "You want some water?"

"Sure, thanks." Doing my best to follow the subject change, I joined him as he walked to the detached garage next to the house. It felt good to stretch my legs after letting my muscles get cool listening to Casey tell his story.

He handed me an icy cold bottle of water. We both cracked open our bottles, took long swigs, and headed back to the chairs in the yard.

"Lance is your friend, Billy is your brother?" I steered the story back on track because it felt like there was still plenty to be told. Casey was easy to listen to. He was a bit rough around the edges, but it was evident from the first moment you heard him talk about his boys that he was dedicated, protective, and had a good heart under all the gruff and grumble.

And sometimes it was a lot easier to lose yourself in someone else's drama and problems than to revisit your own.

Plus, I needed friends in my new home. I had a feeling buddying up with the Riggs family would be a really good move. Not just socially and for my business, but in my personal life as well.

Didn't hurt that the guy was hot as hell.

Casey grunted. "Lance is my best friend—fuckin' traitor. Billy was my brother, but he fucked me over all the same."

There were definitely more stories there, but I just cocked a brow and waited.

"When Henry was about four, Missy decided she was done with being a mom, done with small town living, done with me. She left a note blaming me for her being miserable and hightailed it out of here. Lookin' back, I know she planned it—she was a mean and spiteful thing deep down—but I spent way too long blaming Billy for what Missy stirred up." He wiped a hand over his mouth and sucked his bottom lip between his teeth. "I saw the note and headed straight for Billy's. Aside from Lance, my brother was the person I was closest to. Ended up finding Billy passed out drunk in bed while Missy pulled her clothes back on. She left me and the boys that day, never looked back, and things with me and Billy were never the same."

"That sucks, man, double betrayal added to a loss and finding out you're the sole provider for your boys." Damn, no wonder the guy was cranky.

Casey huffed. "Yeah, it was pretty much shit. I wallowed for years and years over losing Missy. Had it out with Billy more times than I could count. He was my flesh and blood—and these days, I really don't think he slept with her...I think that was her settin' shit up to fuck me over even more than just leavin' would have—but I couldn't get over the hurt they both caused me. Billy started drinkin' more and more. For a while, he kept things going with the businesses—which was a good thing because my worthless ass couldn't function for a damn long time." He sighed. "Those are the years I regret the most. When I was there physically, but not really there for my boys. Thank god for Lance. He kept us together. Kept me from doin' myself in over a person I've since figured out was never actually the love of my life. It was all shit and it hurt, but I've learned a lot from it. And Missy actually did me a big favor in the long run." He scoffed at his own words. "Not that it made it any easier."

Casey finished his water and stared off at the tree line where the hill sloped gently down into the orchard.

"What are your top three regrets?" I asked.

He turned his gaze on me, eyes narrowing and lips pursed together. "You some kind of therapist wannabe?"

Laughing, I drained the rest of my water. "No, but I've been to therapy enough to know it's good to talk about stuff, and sometimes the shit we think is the worst turns out to be not so bad when we can reframe it."

"Therapy for what?" Casey asked, just as blunt as could be.

"Shit, life? Being gay, an unhealthy relationship with social media, dealing with toxic relationships, the list is long." Well, there. In case Casey had a problem with me being gay, it was out there.

He studied me for a long moment, wheels definitely turning, and I wished I could see what he was thinking. Finally, he just huffed. "Yeah, therapy is shit, but I guess it's good for somethin' too."

I tapped the empty bottle on my knee. "Top three regrets."

Casey blew out a breath. "Not being there for my boys. The way things went down and ended with Billy. And wasting so much time being a pathetic piece of shit wallowing over the loss of someone I didn't even love. I mean, I thought I loved her, but that wasn't love. That was toxicity at its finest."

I nodded. "I get that." Thoughts of the toxic people I'd gotten involved with flitted through my head. I didn't even really like them, but I liked what I thought they could do for me at the time. "You ever try to look at those things and find some positives in them?"

Casey rolled his eyes. "Fuck off with your fake therapy shit."

"I'm just saying," I said with a chuckle—Casey Joe was a breath of fresh air, and I appreciated his frank talk. "Sometimes it helps to find a silver lining when it comes to the shitty stuff."

Casey popped another sucker in his mouth. "Fine. Silver lining to Missy leavin' was we didn't belong together. We weren't good together. She saved me years of being stuck in a crap marriage." He laughed with no humor. "'Course, I just replaced those years of a crap marriage with years of self-pity."

"Any other silver linings?"

Casey's mouth drew down on the corners. "Can't think of anything good about losin' my brother and watching him drink himself to death. And no one would say it's good to be a shit father."

I shrugged. "Not sure on the brother thing, but I've seen your boys around town. They seem like successful, respectable men. What that tells me is they learned about the family business from you, learned how to be independent, and kept integrity in the Riggs name."

"Those boys are good through and through *despite* of me," Casey grumbled.

"I think they're good because of you. Maybe losing their mom and having a dad who didn't function well for a while was hard, but they had Lance, right? They had to have learned something good from you and him. If they hadn't, they wouldn't be the men they are today."

Casey just shook his head. "They shouldn't have had to deal with that. Missy leaving messed them up. Hell, *I* messed them up. Having Lance around was probably the only thing that kept them from turning out like me and Billy."

I bopped my head back and forth. "Maybe, maybe not. I'm not saying the situation was *good*, but sometimes the best lessons in life come from the biggest hardships."

Casey grunted. "I'll never stop wishin' I'd been better for my boys." He screwed up his face in concentration. "But I *can* say I'm actually glad—no matter how much it hurt them—they didn't have to grow up with Missy in their lives. She wasn't a good influence, and the way we fought would have been really bad for kids to be around all the time."

"There ya go," I said, the water bottle crinkling when I shook it at him. "Now, you wanna tell me what happened to your house?"

"Tit for tat. You first. What wild hair up your ass convinced you to leave California to remodel a piece of shit gym in Small Town, USA?"

Chapter 5
Casey Joe

WHY THE HELL I HAD TO OPEN MY DAMN MOUTH and ask Bryce a question requiring him to stay a while, I'd never know, but that's what my damn stupid ass did.

I mean, the guy was ridiculously easy to talk to... almost like how I spilled my guts when my therapist got me in her office...and I hadn't minded filling him in on my history. The thing about getting to know people in a small town was it was often better to jump in and make sure your version of the story got told before the rest of the damn town had a chance to put their spin on it.

So, I'd given him the run-down on all the shit with Missy and Billy—the Riggs family drama in a nutshell. Honestly, it felt good to hear him say he hadn't heard a lot of bad about me around town. Somehow, the Riggs family name had always seemed to fly just under the radar. Yeah, we had our share of shit show drama, but we balanced it out with being good, honest, hardworking people.

And that meant something to me. Integrity went hand-in-hand with the Riggs name—no thanks to all the outside shit—and I was proud my boys had our name to hold on to.

Bryce shifted in his seat and took his turn staring into the tree line like I'd been doing when I told my story.

Interesting.

Maybe he had some shit in his past too.

And fuck, didn't we all?

"I grew up just a couple towns over. Great family. My sister's a nurse at the hospital up the road. She's got a good life. Great husband, great kids, even has a grandbaby. My parents still live in the town where I grew up. My aunt lives with them too. I stayed with them when I moved back this way." Bryce chuckled and let out a sigh. "It was a good reminder of why it's sometimes better to live close to family but not live *with* them."

"Fuckin'-A, man." I tipped my empty water bottle his way. "I'll fuckin' drink to that. Been livin' with Hudson and Lance since my house burned, and I'm about to take a damn icepick to my ears if I have to hear them fornicatin' like damn Energizer bunnies one more damn time."

Bryce snorted, and I couldn't help staring at his lips as they broke into a grin that filled his entire face. "Damn, man, that's rough. I'm down for some good sex, but I also need my sleep. It being family just makes it all that much worse." He cocked his head. "Lance and Hudson been together long?"

I grunted. "Long enough." Popping another sucker in my mouth, I leaned back in my chair. "Lance left town several years ago. I hated it. I knew why he did it, but that didn't make it any easier to lose my best friend. But he figured some shit out about himself while he was gone, or some fuckin' shit like that, and when he came back him and Hudson ended up talkin' on that damn ClickC*ck hookup app for a while. When they realized they knew each other, one thing led to another, and voila, my ex best friend was bonin' my son."

Bryce's eyes grew comically wide. "Wow. That's a lot to take in." He cocked his head. "Wait, what's the difference in their ages?"

Groaning, I choked out, "Don't make me do the math."

"You just had a birthday, right?"

"Yeah, turned fuckin' fifty-four. Lance will be the same soon."

"And Hudson looks to be in his thirties?" Bryce asked.

"Thirty-three," I mumbled. "Fuck. You sneaky bastard, you were supposed to be tellin' me about what brought you here, not makin' me think about my best friend being some sort of silver fox daddy yankin' my baby boy from the cradle."

"That's a bit dramatic," Bryce said with a wink.

My insides weren't sure whether to get prickly or do a flip-flop.

So, I shrugged. "Then Henry went and got himself a younger guy. There's about ten years difference between him and Jack."

"Six here," Bryce said. When his cheeks flared pink, he muttered, "I mean, I'm forty-eight. Just six years difference." He gestured between us, his cheeks turning a brighter pink. "So, anyway, after I graduated high school," he barreled on with his story.

For a split second, I wondered at the age comment, but I quickly got caught back up in what Bryce was saying.

"I wanted out of that tiny town. While my sister had always wanted to stay there and raise a family, all I'd ever wanted was to hightail it out of there." Bryce shrugged. "So, I headed out west for college. Been out there ever since."

Wrinkling my nose, I prodded, "So, why come back here? Parents sick?"

Bryce shook his head. "No, coming back here has been a long time coming. I loved California, but the last several years, I've had to admit to myself I didn't like who I'd become out there. I got caught up in some shit that wasn't good for me—"

"Don't be bringin' fuckin' drugs to town," I bit out. "Fuckin' last thing we need here is some drug runner."

"Man, shut up. I didn't bring fucking drugs to Haven Grove." Bryce rolled his eyes. "You going to let me tell my story?"

I nodded and waved him on, not hating the little flare in my stomach snapping to life when Bryce gave back as good as he got.

"So, I had a great job, great place, great car, but shitty friends—more like acquaintances—a really unhealthy relationship with social media, and a conscience that kept reminding me of where I came from and the type of person I'd always wanted to be." Bryce lost himself for a moment, his eyes looking beyond the trees.

"Didn't you want to be successful and living your dream?" Not gonna lie, it sounded great, and I was possibly slightly jealous.

Bryce nodded. "I did. That's all I wanted. But I hadn't counted on what I'd have to sacrifice. Could have just kept going the way I was, but I'd lost myself in all of it."

"Got some drama with an ex boyfriend? A long string of exes—do the love 'em and leave 'em thing and had to get out of town?" For some reason, Bryce's mention he was gay had rocked me yet also not taken me by surprise.

Like, it was a punch to the gut, but it felt so good.

And *that* was something I was in no place to analyze.

Bryce snorted. "Not at all. I dated, but not much. Hookups here and there, but I never really connected with anyone. They'd be ready to move on, and I wouldn't be the least bit upset. Or they'd want more, and I'd be completely uninterested."

The intrigue this man sparked in me grew with each passing moment, and I wasn't exactly sure what to do with that.

"So, you saw the gym and decided to move back here and fix it up?" I asked.

"No. Moved back here not really knowing what the hell I was going to do with the second half of my life—but knowing I couldn't keep going like I was out in L.A.—and saw a story on the news about the gym. Went to see it— seriously, was just going to take a look—and ended up with the key in hand."

I snorted and shook my head. "Glutton for punishment. That place needs a lot of work."

"Fuck, don't I know it." Bryce groaned and ran a hand over his face. "And I'm *not* a fixer-upper. Probably be best if I hired someone, but I've not been able to admit defeat just yet."

Before my brain could catch up with my words, I said, "I've done plenty of renovation work over the years, I could help."

Bryce's eyes snapped to mine. "No shit? Like, for real? You really have experience with it? I've got the money to buy what I need, and I could pay you for sure, but I just don't have the know-how to pull it all together."

I shrugged. "Sure, no problem. I'm pretty good with my hands."

Again, word vomit before my damn inactive brain even gave a second thought to what was pouring from the damn hole in my face.

Bryce's eyes traveled to my hands and back to my eyes, trying and failing to hide a smile. "Good to know."

He winked.

Fuckin' winked.

In desperation to change the subject, I nodded toward my house. "So, someone set fire to my house not too long ago thinking they could hurt Jack. Ended up not working since none of us were at the house at the time, but that doesn't change the fact my house isn't livable right now."

"I've got room at my place," Bryce said, and I didn't miss the way his eyes flashed like he couldn't believe what he'd just offered.

I cocked my head. "Where you stayin'?"

"Over the gym. It's a two-bedroom apartment. Nothing huge, nothing fancy, but you're welcome to the second room while you wait on your house to be done."

I wanted so damn bad to refuse his offer.

Wanted to scoff and tell him to shove it.

Didn't want to *need* a new place so badly.

But I did.

Damn, I did.

"I'm not usually one for taking charity—"

"Fuck off," Bryce shot back with a grin. "It's not charity. I'll pay you less for helping me out if you take the room."

Leaning forward, I rested my head in my hands and thought about how many nights I'd lain awake recently, unable to sleep because of all the fuckin' noise Lance and Hudson were making.

"Fuck," I growled. "I really don't want to take you up on it, but you have no idea how bad it messes with your head to have to listen to your best friend and son goin' at it every damn night."

Bryce laughed. "I can't even imagine. So, plan on moving in as soon as you can. And we can take a walk through the gym and figure out a plan for getting some shit done. I think I can be a pretty good help if you can just tell me what to do." He cocked his head. "You have any interest in being one of my first employees when we open?"

I scoffed. "Do I look like some kind of personal trainer?"

He bit his lip, those pretty hazel eyes traveling up and down my body making my skin tingle. "I was thinking more along the lines of a manager. Working with memberships, making sure the other hires are scheduled right, maybe helping me get clients to sign up."

I cleared my throat. "You barely know me. What if I'm a shit person and shittier employee?"

Bryce shrugged. "Then I'll fire you. If we find out we

don't work well together on the renovation, we can part ways when we're done. But we've gotten along fine sitting here, so I don't think it's a problem. Plus, the town has pretty much already vouched for you."

It was weird how his words touched something deep inside my chest. There were days over the years when I'd longed for the chance to take my boys and escape this little town. Maybe if I could have provided them with bigger and better, we would have been happier, healthier, and...hell, I didn't know what else. But moments like this made me realize my life was right where it was supposed to be. Henry, Hudson, and I belonged in Haven Grove.

"I have a certification in Graphics and Design, and I've helped Jack with marketing his cake business," I offered, not liking the vulnerability in my words.

"No shit?" Bryce beamed. "That's perfect. I think we'll make a great team. Now, what's this about cake?"

Chapter 6
Bryce

THE MORNING CASEY JOE WAS SCHEDULED TO move in, I was running around like a chicken with my head cut off. Part of me thought I'd gone and lost my damn mind inviting Casey Joe to stay at my place, but I was also looking forward to it.

Why?

Well, that was a can of worms in and of itself.

A whole damn can of worms.

On one hand, I thought I'd probably like having someone else in the apartment. When I'd been doing the physical training stuff in L.A. for all those years, the job kept me around people. True, none of them were my friends, and I definitely knew what it was like to be surrounded by people while feeling lonely as hell, but at least I was socializing.

Being in Haven Grove meant a whole lot less people, and I found I wasn't the greatest at just making conversation with strangers. Unless you counted the easy way I spent a couple hours chatting with Casey Joe.

On the other hand, asking him to move in made the most sense. It was logical to have him close to the gym if he was going to be helping with the renovation. If he'd had his own house to live in, I wouldn't have offered up the room. But he did actually need a place to stay for a while, so the roommate situation was best all around.

Yeah, he technically *had* a place to stay, but no one should have to listen to their best friend and son going at it every night.

And, if I was being completely honest, he was hot.

So fucking hot.

I was drawn to Casey like no one else I'd ever known. Did I think I had a chance? Most likely, no. I mean, I wasn't one hundred percent sure he was completely straight—some of the looks he'd given me made me question things a bit—but nothing said I couldn't just enjoy looking.

Plus, for whatever reason, I liked talking to him. It was kinda fun having no idea what might come out of his mouth. I'd had my fill of fake people for the first half of my life. Casey Joe was refreshing because he was as real as they came. He said what he was thinking. He didn't try to fake who he was. Didn't try to hide the real him.

I'd lost myself to all the glamour and glitz for so long— not really being a part of it but hiding who I truly was behind it—it did my heart good to be around someone who was as down-to-earth as Casey Joe.

So, I made note to buy a new set of sheets as a spare and set to work putting my extras on the bed in the second bedroom. I straightened up the apartment, ran the vacuum, washed the tiny bit of dishes I'd left in the sink, and started a load of towels all before ten in the morning on the day Casey Joe had said he'd bring his stuff over.

My plan was to show him his room, let him unpack if he wanted to, and then give him a tour of the gym. If everything went as I hoped it would, we'd have a list of projects and a timeline by the time we went to bed.

Thinking about Casey Joe and bed was a bad thing.

A very bad thing.

Thinking of him using the same shower as me, wondering if he slept naked, and imagining what it might be like if he maybe—just maybe—was interested in men was all going to likely be my demise.

Shit.

I hadn't had a crush on any guy in a very long time.

I'd had my pick of pretty much anyone I wanted out on the west coast, and I couldn't ever make that connection.

Then I moved back home, met a foul-mouthed grump of a man, and somehow found myself enamored like a damn cartoon character with hearts in my eyes.

And then I asked him to move into my apartment, work with me day in and day out, and let myself get all kinds of delicious thoughts about him.

Yeah, that sounded like a great plan.

Nothing could go wrong.

Nothing at all.

My phone buzzed, and I smiled when I saw it was Casey Joe. He'd suggested we exchange numbers the other day before I left his place. "Just in case you get home and realize you've been talkin' shit this whole time and really don't want me to move in with you," he'd said.

CJ Riggs: Still got that spare bed?

Me: Yep. Even put clean sheets on it for you.

CJ Riggs: I'm downstairs.

Me: Come on up.

I knew he'd easily see the apartment entrance next to the main gym door. When I heard the heavy door slam shut behind him and his boots on the steps, I unbolted the door and opened it to wait for his head to appear at the top of the stairs.

And there he was.

Blond hair dark enough to be called light brown kept short enough it likely wouldn't get messed up in the wind, blue eyes taking in the narrow, dark hall, and a pinched expression on his face.

"Welcome home," I teased, gesturing him down the hall and into the apartment.

"Why's that hallway feel like I'm walking to my last meal on death row?"

I barked out a laugh, and some of the tension eased from my body.

"Seriously, get some damn lights or something." Casey Joe stood in the middle of the apartment and looked around.

It was nothing like the place I'd had out in L.A., but it was about the same size. And I owned it with the gym, so rent-free was hard to argue with.

"Let me show you around." I gestured toward the left and started through the dining room.

Casey Joe followed me.

I passed through the kitchen. "The bedrooms are back here." I pointed to my door. "This one is me. Sorry, we share a bathroom."

Casey Joe grunted. "I have two boys, and we had one bathroom. I'll survive."

"This one is you." I pushed open the door to his room. "They're pretty much exactly the same. Worst part about them is they're directly above the gym. I can't say whether the noise is bad or not, but if I had to guess, I'd say we'll both be glad the gym isn't open twenty-four-seven."

"I sleep heavy, but I get up pretty early, so I don't think it will be much of a problem. Plus, we'll be the only ones making noise for a while until it's up and running."

For some reason, my damn brain decided to turn his words into some sort of little fantasy about us making noise—and I wasn't imagining the type of clatter a renovation project would make. Clearing my throat, I pushed aside the thought and gestured toward the bed. "Pretty sure the beds are exactly the same. The one in my room is pretty comfortable. Maybe not the height of luxury, but you won't wake up with a crick in your neck."

"I've woken up to pee and puke from the boys more times than I can count. If there's not wet spots, I'm good." The way his own words took their sweet time sinking in and turning Casey's face the cutest shade of red had me biting my lip to keep from laughing. He pointed a finger at me. "Shut it. That wasn't what I meant, and you know it."

"No worries," I said, trying to keep a straight face. "I won't make you sleep in the wet spot."

Casey flipped me off, threw his bag on the bed, and crossed his arms over his chest. "This how it's going to be the whole time? Juvenile innuendo?"

Shit.

"I'm sorry. I was just playing around. I didn't mean to make you uncomfortable."

Way to go, Bryce. Just because the guy is fun to mess around with, don't go making things weird.

Casey laughed. "Have you met Lance and Hudson? They're the queens of innuendo. I'm not offended, I was just givin' you shit because I opened my damn big mouth and stepped right in it." He gestured toward the door. "Show me the rest of the place so we can get started."

I sighed inwardly and gave a nod. "The bathroom is across the hall. Towels are in the linen closet out here, everything else is in the cabinets and drawers in the bathroom. Feel free to use whatever you want or get your own stuff if you don't like what I have."

Casey Joe grunted. "As long as you don't use some pineapple cherry vanilla shit or somethin', I'm good."

Laughing, I shook my head. "No, I mostly use cedar and citrus scents."

"Perfect. Juicy Peach has good soaps and shampoos I like, so I can pick up some next time I go. Not gonna be moochin' off you."

We made our way to the kitchen. "You're not

mooching. You're working off rent for the room by helping me, and I'm paying you a very small sum because it wouldn't be right to let you renovate this place with me for free. And when your house is ready, and you move out, I'll up your pay."

Casey hummed absently. "You plannin' on living in this apartment forever?" He glanced around the kitchen. "If you got yourself a house, you could probably rent this place out for two to four people depending on their set up and needs." He nodded toward the kitchen window. "That's what Lance is doing with the apartment above the DP. He was livin' there, but when he moved in with Hudson, he started rentin' the place out. That's why I was stayin' with them since his apartment already had a tenant."

"The DP?" I did my best not to let laughter cling to my words.

Casey huffed. "Dairy Palace. Full name is the Sweet and Creamy Dairy Palace, but it's usually shortened to DP." He eyed me suspiciously. "Why?"

I shook my head, dying to giggle like a teenager. Surely Casey knew why DP was funny. He had to. Right?

He finally shook his head, and a tiny grin played on his lips. "Go ahead. You can laugh. I'm impressed you kept it in this long."

Laughter burst from me. "Oh my god, for a second I thought you didn't know why it was funny, and I was going to die if I had to explain it to you."

Casey rolled his eyes. "I'm fifty-four years old. I have two grown children. We can assume I know enough about sex to grasp most innuendo and play on words." He chuckled. "If you haven't already, you should definitely check out the merchandise at the Roadhouse. Lots of funny shit on t-shirts, hoodies, stickers, magnets, mugs, even underwear. They used peaches and cream along with DP to make a bunch of dumb shit, but people love it. Anytime they get somethin' new on the shelves it sells out almost immediately."

"That's good marketing," I said. "I want to do some stuff like that for the gym. Tanks, hoodies, t-shirts, mugs, bumper stickers, the works."

"I can definitely help with that," Casey said.

"That would be awesome." I leaned against the kitchen counter. "We can talk more when we get the gym further along, but I was thinking about having a glass case or some shelves behind the check-in desk to display the merch. Water bottles for sure. Maybe we can look at how Hudson, Lance, and Henry have things displayed and set ours up the same."

Casey Joe cocked his head. "Ours, huh?"

I shrugged. "Told you, I'm down with hiring you on to help with memberships and managing the crew if you're interested."

He eyed me like he was waiting for some punchline of a joke. "Why? You don't even know me."

"Look, we can talk about it more later on down the road after we get the gym up and running, but I know people. I've spent several years working with people, and I recognize good, trustworthy folks when I see them."

Casey grunted. "Thought you said you got in with some pieces of shit."

I smirked. "I did. I knew they were pieces of shit when

I got involved. I just didn't care enough to keep my distance. The Riggs family and those involved with you are good people. I can feel it. But no decisions need to be made right now." I pointed to the pantry. "I go through peanut butter and protein powder like water, so I buy in bulk. I try to keep a lot of rice and canned veggies on hand." Opening the fridge, I gestured toward the stocked shelves. "I'm a fan of fresh fruit and veggies. Lots of chicken, pork, and fish. I don't really keep a lot of junk food around the place."

"Fuckin' hell," Casey muttered.

"What?" I asked, turning to see him pinching the bridge of his nose. "What's wrong?"

"I should have known this was too good to be true."

"What? Why?" I seriously felt like I'd been smacked in the face.

"No junk food? Did my boys set you up to this?" He scowled. "Is that what Lance was talkin' to you about the other night? Trickin' me into movin' in and then pullin' this shit?"

I fought the urge to cross my arms over my chest, instead opting for what was hopefully a more neutral position with my thumbs tucked in the pockets of my jeans. "Lance and I definitely didn't talk about any of this. As far as I know, your boys don't know you're moving in here unless you told them."

"Well, I ain't stayin' here if you think you're puttin' me on some goddamn rabbit diet."

My head spun. "Rabbit diet? What the hell is a rabbit diet?"

Casey pointed a finger toward the fridge. "All the green

shit. I'm a grown ass man, and if I want to eat some Twinkies or chips or a piece of cake, I can." He gestured wildly. "Donuts, pie, candy bars, whatever the fuck I want to eat, I can eat, and you can't stop me."

I took a moment to breathe in deeply and rested my hips against the countertop again. "Are you finished?"

"Finished? No." Casey eyed the pantry. "No, I'm not finished. I had a fuckin' heart attack. I could have died. I shouldn't have to be punished with dry chicken and plain rice just because my heart wanted to up and try to give out on me. If you think you're going to control what I'm eating, you've got another think comin'."

Standing as calmly and patiently as I could—which took quite a bit of effort—I watched him and waited.

Finally, some of the tension eased from Casey's shoulders and he ran a hand over his face. "I guess I'm done."

I opened my mouth, but he started up again.

"And I can drink beer if I damn well want to."

I quirked a brow.

He gestured at me to go on.

"Well, now that you've gotten that out of your system," I said, hoping my tiny grin looked wry and not terribly accusatory. "I think we can have a conversation about food." When Casey looked to rev back up, I held my hands up. "I have zero interest in controlling what you eat. You're an adult. If you want to make poor food choices, that's completely on you."

Casey jutted his chin like he was preparing for an argument.

"Honestly, I have no desire to try to change your mind.

It wouldn't work anyway. People only change when they want to change. If you don't want to be healthier, that's on you. No amount of me nagging—or your boys pushing—will change your mind."

He relaxed a bit.

"I keep fresh, healthy food in the house for meals and snacks. If I want something as a treat, I'll go out and get it. I might walk to the DP for ice cream so I can get some fresh air and exercise before and after my treat." I gestured toward the fridge again. "I like to cook, and I think I'm pretty good at it. I make healthy dishes that taste pretty damn good. I'm one hundred percent down with cooking for two—"

Casey's eyes flashed like a tiny dog ready to snap back into attack mode, and I went on quickly.

"—but if you'd prefer to cook for yourself or just have snacks for your meals, that's completely up to you." I pointed to the pad of paper on the side of the fridge. "I think I'd like to keep trips up the road for groceries to once a month—stock up as much as possible when I'm there—and get most of my food at the Juicy Peach if I'm able. You can grocery shop on your own, or you can add things to the list and go with me." I paused and raised a brow. "I *will* draw the line at actually buying the unhealthy snacks for you, so if you want them purchased, you need to get them yourself or go with me."

Casey clenched his jaw and gave a tiny nod.

"So, we good?"

He rolled his eyes and nodded again. "Yeah. Sorry for blowin' up. It's somethin' I do, but I'm workin' on it. Fuckin' therapist says since I couldn't control the heart attack—and other shit in the past—I grasp at things I can control, and one of those things is the food I eat." He huffed. "I know I need to eat healthier and get more exercise. And stop drinkin' so much." He sighed and his eyes got a far away look. "Not sure which is worse, the shit I eat or the drinkin'."

I smiled. "I get it. I promise not to force anything on you." With a wink, I pushed off the counter. "Just remember, you live and work with a personal trainer who happens to be a great cook. Anytime you want to set up some workouts or get some healthy meals planned, I'm your guy."

"So, you okay with snacks?"

Snorting softly, I nodded. "You're a big boy." Letting that topic go, I gestured toward the living room. "There was a couch when I moved in, and it seems to be pretty new, so I just left it. Put up a flat screen, hooked up my games, and that's about it. My old place was decorated better, but I don't know how long I'm staying here, so it didn't feel like I needed to put in too much effort."

Casey's suggestion about renting out the apartment was already something I'd been considering, so I didn't think I wanted to get too comfortable.

"I'm used to minimal décor. My place is country cute, but it's old—totally livable though—and not frilly. My mom had lots of lacey angels, bears with bows, and baskets with geese and apples when I was growin' up. Not my thing," Casey Joe said. "So, I cleared all that shit out. Functional and comfortable is my decoration style."

I smiled. "Look forward to seeing it when you get to move back in."

He winced. "Whenever the hell that might be. Probably ruined a lot of shit I'll have to replace."

"That's what insurance is for."

"Doesn't make it any less aggravatin'."

"True that." I gestured vaguely back toward the bedrooms. "There's a hookup for a washer and dryer, but it didn't come with one. For now, I think I'm going to use the ones in the gym. If I decide to stay here, I'll get a set— or maybe I'll get a set to entice renters—but for now, I think I can deal with washing clothes downstairs if you're good with that?"

Casey nodded. "Not like I have a fashion reputation to uphold. As long as I have clean underwear, I'm good to go."

Nope. I wasn't going to let myself think about Casey Joe in his underwear.

"You wanna take a look at the gym and see about getting a plan put into place?"

He checked his phone. "Yeah, let's take a look. Then we can grab lunch and figure some shit out. I told Jack I'd try his new cake before he debuts it at dinner tonight."

We walked out the door, and I locked it behind me. As we headed down the stairs, I said, "Jack is the younger blond who is dating your oldest?"

Casey Joe smiled. "Yeah, he's somethin'. Got a shitty past, totally deserves his do-over. Came to town just runnin' from his demons. Found Henry, and things just clicked. They took their time, neither of them really settin' out lookin' for anything serious, but there was no way they weren't gettin' together."

"And Jack has the cake part of the Roadhouse?"

Casey puffed up like a proud father. "Let Them Eat Cake is his part of the menu. He has a real talent. Cakes are the best I ever had, and he decorates them real nice, but he's most skilled at matchin' cake flavors with meals and drinks."

"And Henry creates the menus and drinks at the Roadhouse?"

We'd taken the tiny hallway from the apartment stairs to the back entrance of the gym. The door opened into the laundry room and employee break room. Through a door to the right was the gym manager's office which was where I planned to do most of my work when I wasn't out on the floor with clients.

"Yeah." Casey's eyes gleamed. "Henry's always been the silent, grouchy type. He's not actually a grump, but he can come across that way."

I huffed out a laugh.

"What?"

Shrugging, I bit my lip before saying, "Just wondering where he got that from."

Casey's eyes flashed, and for a moment, I thought he was pissed. But then he just chuckled. "Well, the grouchy part came from me, but definitely not the quiet part." He shook his head, a tiny grin dancing over his pretty lips. "Even as a kid, he was so serious, always takin' care of Hudson and me. He does a great job plannin' the meals, and he's amazin' behind the bar. The cake and cocktails are a lot of fun, and a lot of folks have come to try out the cake flights."

"Cake flights?"

"You know how you can get wine flights or beer

flights? Well, Jack does cake flights paired with cocktails. It's a huge hit."

"Damn, that's genius. I'll have to give it a try."

"Now that you're part of Haven Grove, you can be an official taste-tester since you've got a Riggs family connection."

Something tugged at my heart. Did I? Have a Riggs family connection? Aside from my own family, I hadn't felt connected or genuinely *welcomed* just as I was in…well, pretty much my entire adult life. All those years of faking it, pretending to fit in, hiding myself behind the glitz and glam just to have the right crowd to hang with had worn me down and dulled something deep inside.

But now? After a short time in this tiny little Podunk town, I had a respected member of the community metaphorically taking me under his wing and telling me I belonged. That was pretty heady stuff.

I cleared my throat, trying to stave off the wave of emotion. "And Hudson runs the orchard and the store?"

"Basically saved the orchard single handedly—fuck knows I wasn't a damn bit of help—and kept the Juicy Peach goin'. He does other shit around town—massage, handy man, shit like that." Pride in his sons was heavy in Casey Joe's words. "He and Lance partnered up to share promo between the ice cream shop and the Riggs businesses. The two of them are really good together." He huffed and rolled his eyes. "If you ever tell them I said that I'll deny it."

Chapter 7
Casey Joe

"CASEY IS REALLY GOOD WITH STUFF LIKE THAT," Jack said as Bryce and I sat at the bar savoring slices of Jack's newest cake along with matching cocktails expertly mixed by Henry. "He taught me how to change the oil in his truck, he'll help you get the gym ready in no time."

"I'm not a licensed contractor or anythin'," I started, but Bryce shook his head.

"You're a thousand times more in the know than I am, so I'm already feeling much better about getting these projects started."

We'd taken inventory of the gym before lunch. With a notebook in hand, we'd jotted notes and lists of supplies we'd need. There was a lot to do before Armstrong Health & Fitness would be operable, but the inside of the building wasn't as rundown as I'd expected it to be. It needed a major cleaning and overhaul, but we'd get it in tip-top shape.

I couldn't put my finger on why I felt as comfortable

with Bryce as I did with Lance and my boys when I'd just met the guy—especially when I didn't click with most people very easily—but it had been nice to have someone to hang out with. Not gonna lie, it kinda sucked to be the odd man out with Hudson, Lance, Henry, and Jack all paired up.

Was it confusing the shit out of me trying to pinpoint why Bryce was so easy to talk to?

Hell, yeah.

Had I decided to not question it?

Also, yes.

"Speaking of projects," Henry started, his eyes landing on Jack in a *go on* gesture.

Jack's cheeks pinked. "It might be stupid."

"It's not stupid. I think a lot of people would be interested."

Jack brought his collar up to rub over his chin—a nervous gesture he'd stopped doing *as* much, but something he still did from time to time if he was feeling anxious—and took a deep breath. "Okay, fine. I was thinking about starting something...kinda like a club...not any specific theme or anything. Like for socializing. Or something." He took another breath. "I don't explain it right."

"For baking? Or like a book club or somethin'? The church has a Bible study and a yarn club for knitting and crochet," I said.

Jack nodded his head. "Kinda like that, but without a single focus. So, just a group of people coming together to socialize. No assigned book. No verses to read and analyze. No patterns or recipes or projects. Just people from around town who want to grab a drink or snack and sit around chatting." He shrugged. "Maybe we'd do some special fundraising or volunteer type stuff when we see needs arise. And we can talk about anything and everything—books, recipes, movies, hobbies, all of it." He ran the shirt collar over his chin again as he worried his lip between his teeth. "I don't know, I just thought it might be fun. I'm comfortable enough in town now to want to get to know people better. I figure other people might like the chance too."

"I like the idea," Bryce said. "I don't know anyone, and in my line of business it's best to get to know people if I want to bring them in and have them trust me with their health and fitness."

I loved that Jack had come up with this idea. Not because I liked the idea of socializing just for the sake of socializing, but because he was spreading his wings, and I was proud as hell. "Where would you hold it? How often? Food? Drinks? Membership?"

Jack gave me a relieved smile. "The outside dining area when it's not too hot or too cold. In the hottest and coldest months, I think we can make it work inside the Roadhouse. Depends on how many folks come. I was thinking folks could bring in snacks if they wanted. We'd do samples from time to time. Offer discounted drinks and food for those who want to order." He cocked his head. "I don't think membership will be required. Maybe donations if people feel like they want to help out, but I don't want anyone to be left out just because they can't pay a fee."

Jack might not have been my flesh and blood, but

somehow, he'd ended up just as generous and big-hearted as both my boys.

"If it gets too big," Bryce said, "may be able to move it to the church or the school. Maybe have it at different times on different days so a variety of people can join in. The gym doesn't have any kind of outside area yet, but at some point it might. You'd be welcome to that space once we get it set up."

"Yeah," Jack said, nodding, "those are good ideas. I was thinking maybe every other week? And I think it should be pretty casual. No set agenda, just milling around and talking. If we see it needs more structure, we can always adjust."

"I like it," I said. "Probably not somethin' I'd attend on my own, but if we're puttin' the Riggs name behind it, I'm down to help with it." Honestly, I wasn't one for organized socializing, but for Jack, I'd make an exception. I liked talking to folks around town, so it wouldn't be hard to meet up, eat some cake, and shoot the shit.

"Tell 'em what you want to call it," Henry said with a hint of teasing in his words.

Jack's cheeks pinked again, but he smiled. "The Lemon Drop Social Club."

I laughed, and Henry grinned as he leaned over the bar to press a kiss to Jack's lips.

Bryce looked confused.

"Peaches are our bread and butter here in Haven Grove," I explained. "But this one," I put an arm around Jack and ruffled his hair, "is all about lemon. Especially Lemon Drops, so it's a perfect name."

Jack shrugged. "I like peach, I just like Lemon Drops better."

"It's a good name, I like it," Bryce said. "Count me in for participating. Do you think we'd need any rules or anything like that?"

Jack pursed his lips. "I think maybe a couple ground rules like being polite, respecting different lived experiences, no drinking and driving, stuff like that. If we find out loose rules aren't going to cut it, we can put something more official into place."

"I think," I started, "you probably need to do somethin' along the lines of no hate of any kind. Let Preacher Holmes and his minions know they aren't welcome if they're going to be spewing anythin' other than acceptance and love."

Bryce gave me a look I couldn't decipher.

"What?"

"Nothing," he said with a shake of his head.

We talked a bit more about Jack's new endeavor, finished off our cake and cocktails, and headed out the door.

The day was bright, the sun warm, and a hint of crispness danced on the air. Fall would be here before we knew it. Which meant cold, snow, and ice would be just around the corner. But for the time being, I took a deep breath and enjoyed the heavy, fragrant scent of summer's last hurrah on the breeze.

"I love that everything is pretty much within walking distance around here. Makes for good exercise, less wear and tear on my car, better for the environment," Bryce paused and took in a deep breath, "...plus, the sunshine and fresh air are good for the soul."

"It's nice when it's not blazin' hot, freezin' cold, or pourin' rain," I groused. "Fall and spring are the best times in Haven Grove, but summer's not too bad. Humidity will kill ya, and the thunderstorms can be wicked."

"Get many tornadoes lately? I remember sitting in the basement at home quite a few times as a kid," Bryce said.

"Thunderstorms—bad wind, hail, lightning...a strike nearly took Hudson out in the orchard not too long ago... those are more prevalent, but we get our fair share of tornadoes being in Tornado Alley. It's been a while since Haven Grove dealt with any twisters, but a few have gone through just about every spring in towns and counties all around us." As we reached the gym, I pulled the door open. "I remember a few far into the fall, too."

"Tornadoes scare the fuck out of me."

"You lived in a place that had earthquakes. No warnin', just *bam* your whole world is shakin' the shit out of everything."

Bryce chuckled. "Yeah, those are shit too. Had plenty of little ones in my time out there. Only maybe one *big* one. Hurricanes, earthquakes, tornadoes, fires, they're all so damn destructive. For some reason, a tornado scares me the most."

"Well, we're lucky we get good internet service for the most part here in town, and our warnin' siren seems to work right. We'll at least get a heads up if one's headin' this way." I picked up the notebook and tore a page out.

"You have a basement?"

"My house and Hudson's have storm cellars. Henry's got a cellar attached to the Roadhouse." I tapped a pen against the paper. "In here?" I glanced toward the huge windows and winced. "Not out here. Inner most area is probably the locker rooms or where the washer and dryer are."

Bryce shivered. "Let's hope we never have to find our safe space."

I gave a nod and turned my attention to the paper. "Let's make a list of things we can probably order through Hudson at the store and things we'll need to go up the road for. We can use my truck for any of the big things. You good with orderin' today, a shopping trip tomorrow, and getting' started day after?" I gestured toward the run-down area. "I'm itchin' to get this place fixed up. Gonna look real good with equipment and clients."

"Sounds good. Think we can do some cleaning today? Thought we could at least start making piles of shit that need to go."

"Yeah." I scribbled on the notepaper. "We can rent a dumpster. I know a guy who will give us a good deal."

Bryce cocked his head with that same look he gave me at the Roadhouse.

"What? Why you keep lookin' at me like that?"

He shook his head. "You're not the asshole you want people to think you are."

I scoffed. "Don't *want* people thinkin' nothin' about me. What they think is their own business."

Bryce shook his head. "No, you hide behind being cranky. You keep up a façade while spewin' shit without a filter. But you're a good guy. Might be deep, deep down, but the true heart of Casey Joe Riggs is good and gentle."

"Fuck off," I grumbled.

Bryce laughed. "You know, I'm really surprised you're as accepting of your boys as you are."

My papa bear bristled immediately, and I crossed my arms over my chest. "What the fuck's that mean?"

He held up a hand. "I'm just saying, most of the people I grew up with fall into two categories. Those who left our small town and experienced more of the world usually ended up being more accepting and open-minded. Those who stayed in or around the area are a lot more likely to be pretty damn bigoted." Bryce gestured toward the windows. "You grew up here, so I would have guessed you fell into the second category, but you don't."

All the bluster left my sails, and I cleared my throat. "Yeah, well. I grew up with bigots for parents. Honestly, probably would have ended up that way myself if it hadn't been for my boys. Not gonna lie and say there's nothin' in my past I'm a bit ashamed of—I'm not perfect, and I did and said some things that weren't right." I shook my head. A brief flash of memories from way back then—when I felt things I didn't understand, when I knew damn well I didn't have a soul I could tell or ask questions—played through my mind. "I buried a lot back then. If I ignored it, it didn't exist. My parents were doin' enough hatin' for all of us—if someone didn't look like us, love like us, worship like us, speak like us…well, you get the picture. I lost myself in my own drama for so long, I really didn't have the energy or time to hate—too busy raisin' my boys and drownin' in a broken heart. When my boys came out to me in their own ways at their own times, deep down, I knew I had two options. I could carry on the hate I'd grown up with or keep on lovin' my boys the way I had since the moment I knew they existed. Hudson being gay and Henry being bi and demi didn't change a single thing about how much I loved them. I was maybe a little confused and unsure in the beginning, but I asked questions—probably too many if the boys were to tell it— and I educated myself."

I also let tiny bits of wondering, doubt, fear, and hope trickle into my own life, but those came slower than a snail's pace and were things I wasn't sure if or when I'd ever be ready to examine any further than my therapist's couch.

But then I caught Bryce's eyes on me. His curiosity, his genuine interest, the true connection I already knew I had with him. And a sliver of my soul wanted to pour it all out. Tell him about my past. Spill everything I'd been exploring about myself. Ask him about his own journey.

Instead, I took a cleansing breath and returned to my story. "If it weren't for my boys, I might have turned out to be a bigoted, racist, homophobic asshole. But I wanted better for them. I wanted better for *me*. I know I'm a privileged, cis white guy. I know I have the same implicit biases as the next person, but I try to keep learnin' and keep betterin' myself." I shrugged. "Most people seein' me or meetin' me for the first time probably think I'm a homophobic, racist, sexist asshole. I don't mind them makin' that judgement. And I don't set out to prove them wrong, but I do try my best to live in a way my boys can be proud of when they look back at their time with me." I huffed out a humorless laugh as I leaned my elbows on the counter. "I screwed up so much in so many other ways, the least I can do is give them that."

The warmth of Bryce's hand on mine took a moment to register, but then I froze. My eyes bore holes into the place where his skin burned against mine. "You've spent too long carrying that load—"

I cleared my throat, pulled my hand from under his, and scribbled some nonsense on the notepad. "Need to get over to see Hudson if we're going to get this order placed."

"Case—"

"Probably get some junk piles started, and once we get a dumpster delivered, we'll be good to go."

Bryce sighed. "Yeah, sounds good. Let's get going."

Chapter 8
Bryce

"Oh my god," Hudson crowed as he walked through the gym doors. "Is this a gym or music time at the senior citizen center?"

"Shut the fuck up," Casey shot back. Standing from his current project, which consisted of replacing and patching drywall, he pointed a finger at his youngest. "Don't come in here with that shit."

"Carrie" by Europe played from the speakers of an old boombox style radio, cassette, CD player we'd found in a closet while cleaning out the junk. We'd spent a couple days clearing out shit we didn't need before we could really get started on the renovation.

Things had gotten a bit weird with Casey Joe for a moment, but he seemed to want to ignore things—which appeared to be one of his finely-honed skills if I had to guess based on the short time I'd known the man—and I was fine with following his lead for the time being. We'd found a pretty good routine living and working together, and I wasn't about to push any boundaries. At least not yet. I considered the guy a friend, but I wasn't going to overstep.

"If you're playing that on a tape, I'm going to call the nursing home and see about getting you a room," Hudson went on, his smile huge, and his blue eyes sparkling.

"Get your child," Casey Joe bit out as Lance came through the doors. "I won't be disrespected."

Hudson cackled. "I can't help it. Old people music creeps me out."

Lance rolled his eyes. "This isn't *old people* music. We aren't *old*."

"Whatever you say, babe," Hudson said, smacking a kiss to Lance's lips. "Y'all might not be old, but this music is a total downer."

"He's not wrong," I said with a wink for Casey Joe.

"Sorry, I popped a—" he glared at Hudson, "—fuckin' CD in and hit play. Wasn't trying to set the damn mood."

"Well, get yourselves in a social mood because Jack is really nervous about his first Lemon Drop meeting, and he's being cute as hell." Hudson glanced around the gym. "I'm so pumped for when this is open. Swear, I'm gonna be your first client."

"Double chargin' you for a damn membership," Casey groused. He made one more swipe of spackling. "Better call it if we're gonna get cleaned up and over there in time."

Jack had let his social club idea take hold, and he'd been making plans left and right ever since. He'd opted for

a soft type launch with very little fanfare. A few signs at
the Roadhouse and around town, plus a newsletter
announcement to those who were local was all the
advertising he'd done. Part of me worried he'd have way
too many folks show up, and part of me worried he
wouldn't have any.

Everyone loved Jack. Everyone loved Henry. Hell, the
Riggs family was pretty much universally loved in and
around Haven Grove, so I didn't think Jack would have
much trouble getting people to come to his shindig, but I
still wanted to be there to show my support in case the
word hadn't gotten around town for this first one.

Being in Haven Grove, feeling so welcome and
comfortable so quickly, was a huge difference for me. I'd
been right on the edge of popular back in high school. In
college, I pretty much toed the same line. I fit in fine with
pretty much all the groups of people, even if I never really
felt like I belonged to any of them.

Once I was on my own and building my career, things
pretty much continued the same way. I was kinda like a
chameleon with all the people I interacted with on a
regular basis. I adjusted to what they needed me to be. I
played the part. I put up the façade. They either never
caught on I wasn't really one of them, or they just didn't
care. I was good for their image, and in ways that counted
the most—or the least, depending on how you looked at it
—they were good for mine.

But never once did I feel like I belonged with them.
Never once did I feel like I was welcome or safe. I'd gone
forty-eight years just coasting through life, barely

skimming the surface of relationships—never digging deep into anything real—and I wanted more.

Of course, it had taken me half my life to realize and admit I wanted more.

But there I was.

Coming back home had done something for my heart I hadn't realized I needed. Moving to Haven Grove had been the reset I so desperately longed for. Meeting the Riggs family and folks around town was a fresh start, and my soul was absolutely giddy with the idea of having friends to spend the next half of my life with.

To *build* a life with.

"We just wanted to stop by and—"

"Give us shit about our music?" Casey Joe interrupted Lance.

His best friend smiled and wrapped his arm around Hudson's waist. "*I* wanted to see the progress on the gym."

"I wanted to see the progress *and* give you shit," Hudson said. "Just so happens you were playing elderly music. You make it so easy sometimes." He snapped his fingers. "Oh, shit. I forgot. Henry wanted me to ask about your appointment. It's this week, right? You want one of us to go with you?"

Casey Joe scowled. "I'm fifty-fuckin'-four. Think I can drag my sorry ass to a doctor appointment without my boys holdin' my hand." He put the lid back on the spackling. "Can even wipe my own ass if you can believe that," he muttered.

"We just wanted to make sure you knew we're willing

to go," Hudson said, only the slightest tinge of hurt in his voice.

"That's what friends and family do for each other." Lance gave Casey a none-too-happy look.

Casey shoved a Dum Dum in his mouth and grunted. "Yeah, yeah. I know. But I'm good. Thanks."

"You'll let us know what they say about your numbers, right?" Hudson asked. "You've been following the doctor's advice on food and exercise?"

"Made it this damn fuckin' far in life, pretty sure I can make it at least a few more years. I'm done talkin' about fuckin' medical shit," Casey Joe growled around the sucker. "We'll see you there." He gave a wave and headed toward the back where I assumed he'd stomp up the stairs to our apartment so he could get ready.

I glanced at Hudson and Lance. "Seems he's…"

"An asshole who gets super anxious about doctor appointments because he's worried he's dying, but he's not been willing or able to commit to healthier eating and exercise?" Hudson offered. "Yeah, seems he is." He ran a hand over his eyes. "I offered to run with him. I offered to do weights with him. I mean, it's good he's stopped smoking—like, really good; I never really thought he'd be able to do that—but I know he's still eating like shit and drinking too much."

"He won't change until he's ready," I said. "But I'll work on things on my end."

Hudson and Lance both looked at me like I'd grown two heads.

"What?"

"Why would you be willing to help someone you

barely know? Especially when he's such an asshole most the time?" Hudson asked.

I shrugged. "When you grew up in the small-town way of life, and you move away, you find yourself missing parts of it. I didn't realize how much of it was still engrained in me until I came back." I glanced toward the back of the gym. "You all have been good to me when you didn't really have to be."

"You're a good person," Lance said with a smile. "Believe me, small towns know. Small town hospitality is something given to most without question, but everyone recognizes when there's something special about a newcomer."

"Probably smelled the small town on you," Hudson teased. "Like dogs. We recognize our own."

I laughed. "Well, I'm grateful for it. Casey is someone I consider a friend."

Hudson and Lance exchanged a look before giving me raised brows.

"What?"

"My dad doesn't have a lot of friends."

I huffed out a laugh.

"No, really. Casey doesn't have a lot of friends. I'm here because I knew him before. But most people won't put up with his shit," Lance said.

"He's not that bad."

Their eyes remained fixed on me like they were waiting for the punchline of a joke.

"He's not." I looked toward the back again. "He's a grump, and he has a foul mouth, but his bark is worse than his bite. I kinda get it, though. He's had a lot to deal with, and his health is something scary. I can't imagine having a heart attack and not knowing if I was going to live or die." I shoved my hands into the pockets of my work jeans.

"Yeah, but he was an asshole before his heart attack," Hudson said. "Kinda even more of one." He gestured between him and Lance. "We put up with him because he's family, we love him, but a lot of people won't deal with it."

Lance nodded. "I mean, the town pretty much loves him, but most of them have known him as long as we have. Anyone he's tried to..." His words trailed off. "Well, I don't know that he's dated anyone, but I know he doesn't do well getting to know people or letting down his guard."

"Maybe that's why we hit it off. No expectations. No guards up or down."

Hudson shrugged. "If you say so. I'm glad he hasn't run you off. Not sure what's gonna happen if you tell him he needs to eat healthy though."

I laughed. "Oh, I already took the brunt of that misguided conversation. You know the saying about when you know better, you do better? Well, I know better now." I winked. "I know he likes snacks and shit. I'll try to have some healthier options for him. Or maybe try to fill him up with healthier meals so he's not hungry for the junky snacks."

Lance nodded toward the expanse of unrenovated gym. "Maybe once this is up and running, he'll be more willing to work out. We can all make it a point to get here and put in the work, that way he can join us if he wants."

Hudson sighed. "I know he has to be willing to do it himself, we can't force him to. The heart attack scared him so bad he stopped smoking—even though I have to say I won't be at all surprised if he starts back up—but he's not taken the other steps." He shook his head, shoulders slumping. "Baby steps I guess, but I worry he doesn't have the luxury of baby steps if he doesn't take control of shit."

Lance pulled Hudson close to his side and pressed a kiss to the younger man's temple. "We'll keep at it." He glanced at me. "See you there?"

"Yeah, we'll be there. Just gotta shower."

Hudson and Lance left, and I locked the door behind them before heading to the back. I stopped dead in my tracks when I found Casey Joe with only a towel around his waist holding up a pair of my jockstrap style underwear.

He needed to put on some weight, but his back was broad; firm and sinewy, hard lines, and soft shadows. At fifty-four, he looked damn good. Maybe not body builder fit, but the wide shoulders, thick torso leading down to a trim waist, and solid thighs under the white terrycloth were all definitely enough to have my imagination getting all sorts of lusty.

I must have made a sound—oh god, I hoped it wasn't a whimper—because Casey whirled around with my underwear in his fist.

"What the fuck is this?"

"A jockstrap." I grabbed it from him and shouldered past to get the rest of the laundry from the dryer.

"But for what?"

"It's called underwear. Most people wear it under their

clothes." One thing about whatever Casey Joe and I had been building, I wasn't one to back off when he got mouthy. I gave it right back, and I truly thought it was one of the reasons we'd kinda hit it off right away.

His family wasn't *scared* of him, but they sometimes let him get by with shit. Folks around town were maybe slightly hesitant when Casey was running his mouth. Those who loved him thought it was...endearing? Those who weren't a fan used it as a reason to keep their distance.

But me? Hell, no. I liked the guy. I enjoyed spending time with him. We'd figured out we were pretty good roommates and co-workers. But there was no way in hell he was going to shoot off at the mouth and get me to back down.

Throwing the last piece into the basket, I slammed the dryer shut. We'd opted to throw our clothes in together recently since neither of us were doing huge loads of laundry. I hadn't thought about Casey seeing the jockstrap or any of my other underwear.

"Most people wear boxers or briefs or even boxer briefs." He frowned. "Don't they?" Casey pinched the bridge of his nose. "Hell, I had the misfortune of once seeing Jack in this skimpy little pair of pink bikini shit." He winced. "Don't know what's wrong with regular underwear."

"These are regular underwear." I shook the jock. "People can wear whatever they want. Damn man, what would you do if I was one of those guys who likes silk or lace?"

The look on Casey's face had me snorting.

I tossed the jock in with the rest of the clothes and hefted the basket.

"Wait, what? Do you?" Casey crossed his arms over his broad chest as I turned with the basket, and I tried my best to avoid looking at the smattering of crisp, brown hair over his pecs, down his abs, and disappearing under the towel.

"No, I stick to mostly boxer briefs, jocks, and the occasional bikini depending on..." I paused and considered my words. "...things."

"Things?" Casey Joe scowled. "What things?"

I turned to go, and he grabbed my arm.

"No. What fuckin' things?" His skin burned on mine, and we both looked to where our bodies joined. "I'm askin' for damn real. What fuckin' things? I'll be damned if I'm doin' underwear wrong. I got some boxers, and I got some briefs. I wear them until I'm almost out, wash 'em, and start over. And now you tell me I gotta think about silk and lace? Jocks? And certain times I need to wear certain types? Never thought about which ones to wear when; just put on whatever I grab."

Taking a deep breath, I put the basket back on the dryer. Letting the breath out slowly, I turned toward Casey. "Don't ask questions you don't want the answer to."

He snorted. "If I didn't want the fuckin' answer, I wouldn't've asked the fuckin' question."

I rolled my eyes. "Fine. Sometimes I wear certain underwear depending on what type of...activities I think I might be getting up to."

"Like basketball? Or working out?"

"Sometimes, or sometimes other things."

Casey stared at me.

I stared back.

And sighed.

"If I think I might have reason to be seen in something a bit sexier, or I think I might want something that provides easy...access..." I let my words trail off.

For a moment, my words had zero effect. And then realization flashed over Casey's face, and I had to bite my lip from laughing.

He appeared to be thinking over my words for a bit, but then he said, "Wait. You just wore those? Who was seein' your fuckin' drawers? Easy access? Who the fuck you givin' easy access? You on that ClickC*ck app? You gotta be damn careful with those guys. Hudson and Lance have told me some stories."

At that point, I did laugh. "Calm the fuck down. I wore them recently because I was out of clean laundry. But I like the way my ass looks in them. Some days are made for jocks, some days are perfect for bikinis, and some days are just right for whatever I grab from my drawer." I grabbed the basket and headed toward the back door. "Come on, we're going to be late."

A split second later, Casey Joe was following me up the stairs. "Wait, what do you mean you like the way your ass looks in them? Doesn't an ass in a jock just look like an ass in a jock? What do they do for your ass?"

I just chuckled as we made our way through the door. "Hurry up with your shower." I walked into my room, letting the door click closed behind me, and moving quickly to close the bathroom door between our rooms.

"Damn it, Bryce!" Casey Joe yelled from the hallway. "What do they do to your ass?"

I hoped he took a long enough shower for me to deal with the damn problem he'd caused in my pants by talking about ass and underwear.

Chapter 9
Casey Joe

WE GOT TO THE ROADHOUSE BEFORE THE EVENT was scheduled to start. Figured it would help Jack if we were there to help instead of showing up with the crowd.

Luckily, we'd walked over because I needed some time to clear my head and work out some energy.

Bryce's jock had thrown me for a loop.

I knew what a damn jockstrap was. Hell, I'd played sports. My boys had played sports. That wasn't the problem.

The problem was my brain couldn't wrap around Bryce wearing a jock outside of a sporting event. When he told me the *why* behind wearing that type of underwear, I'm pretty sure major synapses inside my gray matter ceased to exist.

Images from middle school and high school flashed through my mind. Back then, confusion, fear, longing, and curiosity blanketed my thoughts as heavily as the thick steam from the locker room showers.

And, if I was being honest, that same soup of emotions—

Nope.

Not going there.

There was no damn reason for me to be thinking about underwear or asses.

Not back then.

Not currently.

And definitely not when it came to Bryce fuckin' Armstrong.

"So, I was thinking we'd have everything outside since the weather is nice," Jack said as he carried a covered tray to the outdoor dining area. "I have pitchers of sweet tea, unsweet tea, lemon cucumber water, and sangria." He winced. "Is that all too summery? Should I have gone with more fall-ish drinks?"

"Summer is still holding on," Lance said. "I think you're fine. You can switch things up next time."

Jack relaxed and nodded. "The bar out here is stocked for pretty much anything as long as it's not too terribly complicated." He gestured toward the table. "I decided on a peach chiffon cake with raspberry preserves, a key lime and dark chocolate cake, and a brown butter caramel cake. I don't think we'll have so many people we'll run out of cake."

"Oh, you sweet, sweet child," Hudson crooned as he pressed himself to Jack's side and wrapped him in a hug. "You could have zero guests show up, and you'd still run out of cake. Just let me loose with a fork."

I smacked the back of his head. "Don't be greedy. We all get some."

I knew damn well I needed to watch what I ate. I was still consuming way too many sweets. I'd done pretty decent with cutting down on the fried, fatty foods, but snacks were my weakness. Chips, honey buns, *cake*. Part of it was because it all tasted so damn good, and part of it was my brain telling me no one got to tell me what I could or couldn't eat, and if I wanted to eat junk, I could.

Add in the fact I'd kept up with trying to kick the cigarettes, and snacks were damn hard to get rid of.

"Everyone can have a full-size piece of one cake or a sample-size of all three," Jack said. "There's plenty." He walked around the open area. "I think there's room for everyone. People can talk, we'll have music playing, drinks. Henry made a great veggie and fruit spread." He turned panicked eyes my way. "Oh god, what if no one shows up, and I look like a total loser with all this food and no one wanting to socialize?"

"Fuck 'em. We can all socialize. We don't need nobody else." I grabbed Jack and ruffled his hair.

"Yeah," Hudson agreed. "Just don't let Dad pick the music or everyone will ask for their senior discount and leave early to get home to watch the early news before soaking their dentures and heading to bed."

"Go home," I groused. "Children aren't welcome at the Lemon Drop Social Club."

Hudson laughed and dodged the arm I sent out to grab him.

The anxiety on Jack's face eased, and a grin softened his face when Henry came outside with a very large platter of veggies, fruit, cheese cubes, and dips.

"Mmm, I'll try the cake, but that looks amazing," Bryce

said. He truly looked like he was almost drooling over carrots, broccoli, and strawberries. "Oh my god, is that a cream cheese dip?"

"Yep, there's a brown sugar one and a strawberry one," Henry said with a tiny grin under his beard. "And a garden pesto dip for the veggies that's to die for."

"It's sooo good," Jack said as he stole a carrot and dunked it in the dip.

"Damn, man. Leave some for us, and no double dippin'." Glancing around for a bowl of chips or pretzels, I gave up and snatched a bell pepper. The dip looked like ranch. "What the fuck is a pesto?"

"Basically, just basil, pine nuts, olive oil, and garlic," Henry said. "I made the dip from mayo, sour cream, pesto, and lemon juice. I think it's best on veggies and pretzel sticks."

I took a bite and chewed.

Henry eyed me. Jack bit his lip.

"Well?" Bryce asked. "Is it good?"

"Be better on a chip," I said, "but it's good." I reached for a carrot. Fuckin' rabbit food. But the pesto dip was fuckin' delicious—not that I was gonna tell them that. Almost like a bag of chips—like when you can't stop reaching back in for more so you can keep the crunch and the flavor coming—my taste buds savored the dip and begged for more. "I could eat it if I had to."

Henry huffed and shook his head. Jack grinned like a parent proud of his kid for eating all his green beans. And Hudson shouldered his way in front of me to dip another carrot into the dip.

"How 'bout we save some for everybody else?" Lance suggested.

I grabbed one more carrot and scooped up some dip. "Anything we can help with?"

Jack glanced around and shook his head. "No, I don't think so. As long as people show up, I think things should run pretty smoothly. Maybe if you see people not really socializing, you can pull them into conversation?"

"Do you want to say a few words at the beginning just to make sure everyone knows what's going on? Set the expectations?" Lance asked.

I'd helped Jack with the flyers, so I knew he'd explained the point of the Lemon Drop Social Club, but I also knew people didn't pay attention worth a shit.

Jack bit his lip and pulled the collar of his shirt up to rub along his chin. "Yeah, that would probably be for the best. Does anyone want to help with that?"

"Maybe we all can back you up?" Hudson asked. "You start it off, and we'll add in anything you might miss? We can see if anyone has questions and go from there."

Jack smiled and looked relieved. "Yeah, that sounds good. I just don't want people to think this is stupid."

Henry put his arm around Jack. "It's not stupid. It's a good idea."

"People like to chit-chat," I said. "I think it will be really popular."

Over the next several minutes, folks began to arrive. Everyone was greeted, shown the food, drinks, bar, and tables. People immediately got themselves water, tea, or drinks from the bar. A few filled plates, while others found seats.

About ten minutes after the official start of the event, Jack cleared his throat. "I wanted to take a minute to tell everyone thank you for coming."

Conversations paused, and the Riggs crew gathered behind Jack as he addressed the guests.

"Most of you know me," Jack continued. "I haven't been in Haven Grove for long, but it's been more of a home for me in the short time I've been here than any other place I've had the misfortune of living."

Henry put his arm around Jack's shoulders, and Jack's eyes lit up like the gentle touch energized him.

"I wanted to start something that would give people the chance to just visit. Maybe one day, we'll raise money for something important or get a group together to volunteer for something. But for now, I just want people to get to know each other and spend time together. There's no set agenda. Talk about books, hobbies, cooking, weather, whatever." Jack glanced at Henry.

With a soft smile that seemed meant only for Jack, Henry went on. "We didn't want to set a lot of rules or regulations. For the time being, keep things civil. Treat others the way you'd want to be treated. The Lemon Drop is open to anyone and everyone, but we won't tolerate bigotry of any kind."

I cleared my throat. "In case you're not sure what bigotry includes, let me clarify." Swiping my phone screen, I read from the bit I'd pieced together from some online definitions. "Bigotry can include, but is not limited to, intolerance, prejudice, discrimination, hostility, and stereotyping based on race, religion, gender, sexual orientation, or gender identity." I put my phone back in my pocket. "Basically, don't be a hateful dick, and everything will be just fine. But if you want to be an asshole, you'll be asked to leave."

As my gaze swept over the gathered people, I recognized most and knew they wouldn't bring problems to the group. Only a few folks in town would raise red flags for me, but I thought it was better to make the blanket statement right away rather than have to bring it up if a problem cropped up later.

Jack clapped his hands together and went on. "If you haven't yet met Bryce, he's the new owner of Armstrong Health & Fitness. Be sure you make him feel welcome, and chat with him about his plans once the gym opens."

I didn't think Bryce had known Jack was going to introduce him like that, but he just smiled at Jack, gave a quick wave, and said, "Thanks for the friendly welcome to Haven Grove. I grew up not too far from here, still have family around these parts. Does a person good to come back home. Casey Joe's been helping me with the gym, and we hope to have it up and running in the new year if not before."

Hudson stepped next to Jack. "One thing Jack is too modest to mention is it costs a decent amount of coin to provide drinks and food for something like this. Jack's idea for this little club was to have it be free for as long as possible. However, if you appreciate the drinks, food, and atmosphere, please be sure to pop a small donation in the jar at some point during the evening."

Henry cut in. "And the bar drinks aren't free, but they *are* discounted just for this group. All bar tips will go toward the next Lemon Drop event."

With all the *official* business taken care of, the group returned to visiting, mingling, and getting food. We were about half an hour in, and things looked to be going exactly as Jack had hoped.

This was good. As much as I'd usually rather scoop my eyeballs out with a rusty spoon than make small talk with random folks around town, the vibe in the outdoor dining area was upbeat and easy. If it meant something to Jack, I could definitely make myself participate every other week.

Hell, the pesto dip alone was likely enough to bring me back.

And the cake was an added bonus.

At one time, the bar would have been a strong pull, but I'd recently had a bit of a breakthrough with my therapist about my reliance on alcohol.

The conversation had been terrible, and I'd hated every single second of it.

I hadn't left with any big plans or promises, but the whole thing had flipped a switch in me. I'd realized just how often I got through a day by drinking, and something deep inside sparked to life with a challenge.

I wasn't naïve enough to think I could just stop cold-turkey, but for the time being, I was feeling pretty determined.

After all, I'd almost died. Alcohol might not have been *the* culprit to my heart attack, but it had likely played a part. If I planned to stick around to see my boys live their lives, the alcohol needed to be gone.

Yeah, yeah, a ton of people had been telling me that since before the heart attack, but I was a belligerent

S.O.B., and telling me to do something was the quickest way to make me refuse just on principal.

Again, my therapist said I was grasping at control in whatever ways I could get it thanks to my past and my health condition.

So, anyway, I'd promised myself I'd stick to tea instead of alcohol at the Lemon Drop, and so far, I'd done well. There was no way I could drink unsweetened tea. I'd found out the hard way that Bryce preferred his iced tea unsweetened when I almost choked to death on the dirt water he had in a pitcher in his fridge. But I'd agreed to swap out real sugar for monk fruit sweetener in my iced tea, and I had to admit it wasn't half bad. Skipping the sugar actually made me feel slightly better about the amount of sweet stuff I was putting in my body—next thing to cut was the damn suckers...if only sugar-free ones came as cheap as good ol' Dum Dums.

Henry eyed me as I walked past the bar.

"What?" I grunted.

"You want a drink?" he asked all tentative, like a man disarming a bomb.

And fuck if that didn't sting.

Hell.

Had my drinking forced everyone to walk on eggshells around me? Fuck it all the way to hell and back again. The last thing I wanted to do was to make my boys and friends have to tiptoe around me.

Shame, guilt, and regret washed over me as a tiny voice whispered, *"You've been doing this to them for years, but now that you've decided it's for the best to cut the shit, it's all good?"*

Nope. Wasn't going there.

I wanted a life with my family and friends. I wanted a life period. It maybe wouldn't be worth living without my boys, but I knew I had to make changes if I was going to be around for them.

"No," I said, raising my iced tea. "I'm good."

I hadn't told anyone I'd set a goal to cut back on the alcohol. I didn't need all those eyes on me. The weight of their expectations.

Honestly, there wasn't a single time in my life when I could remember attending any type of social event—and, let's be honest, I could convince myself a lonely evening by the firepit was a social event—without plying myself with some sort of alcohol.

The whole situation had me a mix of anxious, proud, on-edge, and waiting for the moment when I fucked up. When one word or action from someone would remind me of all the shit in my past and have me reaching for something to dull it all.

But so far, the iced tea, veggies and fruit, and cake had kept me satisfied. Bryce had been by my side for much of the evening, letting me introduce him to people he hadn't yet met, keeping the conversation going when I might have crept toward being a bit too prickly. At one point, I nearly stopped breathing when he patted my jeans pocket, but I quickly realized he was suggesting a sucker.

And damn if he wasn't right. The cravings were lessening in frequency, but they hadn't decreased in severity. The little globe of sugar helped, but the cardboard stick seemed to be the part that eased my tension the most. I missed the long drag on a smoke, the instant rush the nicotine provided, the all-over wash of calm, but I'd realized after I quit smoking that having something to do with my mouth and hands was one of the hardest habits to break.

A flash of conversation danced through my mind from a few nights before.

"I wish I could get rid of the suckers," I'd said, rolling the stick between my fingers. *"Feels like I'm rottin' my damn teeth out. Lance says it's better to lose my teeth than die, but they constantly feel furry like they're wearin' little sugary fur coats."*

Bryce had laughed. "What if we got you some sugar-free candy? Jack had some kind of lemon drops the other day, and they didn't have the bad kind of artificial sweeteners."

"It's the stick. It's like my brain and body have accepted they aren't gettin' the nicotine, but I can't get past needin' something to do with my mouth and hand."

The look Bryce had given me had lasted a beat too long, and I'd been forced to replay my words. When I'd huffed and rolled my eyes, Bryce had grinned like a loon. "I'm just gonna put it out there," he'd said, "in the interest of your health and being a good friend, I'm always willing to help with mouth and hand activities."

"Fuck off," I'd said around the sucker, but I hadn't been able to keep the laughter from my words. *"I used to smoke about a pack a day, pretty sure ain't no one want to deal with that many blow jobs a day."*

"Don't knock it 'til you try it," Bryce had teased.

I snorted and chomped on the sucker, preferring the crunchy sugar and possible broken tooth to the potentially dangerous images Bryce's words had ignited in my mind.

"I'd like it noted for the record," Bryce went on, *"that you didn't say no."*

"I'm not blowin' you every time I need a smoke."

Bryce had smiled and waggled his brows. "Who said anything about you blowing me?"

His words sent a jolt through me as I considered what he meant.

Fuck.

"Offer stands," he'd said with a wink before he went back to applying painters' tape to the walls.

I eyed the cake, but the sucker had coated my mouth in such sweetness, I didn't know if I could stomach the dessert. The carrots wouldn't have ever been my top choice, but the dip was damn good, so I scooped some of the pesto shit into a bowl and placed about ten carrots off to the side.

Luckily, I could stand to gain some pounds if I was going to turn it back into muscle—that was my plan once the gym was open—because I was basically eating my weight since I stopped smoking. But carrots were good for you, right? My ticker might not be the healthiest, but I'd have the best damn eyesight in Haven Grove as long as they kept plying me with that damn dip.

Bryce came over and snagged a carrot just as the Roadhouse door opened. Two people walked from inside the restaurant to the outdoor dining area.

An older lady I recognized as the tenant in Lance's apartment and another older woman completed the duo.

Nothing struck me as significant about any of them, but Bryce whispered, "Holy shit," as he sucked in a breath, began coughing on what I assumed was a carrot trying to kill him, and choked out, "Dizzy?"

Chapter 10
Bryce

"YOU OKAY?" CASEY JOE ASKED ME AS DIZZY beelined toward me.

I cleared the chunk of carrot from my throat. "Yeah, just took me by surprise," I replied as the short, round fireball who looked just like her sister opened her arms and wrapped me in a tight hug.

"There's my Brycey," she cooed, leaning back to look up at me and pat my cheek.

"Dizzy?" I couldn't help the shock. "What in the heck are you doing here?"

True, she and my parents didn't live far away from Haven Grove, but I hadn't expected her to show up at Jack's social club.

"Heard about this fancy little cake place a while back. When Barb told me she'd moved here, I knew I'd need to come visit and check out the cake." Dizzy gestured toward the older woman who'd arrived with her and was chatting with Lance and Hudson. "But when she told me about this

Lemon Drop Social Club, I all but ran my fat ass over here." She slapped her backside. "And let me tell you, that's not easy when your legs are as short as mine."

I gave her another hug. "Well, it's good to see you. Let me introduce you." I turned toward Casey. "This is my roommate, Casey Joe. He's helping me renovate the gym." Something weird pulled in my gut as I spoke the words, like I wanted to say more about Casey, but not knowing if I had that right. "Casey, this is my aunt, Delores. She was Dezzy most of her life, but my sister always called her Dizzy, and it's stuck ever since. She's my mom's sister."

Casey Joe, for all his grousing and cursing, was the type with manners instilled deep down, and he offered his hand for a shake. "Nice to meet you," he started, but Dizzy slapped his hand away and wrapped him in a hug.

His slight grunt and the way his wide eyes stared at me over her head made me smile. He liked people to think he was gruff, but my spitfire aunt had just hugged the fight right out of him.

"So good to meet you," Dizzy said. "If you're friends with my Brycey, you're fine by me."

Casey Joe mouthed, "Brycey?" over my aunt's head with a grin.

I huffed and rolled my eyes. "Come on, you can meet everyone else."

We made our way to Hudson, Lance, and Barb. Before I could even make introductions, Dizzy interrupted.

"This is my friend from way back in elementary school, Barb Jackson. I believe you know her from renting an apartment over an ice cream shop?" Dizzy patted her friend's shoulder.

Greetings were given, and I introduced Hudson and Lance to my aunt before motioning for Henry and Jack to join us. Another round of introductions was made, niceties exchanged, and Dizzy hooked her arm in mine.

"Okay, let's take a look at these cake options," she said as she pulled me toward the food.

Jack absolutely glowed as he described his cakes to Dizzy and Barb. Everyone took slivers of cake, and we all made our way to a table. Dizzy and Barb raved over Jack's cake. The kid was seriously adorable the way he blushed and preened under their kind words.

I noticed Casey Joe going to town on the carrots, peppers, and dip—leaving the cake untouched for the time being. The way his knee bounced, and his hand shook didn't escape me. I knew him well enough by now to recognize a cigarette craving.

Grateful no one at the table had gotten cocktails since I had a feeling Casey would have struggled to abstain from both alcohol and nicotine, I reached into my pocket and pulled out a rubber band.

"Meant to give this to you earlier," I said, hopefully quietly enough only he could hear. I purposely didn't linger at his ear, but the man's scent was intoxicating all the same.

Casey looked at the rubber band, glanced up at me, and scowled. But after shoving another carrot in his mouth, he yanked the stretchy band over his hand. It fit snuggly on his wrist, and he immediately snapped it.

"Ow, fuck," he growled.

"What's wrong, dear?" Dizzy asked.

Casey Joe's cheeks pinked. "Sorry." He held up his

wrist. "Tryin' to quit smokin'. Been chompin' on Dum Dums like there's no tomorrow, thought I'd maybe try this to help redirect the cravings and avert the rotten teeth."

Dizzy nodded. "I've heard of that working for many people. Good for you. It's never too late to do what's best for your health and well-being."

Casey Joe stared for just a moment too long before shaking his head as if to reset himself. "Yeah, guess so. At least that's what my doctor says. *Smokin' bad, veggies and exercise good.*" He forked up a bite of cake like a petulant child just daring someone to say something to him.

"Oh, if you're trying to shape up and get healthy, you've found the perfect guy for the job." Dizzy beamed at me. "He's the best."

"We'll be fitting in some workouts once the gym is ready," I said in hopes of satisfying my aunt without provoking a tirade from Casey.

"Speaking of the best," Dizzy went on as if I hadn't even spoken. "A friend of a friend has a cousin who has a nephew—"

I groaned. "Not this again."

Dizzy shushed me. "This one is better than the last, I promise."

Running a hand over my face in hopes of some patience, I said, "The last one spent the entire dinner regaling me with stories of every single man he'd ever dated and extensive reasons they were wrong for breaking up with him."

Dizzy waved me off. "Never you mind that, this guy is perfect for you."

"Have you even met him?" The way her cheeks pinked

answered my question before she could. I groaned again and rolled my eyes.

"You deserve to meet someone, fall in love, and be happy."

"I *am* happy," I argued. My aunt meant well, but she had a long track record of setting me up with people simply because we were both gay. So far, she'd mentioned about twenty guys, and actually attempted three set-ups. In the end, all three had stolen hours from my life I'd never get back.

One guy was attractive, but a fence post had more personality.

The second guy had been very sweet and easy to talk to, but he'd been looking for something a lot more serious and permanent than I'd been ready for at that time.

The third guy was the storyteller.

Dizzy was oh-for-three—and none of the other seventeen had even come close to making the cut based on the details she'd provided—and I had very little faith this current guy would turn out any better.

"But *are* you?" Dizzy crossed her arms and narrowed her eyes. "You aren't getting any younger." She patted my arm. "I just want someone else to love you as much as we all do."

I sighed. "Yes, I *am* happy." It wasn't that I was against meeting someone and falling in love. I actually wanted that to happen if it was meant to be. I just didn't think I had it in me to lose another evening of my life to one of Dizzy's well-intentioned-but-terrible set-ups.

"When was the last time you went on a date?" my aunt pushed.

Damn woman was like a kid picking at a scab.

"I—"

Casey Joe cleared his throat. "Haven't had a whole lot of time for goin' out since we've been workin' so much on the gym, but I promise I'll take him somewhere real nice when we're all done."

Almost gave myself whiplash as my eyes flew to Casey. Shit.

Did he know how that sounded?

"Oh," Dizzy said, eyes wide as she glanced back and forth between us. "I didn't realize…"

Casey shoveled another bite of cake into his mouth. "We'd planned on keepin' it quiet for the time bein'. Small town gossip and all that. You know how it is."

What the hell was he doing?

I tried to catch his attention.

Abort! Abort!

"Well," Dizzy said, leaning in to whisper like she held the world's most important secret. "You don't have to worry about me. I can keep my mouth shut." Then she did a little shimmy in her seat. "Ohhh, this is so exciting. I just knew the moment I saw you two together there was something special between you."

Casey chomped down hard on another carrot as he gave a hesitant grin.

I forced a smile and tried not to snort at the look of amusement and wonder lighting up Lance and Hudson's faces. "Appreciate it if you keep it quiet for now. We've got a good friendship, and we don't want to mess that up if this doesn't work out."

"Oh, of course." Dizzy nodded solemnly.

There.

I set us up with an out.

We could "break up" a bit down the road, tell Dizzy we'd decided we were better off as friends, and she'd be none the wiser.

When my aunt turned to Jack to ask something about the brown butter caramel cake, I gripped Casey Joe's elbow and gritted out, "Can I talk to you a second?"

He glanced at where my hand held his arm, but shrugged, and popped another carrot in his mouth.

I stood, hoping Dizzy was too into Jack's description of browning butter, and walked toward the side of the Roadhouse. By the time Casey Joe sauntered his way over, I was pacing by the steps to Jack and Henry's apartment.

"What the actual fuck, Case?" I asked.

"What the fuck, what?" Casey asked.

"You just told my aunt we're dating."

"Yeah, so?" Casey Joe shrugged. "Got her off your back, right?"

"You don't care that anyone within earshot now thinks you're gay and dating me?" I wasn't in a full-blown panic.

Yet.

He shrugged again and gave tiny snaps to the rubber band. "First of all, if we were datin', I wouldn't necessarily be gay. I could be bi or pan."

I sighed and ran a hand over my face. "Okay, that's true. Sorry."

"Second, this town knows I have two queer sons. They know my best friend is bi. The whole damn town knows my shit history. Them thinkin' I'm bi and datin' you wouldn't even be a blip on the radar of my life." Casey leaned up against the wall of the Roadhouse and propped himself up on a bended knee with a huff and shake of his head. "Woulda made things a lot easier way back then," he muttered.

"What?"

"Nothin'. What's got you so worked up?"

"Dizzy thinks we're dating!" I hissed, gesturing wildly toward where we'd come from.

"Damn, here I thought I'd get a fuckin' thank you for haulin' your ass out of what sounded like another shitty blind date." He tapped a big boot against the wall and snapped the rubber band again and again. "Sorry if I fucked things up. It didn't sound like you wanted her to set you up."

I moved in closer and took his wrist. Rubbing a thumb over the bright red skin, I sighed. "I didn't. I appreciate the save. But now she's going to expect us to be a thing, and I don't want to put you in that situation."

Casey stared down at where my thumb absently caressed his wrist. "How bad can it be? It's not like she lives here. We can tell her we decided we'd be better off as friends."

Unable to tear my eyes away from where we touched, I nodded. "Yeah, I guess. We'll give it a bit, and then we can tell her the next time we see her."

Just as I started to drop Casey's wrist, he gripped my forearm, his big hand heavy and warm against my flesh. "Would it really be that bad?"

"Huh?" Every brain cell was MIA.

"Datin' me," he said, leaning in close enough I could

smell him—citrusy and fresh mixed with something uniquely Casey Joe. "Would it be that bad?"

His words punched me in the gut, taking my next breath as my mind tried to process his words.

Fuck no, it wouldn't be that bad.

Not at all.

This cranky man with no filter had somehow become one of the most important parts of each and every one of my days. I'd be more than okay with the two of us trying to make something of the connection we'd already established.

I shook my head.

Clearing my chaotic thoughts? Answering his question?

Honestly, I wasn't sure.

"Damn right it wouldn't," Casey mumbled, his breath fluttering over my ear before he pushed off from the wall and walked back toward the gathering.

With every single part of my brain scrambling to make sense of what had just happened, I followed.

And arrived just in time to hear Aunt Dizzy say, "Well, you boys will just have to come to dinner soon."

Fuck.

Chapter 11
Casey Joe

WHAT THE FUCK HAD I DONE?

The toe of my work boot tapped double-time as I waited for the damn doctor to see me the day after I purposely let Bryce's aunt think we were dating.

I had a love-hate relationship with doctors.

On one hand, they'd helped to keep me alive back when my damn heart wanted to take me out.

On the other hand, I hated all the changes they wanted me to make.

Yeah, yeah, I knew the changes were for *my* benefit, and if I wanted to keep on keepin' on, I needed to follow their advice.

Didn't mean I liked sitting in the damn waiting room.

Waiting.

Waiting.

And fuckin' waiting some more.

Why was it so many places demanded *I* had to be on time or risk them cancelling my appointment or charging me a fee, but they could damn well keep me waiting until my dick shriveled up from old age?

I snapped the rubber band on my wrist.

Fuck.

I knew damn well my check-up wasn't going to go well.

I'd known it for weeks.

Was I doing a good job with cutting out the smokes and not drinking as much?

Fuck yeah, I was, and I honestly thought I should be getting a bit more praise for what a damn good job I was doing.

Did people think it was easy to just drop a lifetime of cigarettes and drinking?

You know damn well you've got more of a problem with alcohol than what drinking a little less is going to help, an annoying little voice at the back of my head nagged.

I tapped my boot harder and faster.

And you know you haven't exercised worth a shit, and you're still eating pretty much like garbage, the voiced continued to bitch.

I snapped the rubber band so hard it brought tears to my eyes and fought the urge to stomp my boot heel.

Yeah, so what? I wasn't doing as well as I should have been. It wasn't great, but it was better than nothing.

All this shit was why I'd gone and told Dizzy that Bryce and I were dating.

I was stressed, I wanted to help a friend, and I wasn't thinking clearly due to wanting a cigarette and a beer.

Period.

End of story.

The bitchy little voice in my head cackled.

Mmhm, okay. Go ahead and tell yourself whatever lies you think will help you sleep better, big guy.

"Shut up," I muttered, snapping the rubber band before giving up. Unwrapping a sucker, I shoved it in my mouth. Probably would end up with scars on my damn wrist from the band along with my fuckin' teeth rotting out.

But I knew the fuckin' voice in my head was right.

And that knowledge fuckin' terrified me, while at the same time had my heartbeat racing in a way that had nothing to do with my cardiovascular health.

Deep down—no masks, no bullshit, no lies—I was looking forward to having an excuse to be close to Bryce outside of working on the gym and living together.

A few "dates" for Dizzy, and we'd let the farce run out with the claim of *staying friends*. She'd leave Bryce alone for a while, he'd get a reprieve, and—well, what was I getting out of it?

What, indeed.

Fuck if I knew.

Mmhm, keep up the lies, you big lunkhead. How you going to deal with the "breakup"? You think you can just enjoy a few fake dates and then go on your merry way? And how you going to feel about Bryce finding someone new after you two split up?

A fist gripped my heart, and it had nothing to do with how well I'd been taking care of myself. The thought of pretending to date Bryce, pretending to break up, and him dating other guys for real had my stomach churning.

My brain rolled its eyes and said, "*This* right here is exactly why you should've left damn well enough alone."

But my heart sighed, butterflies flitting through my chest, and said, "We *just* found him, we can't let him go so soon. Maybe the dating doesn't have to be pretend? Maybe the eventual breakup doesn't have to happen?"

Fuck.

What the hell did any of this shit mean? Did I want to date Bryce?

Or was the better question *why* did I want to date Bryce?

I hadn't dated anyone since Missy. I wasn't cut out for dating or relationships.

Or maybe you've just needed time, and no relationship was going to be right for you until he came along.

A blast of old memories—emotions and fears punching me right in the gut—washed over me. The confusion, the longing, the disgust, and the wishing for something I knew I'd never have because my situation would never be right for that.

But now?

Now I was a grown ass man who cared less than nothing about what people thought of me. So what if I wanted to start something with someone? *Anyone.* Who the fuck got to have any concern about my personal life?

Maybe you need to figure out your physical and mental health so you can be around to have a personal life, the voice whispered.

And there it was.

The waiting room door swung open at the exact moment my hand ran from my eyes down to my mouth, and my heart caught in my throat.

Whether because I was terrified the doctor was going

to give me bad news or because the soul-deep truth I'd spent most of my life fighting and hiding was tiptoeing toward the light—all because some fuckin' health nut with a gorgeous smile came to town and somehow found the patience to put up with my shit—I didn't know.

Didn't know if I *wanted* to know.

Wasn't sure how to process any of it.

But as I followed the nurse to the exam room, a boulder shifted deep in my chest, certainty sparking all the way to the core of my damn soul. Why right then and there? Maybe I'd never know, but something big had happened in a part of my being that was very unfamiliar to me—a transformation that seemed to come from out of the blue—or maybe it was something that had been building for decades, just waiting for the right moment.

As we continued down the hall, the fluorescent lights were too bright, but the clarity shining through me was abso-fuckin'-lutely crystal clear.

It was time to make a real change in my life.

Yeah, it had been time for years and years, but better late than never.

Right?

Fuck. I sure hoped I was right.

If I wanted to be around for fifty more years, I couldn't keep living the way I was. The food wasn't worth it. The smokes and drinking weren't worth it.

The exercise was going to suck major donkey dick.

But there in that office hallway, the overwhelming scent of antiseptic and latex making me want to gag, I knew without a shadow of a doubt things had to change if I wanted to keep on living the life I'd been given.

Shitty as it maybe was at times, this life was *mine*, and something deep inside me had shifted. While I'd never *wanted* to give up, a million voices in my head had spent most of my life telling me it would just be so much better, so much easier.

But a switch had flipped in that waiting room.

I wanted to fight because I planned to be around for a lot longer.

For my boys.

For me.

And maybe for whatever you haven't yet let yourself admit might be possible with Bryce?

I sighed as I dropped into the chair. "Fuck if I know," I muttered.

"I'm sorry, what?" the graying nurse asked with a quirk of her brow.

I shook my head. "Nothin', just talkin' to myself. Let's get this shit show on the road."

Less than an hour later, I slammed my truck door and revved the engine.

Fuck.

I didn't know why I was acting surprised. I'd known damn well going into the appointment the doctor was going to say my numbers weren't where he wanted to see them.

It wasn't like I thought I'd sit down, and he'd tell me my numbers were comparable to those of a healthy twenty-five-year-old, and I didn't need to see him for the next ten or so years.

"Mr. Riggs," the rail-thin, bespectacled man had started. Doctor Adam Rahim was younger than me, probably closer to Hudson's age. I had no clue how he'd ended up smack dab in butt-fuck Midwest, but I knew he was top of his graduating class, and he was a well-respected doctor.

Yeah, I'd looked him up.

So, sue me.

The man was smart. He was right there, keeping up with all the cutting-edge heart health technologies.

That didn't mean I had to like what he said to me.

"Mr. Riggs," Dr. Rahim tried again as he scanned through the papers in his right hand, his left hand tapping the edge of the file folder on the desk.

I crossed my arms.

When Dr. Rahim glanced up at me, his eyes softened. "Why don't you tell me about the progress you've made."

His words were a pin to my defensive anger. Slumping in my seat, I let out a long breath. "Fuck, Doc. I don't know. I knew it would be hard, but I didn't know just how hard. I'm going insane without the smokes. Usually, I'd drink to numb the cravings, but I can't do that either. I'm in therapy, and it's helpful but also a bunch of shit." I pinched the bridge of my nose. "I *know* I have to do better with what I'm eating, and I have to get more exercise." The stinging heat of tears pricked at my eyes.

Fuckin' hell.

"Mr. Riggs," Dr. Rahim started. "Quitting smoking cold turkey is very hard to do. You're likely through some of the worst cravings, but a patch or something might—"

"No, feels like I've done too much to get to this point. I'll keep pushing through."

He nodded. "If you change your mind…"

I returned the nod. "I know I've sucked ass at the diet and exercise, but I'm ready to change that."

Dr. Rahim cocked his head. "What changed from last time? You were very much against it when we last spoke."

My cheeks pinked. "Yeah, I know. Sorry, I'm an asshole." When he didn't disagree, just smirked, I huffed out a laugh. "I don't know exactly, but things feel different this time. I don't know if I can make all the changes on my own, but I'm willing to try this time."

"It's okay to start small," Dr. Rahim said. "We can provide resources for a dietician and physical fitness coach—"

"Nah," I said with a smile. "I think I've already got the inside scoop."

The rest of the appointment had been a blur of numbers I mostly didn't understand. Dr. Rahim had agreed to see me in three months to check on my progress. If my bloodwork and a stress test weren't looking better, I'd have to answer for it.

But as I climbed the stairs to my temporary home above Armstrong Health & Fitness, I couldn't help the bloom of hope fluttering in my chest.

"Hey," Bryce said. "How was the appointment?" The look on his face told me he'd expected grumpy Casey.

"It was shit," I said. "And I want a cigarette, a beer, and a large pizza. In that order."

He eyed me warily.

"But I think I'm gonna go for a run instead. You wanna come?"

Bryce stared at me for several beats, those pretty hazel eyes blinking slowly. "Um, sure." He gripped the back of his neck looking sheepish. "And Dizzy invited us over for dinner."

"Perfect," I said. "It will help me keep my mind off this shit."

In the next twenty minutes, we changed into running clothes and headed down the stairs. The run was awful, and I had no doubt I was one more stride away from dying. I appreciated Bryce taking it easy on me, but the stop at Hudson's place was likely the only thing that kept me from meeting my maker.

"Do you want to stay for dinner?" Lance asked as he and Jack set the table, and my boys rough-housed over the grill. "We have plenty."

Henry had extended the invite a few days earlier, but I'd declined because I'd been in a foul mood.

What was new?

"No, we're having dinner at Dizzy's," I said before taking a long swig of water.

Lance eyed me. "So, what's up with that?"

I shrugged. "She thinks we're dating."

All four of them paused to stare at me.

"It's just a bit of pretend," Bryce said, his cheeks a delicious shade of pink.

I tossed the bottle toward the trashcan. "Thought I'd get her off his back with the terrible blind dates."

Bryce eased a bit of the awkwardness by carrying the plate of hot dogs and burgers to Henry and Hudson, and Lance took that moment to grab my elbow and steer me around the corner.

"What's up?" he asked.

I shrugged again. "Nothin'."

"No, you don't get to act like a petulant toddler. Are you into him?" I'd known the man almost my entire life, I knew when he was flabbergasted.

"Would that be a problem?" I shot back.

Lance pushed me. "Shut up, you know it wouldn't be. I'm just...I didn't...when did you...?"

I chuckled. "Shit man, I get it, words are hard."

He pushed me again. "Back to my question. Are you into him?"

I sighed and let my gaze travel to where Bryce laughed with my boys.

"I don't know," I admitted. "I know I've got a lot of shit to fix, but I know I'm not *not* into him."

Lance did a long, slow blink. Then he shook his head as if clearing away a fog. "As long as you're happy, that's all that matters."

"And healthy," Jack added, popping around the corner with a grin but very serious eyes. "You have to take care of yourself."

I nodded, my throat suddenly thick with something I wasn't yet able to put a name to. "That's the plan."

"What's the plan?" Hudson asked as the three of them joined us on the side of the house like it was completely normal for us to just stand in the little area chit-chatting.

I cleared my throat. "Um, my appointment wasn't great, but I'm gonna do better this time."

All five men stared at me as if waiting for a punchline.

"Fuck off," I muttered. "For real. I get it. I have to do better." I gestured wildly toward the general vicinity of where we'd been running. "I was runnin' wasn't I?"

"You've been doing a great job—" Hudson started.

"Nah, I need y'all not to fuckin' baby my ass. I'm unhealthy as shit, and I know it." Something cracked in me as Henry pulled Jack to his side and rested his chin on top of his pretty blond head. Blinking back the sting of tears, I went on. "I have a problem, but this time, I really do plan to do better. Everything has to change. Smoking, drinking, eating, exercising, all of it."

"We'll all be here to help," Bryce said, his hand warm and firm on my shoulder.

"Damn right we will," Lance agreed.

Henry and Hudson stepped forward to hug me, Jack getting squished between our bigger bodies with a squeal.

Feeling like I'd just accomplished something huge—although, I had no clue why telling them I was going to work on all the shit was so monumental...maybe because now they all knew and they'd be looking out for me, there was no escaping it even when it was hard—I took a deep breath. "We gonna finish this shit-ass run or what?" I asked Bryce.

He smirked. "Let's do it."

We all agreed we'd see each other before the big Fall Fest, and then Bryce and I took off at a slow jog toward home.

Chapter 12
Bryce

Dizzy shot a sly smile and a wink toward my parents as Casey Joe and I leaned against the porch railing after dinner. "You boys sure you don't want more dessert?"

Casey's arm around me was a comforting and confusing weight. Warm and protective, but I had to remember it was all a farce. "I'm gonna pass but thank you. Everything was delicious." A quiet thrill shot through me when he spoke. Casey Joe was a study in contrasts. Gruff and full of piss and vinegar on one hand, but quick to soften his words and answer Aunt Dizzy politely when needed.

I liked that I got to see both sides of him.

And for a while, I got to call him mine.

Danger! Danger! Abort! Abort!

There was no reason to let myself savor the fake dating. The more I enjoyed it and allowed myself to let it feel real, the worse it would hurt when we stopped pretending.

But that didn't mean I couldn't lean into Casey's warm body.

Dizzy sighed and pressed a hand to her chest. "You boys just warm my heart."

Guilt washed over me. Maybe I'd be the one who ended up getting hurt, but it really wasn't fair to my family to lie.

Mom, Dad, and Dizzy had all loved Casey Joe right from the start. How easy it would have been to bring him home for real. Except for the whole part about him not being into guys.

Flashes of Casey's eyes sparking with heat, his nostrils flaring when I teased with innuendo, and the soft feather of his breath against my ear when he'd whispered, "That's what I thought," the other night all fought for space in my head.

Okay, so I wasn't one hundred percent sure he wasn't into guys.

Or wasn't into me specifically.

But that didn't mean I could assume.

We'd started this thing—no, Casey Joe had started this thing—only to get Dizzy off my back. That's all it was. If he wanted it to be something more, he'd have to be the one to make the next move.

We each finished one last cup of coffee—I'd noticed Casey relied a lot on coffee when the rubber band and suckers just weren't cutting it—and enjoyed small talk with my family. When we finally walked our mugs to the sink and said goodbye, it hurt my heart to see how easily hugs were given.

Damn.

How could something so fake feel so right and real?

Maybe it isn't as fake as you think it is.

Or maybe it was just stupid wishful thinking that was going to end up hurting like a bitch when it was all over.

As we walked down the steps and toward Casey's truck, I shifted to move from under the weight of his arm. But Casey turned to nuzzle my cheek and whispered, "They're all still watching. Just give it a bit."

Butterflies fluttered in my chest even as my stomach soured.

Casey Joe was the realest person I'd ever met, and he fit into my family seamlessly—and I with his, if I was being honest. But instead of having something real and good, we were just playing games.

I didn't like lying. Didn't like faking a relationship.

The sooner we let everyone know we'd opted to just be friends, the better.

Or maybe...

My mind drifted back to my earlier thoughts. With the heady, citrusy-fresh scent of Casey's warm body drifting around me, and the memory of his soft coffee-scented breath tickling my cheek, I couldn't help but think maybe it wouldn't be such a bad idea to at least let him know—*for real* this time, no messing around—I was ready and willing in case he *wanted* to make the next move.

If he wasn't on the same page, we'd navigate it swiftly. I maybe hadn't known the man for long, but I was confident Casey Joe wasn't the type to let a little awkwardness derail the friendship we'd been building.

So, it wasn't a hem-hawing around situation. The decision was solid in my head. I was going to let Casey know—upfront and without any teasing innuendo—that I was interested. I just had to find the right time.

And hope like crazy I wasn't ruining the most real friendship I'd had in my entire life. Maybe it was risky behavior—maybe I needed to just be happy I'd found a place in Haven Grove—but the tug in my heart every time I was around Casey Joe was too much to ignore.

If he wasn't into me—or worse, I offended him with my admission—I'd have some damage control to take care of. But I hadn't lived nearly half a century to let something potentially amazing slip through my fingers because I was worried he didn't feel the same.

Fuck that.

I didn't want to get to the end of my life fifty some years from now and regret I hadn't been true to myself. If Casey Joe didn't feel the same, we had a pretty decent friendship to fall back on.

If everything went to complete shit...well, it was something I was willing to risk.

Casey loves Bryce

"God damn, mother fuckin' piece of shit," Casey Joe howled about a week later.

We'd been working long-ass days on the gym, running

in the mornings, lifting weights in the evenings, and cementing our friendship with each passing moment.

He was brash and had a foul mouth.

He was grumpy and shit at subtlety.

But Casey Joe Riggs was the friend I'd been searching for my entire life.

I didn't understand the how or why of it, but we just clicked.

Don't get me wrong, I adored Henry, Jack, Hudson, and Lance. They were great guys, and I was lucky to call them friends. But spending time with Casey—laughing with him, giving him a hard time, watching him fight his demons, just getting to know him—was what had been missing in my life all this time.

And all it took was nearly fifty years of loneliness, digging myself out of a hole I'd made for myself with all the fake glitz, glamour, and social media buzz, and coming back home to Small Town, USA, to find my soul mate.

I truly did believe that was what Casey Joe was to me.

And I still hadn't found the time to let him know how I felt. It was going to happen, I had no doubt about that, but I just wasn't sure how to bring it up.

Or how to deal with the potential fall-out.

Or exactly what I was offering.

Sex?

Dating?

Shit. Everything had seemed so sure and clear a week ago.

Now it was all fuzzy. My head and my heart had a lot of the same feelings and thoughts, but it was hard as hell to figure out when the right time was to tell the guy who

was basically your only friend in your whole life that you
found him attractive and wanted to...

Fuck.

I truly was stuck. I wanted more than anything to offer
to act on the hints I was pretty sure I'd been getting from
him all this time.

But I also didn't want to assume just because I caught
him staring a few times, and his cheeks burned bright
when I made suggestive jokes, that he was into me the
way I was into him.

Double fuck.

I returned my attention to Casey Joe's hootin' and
hollerin' as he hobbled around cussing up a storm.

"What happened?" I asked, putting down the spackling
I'd been using to fill holes in the new drywall.

Casey heaved himself down on a weight bench. We
didn't have anywhere close to all the equipment ordered
or placed in the gym, but we'd set up a sparse
weightlifting area for our personal use. Approaching him
from behind, I caught a glimpse of him in the mirror.

He took my damn breath away. Not just because he
was gorgeous—he was, don't get me wrong—but because
he was a good person who'd been dealt a shit hand. He'd
also quickly become my closest friend.

Casey Joe still needed to pack on a few pounds, but all
the running we'd been doing—despite his griping about
each and every step—had given him a healthy glow, and
the weights had bulked him up. I knew from looking at
him, and some comments he'd made, he wasn't at his
former weight, but he was making a lot of progress.

And I was so damn proud of him.

"Dropped that mother fuckin' damn hammer on my toe," he growled as he held his flip-flop clad foot and studied his bleeding big toe.

I cleared my throat, but before I could even speak Casey pointed a finger my way.

"And I don't wanna hear a single fuckin' word about my boots."

Biting the inside of my jaw, I tried my best not to laugh while I just nodded.

"You were right, okay?" Casey grumbled. "Shoulda put my boots on."

He'd slipped the flip-flops on after a quick shower when we finished our weights earlier. We'd eaten dinner—a healthy one cooked by me and barely a single complaint made by Casey—and debated calling it a day, but Casey had wanted to get a few more things done when we'd walked down to the gym to take inventory of what we needed to do the next day.

Casey had argued going back upstairs to get his boots would take longer than the tasks he had planned.

"Fuckin-A', god damn mother fucker has its own heartbeat," Casey whined.

"If you didn't want to go for our morning run, all you had to do was say so," I quipped, catching his eye in the mirror.

Casey scowled, then his eyes went wide before disappointment washed over his face. "Fuck. Not gonna be able to go for a run. Damn it. Been doin' good." He ran a hand over his face with a sigh.

With my heart in my throat, I placed a hand on his shoulder and kept my eyes connected with his in the mirror. "You've been doing amazing. We'll increase the weights for a while. Give it a day or so, and we'll wrap the toe. Might hurt, but you'll survive a short run." I paused, feeling like *I* was the one with heart issues, but gave Casey a wink. "Plus, I can offer my services for keeping your cardio going."

Casey's eyes narrowed for a brief moment before his nostrils flared. "What the fuck's that supposed to mean?"

Shit.

Laugh it off and pretend it meant nothing?

Or go for it?

I shrugged, my eyes never leaving his. "Just saying I'm not against making this fake dating thing a little more real."

Casey snorted. "Yeah, right. Figured you'd be ready to kick my ass to the curb by now." He stared at me for a moment longer before glancing away.

I swallowed, my spit as thick as tar. "I'm not joking around," I croaked. "If you ever thought about being with a guy, I'm ready, willing, and able."

Casey's face lit up with a mix of shock, anger, and question. Instead of the blow up I thought might have been fixing to detonate, he stood, gave me a nod, and grumbled, "Noted," before hobbling from the gym.

I heard the limping tread of his feet on the stairs up to our apartment.

Trying to fool myself into thinking everything was okay, I finished the spackling.

It was fine.

I was fine.

Everything was *fine*.

Casey's bedroom was closed up tight when I got upstairs.

And the next morning, he was up and gone before sunrise.

Casey Joe: Lance needs help with shit today. Be back later.

Tossing my phone to the mattress, I sighed and ran a hand over my face.

Thinking back to those risks I was willing to take, I pulled the pillow over my head and began planning my damage control.

Fuck.

Chapter 13
Casey Joe

"MAYBE YOU TELL ME WHAT CRAWLED UP YOUR ass." Lance reached for the oh-shit bar as I careened my truck around the corner. "And where the hell we're going."

"Fuck off," I bit out. "Can't a guy just pick up his best friend for a drive? You too god damned far up my kid's ass to take a fuckin' drive?" As the words left me, I realized what I'd said. "Don't fuckin' answer that."

Lance huffed out a laugh. "Don't get me wrong, I'm happy to spend time with you, but you're driving like a mad man. You clearly have something on your mind."

"On my mind?" I gunned the gas. "Wanna know what's on my mind? A drink and a cigarette," I growled. "Fuck it. A six-pack and a whole fistful of smokes."

"Shit, man." My best friend's words were softer, and that pissed me off more. I didn't need no one's damn pity. "Is there anything I can do to help?"

"Fuck off, help me pick up this order, and buy me a large pizza with extra cheese and pepperoni." If I was being honest, the pizza would likely make me sick to my stomach. Bryce had me eating a lot healthier lately, and I hadn't had anything super heavy or greasy in quite a while.

And I didn't *need* the drinks or smokes. It wasn't a physical craving like it used to be. But *damn* the mental and emotional cravings were often even worse.

I'd worked through a lot of shit and come to a conclusion recently—thanks to my fuckin' smug-ass therapist.

I was an addict.

Fuck.

Still couldn't say the words, or even think them, without feeling like I'd been punched in the gut.

Would it be a shock to the people who knew me best?

Not in the slightest.

Wasn't like it was a shock to me.

Just hadn't ever put a label to it.

And I was working through the fact addicts are never *not* addicts.

But accepting I was an addict and always would be wasn't the worst part.

My fuckin' know-it-all therapist—for real, she was super helpful, but *damn*, did she have to be an expert and *right* about nearly every damn thing that came out of her mouth?

Anyway, my therapist wanted me thinking about what my addiction to alcohol, along with the smokes, the piss-poor personality, the inability—or refusal—to get over Missy was helping me avoid.

Fuck that shit.

"Maybe we stop for some coffee?" Lance suggested.

Caffeine wasn't super healthy, I knew that, but it was something I could wean myself from down the road once I finally got the rest of my shit under control.

Or as under control as possible.

My main goal was to get healthier, so I wasn't a walking, talking, ticking time bomb. I'd never wanted to leave my boys, but the changes I'd been making lately had me determined to be around for as long as possible.

I grunted my agreement.

"I think there's a little café up there on the corner. I could eat," Lance said.

"Better watch it, you'll end up on Bryce's health-food menu with me if you're not careful."

Lance just grinned and patted his mostly flat stomach. "Hudson doesn't mind, plus we get all the extra cardio we can manage."

My eyes flew to him as heat flared in my belly with the mention of cardio.

"Fuck, man." Lance grabbed the oh-shit bar again. "Watch where the hell you're going."

His eyes were on me as I parked the truck.

As we walked into the café.

The whole time I studied the menu looking for something healthy.

Fuckin'-A, what the hell had Bryce turned me into?

When the waitperson finally brought a carafe of coffee and took our orders, Lance waited until I had a mug full of black coffee before he finally spoke.

"So, you drag me out of town to run some secret errand," he started, cutting me off when I started to argue.

"I know we're not just on a drive. You said you're picking up some sort of order. But you're being cagey as hell and grumpier than usual."

I grunted.

"What's up?" he pressed.

Shrugging, I savored the strong bitterness of the coffee, not even flinching at the bite of heat against my lips.

Lance studied me and pursed his lips. "Okay, fine. Have it your way."

"I still owe you a few rounds in the ring," I grumbled over the edge of my mug. "Maybe you stop being so damn nosey if you don't want my fist in your face."

Lance chuckled. "Whatever you say, Case." He took a long sip of his coffee. "I want to check out the little store they've got before we leave. Maybe get some teas for Hudson and Jack."

I gave a nod and absently drank my coffee while studying the café's little shop over Lance's shoulder.

That's the way things with Lance and me had always been. As close as brothers—closer maybe in some ways—and we could fight like cats and dogs, but completely comfortable with each other through thick and thin.

"Bryce like tea?" Lance asked.

My eyes shot to his. If I hadn't known the man most my life, I would have missed it. But there was a tiny smirk at the corner of his mouth, and I knew he was doing his fuckin' damnedest to hide a smile.

"How the fuck would I know if Bryce likes tea?"

Lance pressed his lips together and waited.

"What?" I asked, setting my mug down with more force than necessary.

My best friend shrugged. "Just figured you live with him, spend most of your days with him, eat meals with him...thought you might know if he likes tea. Looks like they've got a buy three get one free sale going on."

I reined myself in, determined not to take the bait, and gave a nod as our food arrived. "Yeah, maybe I'll get him something."

We ate in silence for a bit, but I knew it was too good to be true.

"I'm here to listen if and when you want to talk about what's bugging you," Lance said around a bite of omelet.

I stared down at my oatmeal and fruit.

Since when did I enjoy fuckin' oatmeal and fruit?

Lance's words ping-ponged through my head.

Bryce's...offer? Suggestion? Request?

Fuck.

I didn't even know what had happened the night before.

Bryce had said suggestive stuff before. Each and every word stirred up a shitload of *something* deep in my gut, but he'd always laughed it off and made it clear he was just joking around.

Until he wasn't.

At least, he said he wasn't.

Fuck.

The urge to play it off like it was nothing pressed down on me.

But if I couldn't talk about shit with my best friend, who could I talk to?

Sure, my therapist was an option, but the moment I

mentioned anything to her, she would start poking and prodding, and I wasn't sure I was ready for that.

Fuckin' hell, I'd just finally been able to admit I was a god damned addict, maybe I could have a bit of time to adjust to the fact I might be—

Fuck.

Why was it a whole hell of a lot easier to talk about hypothetical sexuality situations with my therapist than to acknowledge things in the stark light of reality?

Maybe I'd found myself attracted to guys at various times in the past.

Mostly in the past.

Okay, not completely in the past.

Perhaps I wanted to explore what I'd slowly been uncovering about myself.

Maybe I'd potentially considered labels that fell into the *not straight* category.

But maybe—*perhaps*—a label wasn't what I needed or wanted.

All that shit had been hypothetical speculation. Sure, my therapist wanted to act like she knew something I didn't know—yeah, yeah, I knew…fuck right the hell off— but it had all been easy to compartmentalize and talk about it like it was someone else.

But then Bryce showed up.

I made a few break throughs.

I started taking better care of myself.

And things slowly started drifting further and further from vague theories to cold, hard reality.

Was it just because of Bryce?

No.

I could at least be honest and not pin all my shit on him.

It just so happened Bryce was one of several catalysts that came along and kicked my ass toward a path forward.

A *better* path forward.

For my health.

For my boys.

My future—something I truly did hope to have.

And then that mother fucker Bryce went and dropped a god damned bomb on me like it was no big deal. Like all the joking around he'd done since I met him had actually been leading up to this point. And he...just threw it right out there like it was a something he offered to his friends all the time.

Sitting there with my fuckin' toe bleeding and throbbing like it had its own heartbeat, and my so-called friend tells me he's willing to—

Fuck.

"Nothin' to fuckin' talk about," I bit out. "Ordered something for the fall fest a while back. Need to pick it up. Didn't want Bryce to see it. Sorry I dragged you away, just thought you could help."

"Don't do that," Lance said. "I'm willing to help, and I'm glad to see you. You don't have to tell me anything, but don't lie to me and act like something isn't bothering you."

"It ain't—"

"Look," Lance said with a hint of weariness, "you already told me you might have a thing for the guy. Is that it? That's what's bothering you?"

Fuck.

As much as it annoyed the ever-lovin' shit out of me
that Lance kept poking, a tiny piece of me—deep, *deep*
down—felt like a little kid with a juicy secret I just *had* to
share with somebody.

And didn't that just fuck with my head?

I glanced around. We weren't in Haven Grove, and I
didn't know anyone in the café, but it didn't feel right
talking about Bryce's offer in public. "Not here."

Lance gave a quick nod, and we returned to eating.

After finishing a third cup of coffee, I decided I might
just survive, and we paid our bill. I took a quick detour to
the restroom while Lance browsed in the little shop. By
the time I returned, he had a basket hooked on his arm.

"Good lord, man."

"It's just tea stuff. I won't cheat on the Juicy Peach, but
this tea is different than what we have back home." He
held up a glass jar of blueberry preserves. "And we've got
all the peaches we can handle, but I'm getting blueberry
and raspberry for Jack. Bet he's got all kinds of recipes for
them." He tapped the strawberry jar. "And I know Hudson
will devour some ice cream with this."

My heart couldn't help but get all warm and squishy at
the thought of my boys and Jack. Henry and Hudson were
the best damn things to ever happen to me, and Jack had
easily landed a place in my heart without even trying.

That fullness in my chest was how I knew all the
changes coming about—bettering my health, figuring shit
out, truly looking forward to a future—weren't just about
Bryce.

Like some damn afterschool special, I'd seen the
fuckin' light, and down the road looked promising

whether Bryce was in my life or not. I had a life-long best friend, two of the best kids in the world, and Jack—my second-chance son.

Didn't mean I wanted to travel down that road without Bryce.

As a friend?

As something...more?

The thoughts had me completely rattled as I browsed the tea selection.

Since the brand was different than what we carried at the Juicy Peach, I grabbed a peach, a lemon, and an apple cinnamon.

"Get another one of the apple for your free one," Lance suggested. "If you don't like it, we'll take it."

"Hands off my tea, fucker," I muttered and rolled my eyes with a huff when Lance laughed at me.

We paid for our items and loaded ourselves into the truck.

Lance waited about one mile before he started back in with his shit. "So, is it just Bryce? Or...?"

I groaned. "Fuck, man."

"Right," Lance said. "Is that what you want to do?"

I missed the joke until the fucker laughed. "Shut the fuck up, that was—"

Lance got his laughter under control and held up a hand. "Sorry, that was bad." He gestured for me to go on.

I didn't.

He sighed. "Good lord, man. Words. They're for explaining and sharing. Use them."

Words didn't come.

Lance clapped me on the shoulder. "So, when I came home and told you I was into guys—"

I grunted. "You mean when I caught you railin' my son?"

He winced. "Yeah, that. And we really were going to tell you."

I ignored that.

"Anyway, when your boys came out, and when *I* figured my shit out, did you know back then or is this a recent development?"

Steamy locker rooms blurred my thoughts.

Flashes of sweaty, naked bodies.

The sinewy strength, solid presence, and hard lines of my teammates.

Girls were—expected. The only realistic option. It wasn't like sex with girls was unpleasant for me. They just weren't—

I took a deep breath and slowly blew it out. "Way back then, I wouldn't even let myself think about it." Shaking my head, heavy memories of so many years of cloying fear and loathing very real in my mind, I went on. "I mean, I *thought* about it, but every single time anything about guys crossed my mind, I buried it deeper and deeper, swearing I'd do better."

"How old were you?" Lance asked.

Huffing, I allowed a bit more of the past to paint images in my head, my eyes focused on the road even though my thoughts were a million miles away. "Probably eighth grade when I had my first crush. The football coach." The tight knot in the pit of my belly loosened slightly. "That was easiest to ignore because it was just a role model, someone I looked up to."

Lance nodded, waiting on me to go on.

"It was a lot harder to ignore in tenth grade when it was the coach's son." I tapped my thumb on the steering wheel. "Sometimes I wish things back then were more like they were today," I mused. "But then I maybe wouldn't have my boys. So, I pushed away the longin' that ate away at me. Did a lot more lookin' at girls and convinced myself I didn't feel somethin' more when I looked at guys. Ended up with Missy."

"So, you're bi or pan?" Lance asked.

I shrugged. "Probably. Not sure I need or want a label. I just know I'm not straight." For a moment, a tight shot of anxiety swirled through me. It was the first time I'd said those words out loud to anyone other than myself in the quiet dark of my dreams. I swallowed thickly, grateful for my best friend. "You know Missy and me were oil and water from the very beginnin'—sure as shit didn't have it in me to worry about thinkin' guys were hot when I was dealin' with a toxic relationship, school, and a job." I ran a hand over my face. "She got pregnant, we got married, and nothin' else had time to surface. When she left, and all that shit went down with Billy, all the hurt and betrayal buried me so far down, it's a wonder I ever dug myself back to the top."

Lance's hand on my shoulder had my throat clogging with emotion. "Now that you're healing, you've got a lot more time to get to know the real you."

I nodded and cleared my throat. "Yeah, somethin' like that."

"You ever think the smoking and drinking and digging yourself deeper and deeper into the abyss were ways to cover up a part of yourself you didn't want to deal with?" Lance asked.

I grunted. "Fuck off."

He chuckled. "Sorry."

Taking a deep breath, I let it out with a whoosh. "No, it's okay. Just the same shit my fuckin' therapist was sayin' the other day."

We drove in silence for a few moments.

As I pulled the truck into the parking lot of a rental place, Lance asked, "So, are you just sitting with this information? Or planning on *doing* something with it?"

Fuck.

That sure as shit was the question, wasn't it?

I grunted and got out of the truck. Lance joined me on the driver side, and we headed toward the entrance.

Lance slapped me on the back. "You don't have to have it all figured out, ya know?"

I glanced at him, part of me thinking he was full of shit, and part of me wanting to beg him to promise me everything was going to be okay.

"Unless figuring it all out is what you want to do," Lance hedged.

I sighed as we reached the door. "Fuck if I know."

Lance nodded. "It's okay. You have time."

Huffing out a heavy breath, I yanked open the door. "That's a bunch of bullshit, and we both know it. I may not know exactly what I want to do with all this shit, but I know I wasted half my life. I'm fuckin' done with that shit for sure."

"Well, then," Lance said with a smile. "This ought to be fun."

Chapter 14
Bryce

I heard him before I saw him.

Was it weird how quickly a bond had formed between us? It was weird, right? I'd gone my entire life without feeling that connection with someone else—wanting to feel it, worried something was wrong with me for *not* feeling it—and then I met Casey, and everything changed.

And I wasn't even talking about a sexual or romantic connection.

Did I want that with him? Yeah. I'd be lying if I said I didn't. I knew some people didn't need or want that type of connection, but I wasn't one of them. At least not when it came to Casey.

And that was possibly going to lead to a lot of heartache.

Would I rather keep things one hundred percent platonic if it meant keeping Casey Joe in my life? Hell, yes.

But at that moment, the invisible thread that seemed

to stretch between us yanked on something deep in my chest as the noise grew louder. The commotion off to the left of my table at Haven Grove's Fall Fest was enough to wake the dead. The addition of Casey's cursing and Lance's laughter from behind the tarp-covered apparatus they were wrestling with had me grinning like a fool and watching them make their way toward my table.

"Whatcha got there?" I nodded toward whatever the guys had been struggling with.

"CJ got you something," Lance said, his eyes sparkling with mirth in the way only a best friend giving his buddy shit could.

Casey Joe grunted. "Just thought it might bring people to the table, maybe help us get some memberships signed up." The way Casey had gone all-in on helping me with the gym and making plans for building up our client list warmed something deep in my belly. He'd probably threaten to punch me in the face if I made a big deal out of it or even hinted he was a good guy under all that gruffness, but he truly was a big softie once you got to know him. Sure, you had to look beyond the cussing and general bad mood, and it was imperative you understood where it all came from, but once you made it there, you were golden. Casey Joe was the best friend a guy could have.

The best friend in question yanked the tarp up to reveal an honest-to-god strongman game complete with hammer, bell, and flashing lights.

"No way," I murmured.

"The name Armstrong and your logo made me think of

strongman," Casey said, a ferocious glare daring anyone to make too big a deal of his gift. "And it's not ours, it's just a rental."

It had been well-past midnight when Casey had gotten home the other night. The next morning, he'd had music blaring in the gym when I'd joined him, and I'd gotten the *back-off-I-don't-want-to-talk* vibe loud and clear.

We'd worked on the gym with music blasting and very little talking for two days. It was comfortably awkward—which made zero sense, but it just was—and we got a shitload of work done while listening to every single song from the eighties and nineties put together.

The few times I'd tried to say something about the day I'd fucked things up, Casey Joe cranked the music, turned his back, or suddenly had something very important to pay attention to.

I wasn't one to let something fester without some good ol' fashioned communication, but something told me Casey was ruminating and maybe needed a little time to organize his thoughts.

So, I let him be.

But not for long because ruminating was one thing, festering was something altogether different.

The day of the Fall Fest dawned crisp and cool. Haven Grove's leaves were about a week away from being in their full glory, but the scent of autumn danced on the breeze, hinting at the biting winds of winter only a few months away.

I'd gotten dressed, glanced at Casey's closed bedroom door, and decided right then and there I'd talk to him before we went to bed that night. Even if he didn't come to the event to help at our table, I was determined to clear the air before another day passed.

The fact Casey had not only shown up to help but had brought a strongman game to draw people to our table had ridiculous flutters warming my heart and made me certain we'd be able to work through whatever awkwardness was between us because of my screw up. My heart ached, and my ego stung a bit, but if apologizing for my offer and promising it would never happen again was the only way to keep Casey Joe as my friend, I was ready and willing.

Lance gave me a smile and a nod—the kind of look that made me wonder if his best friend had told him what I'd said.

Shit.

I wasn't sure if I hoped Casey had told Lance or not. What would it mean if he had? Was it an outraged, disgusted story with threats of never speaking to me again after he punched me in the face? Or had Casey told Lance what I'd offered as a way to get feedback and ideas for how to respond? Did he tell Lance because he was interested? Or because he wanted to reply in a way that let me down easy?

And what had Lance said? The smile and nod had seemed friendly enough. Lance was involved with Hudson, so I wasn't worried about bigoted backlash. But what was the guy thinking?

Something like giddiness sparked in my chest. Feeling like a damn middle schooler wanting to ask the friend of my crush if they'd said anything about me, I returned the smile and gave a nod of my own. The nod was a Midwestern necessity, relaying so much with very little effort. A lift or dip of the chin could mean so many things depending on the situation.

I hoped my nod was taken as *sorry if I screwed up by offering to fuck your best friend, I'm trying to make it right.*

Lance shot a look between me and Casey, slapped his best friend on the back, and said, "I'm meeting Hudson at the store to help him carry things to the table before everything gets started. We'll see you around."

Casey returned the shoulder slap. "Thanks for your help."

And then we were alone.

Just when I started to apologize, Casey gestured toward the strongman game. "Help me get it positioned. We'll get everything set up and then take a walk around to check out all the shit before it gets busy."

"Oh, you don't have to miss everything—"

Casey glowered. "Still plan on me workin' for you?"

I nodded.

"Then I'll be at the table helpin' to bring in memberships." He grunted and pointed toward the edge of the game. "Grab it there. Need to get it moved over some."

The strongman was awkward as hell to move, but we got it positioned in a spot where there was plenty of room for a line and swinging the hammer.

"Keep all the paper stuff in the folders for now," Casey suggested. "Don't want them blowing off the table." The day wasn't windy, but the occasional autumn breeze ruffled through the booths.

"We can use the swag as prizes for the game. If they ring the bell, they get a month free maybe," I suggested.

"Yeah, that's a good idea. Lance and I tried to ring the bell when we picked it up," Casey said, nodding toward the strongman game. "It's easier said than done."

"Good," I said with a chuckle. "Don't want to be giving away too many free months. But it needs to be attainable so people see others win or at least get close so they'll come try it out." I glanced at the table. It looked good. A mix of excitement and nervousness swirled through me. Haven Grove was ready for a gym—tons of people had told me they were definitely signing up for one of our membership choices. I knew opening as the colder months set in was optimal on one hand because many folks don't like to battle the cold to get their workout in. On the other hand, a lot of people go into the winter months ready to be comfy cozy and surrounded by yummy food. So, it was a slight gamble, but waiting until spring wasn't something I was patient enough for. "I think it looks good."

Casey Joe studied the table and gave a quick nod. "The QR code on the flyers and the banner go to our landing page where folks can find the link to the gym's website along with our social media. Everything is up and runnin' so anyone lookin' at our shit will see some decent videos along with progress on the renovations and membership choices."

"Thanks," I said. "Seriously, your help with all of this has saved me a lot of time." I gripped the back of my neck.

"Not gonna lie, I kinda hate social media, so if you can keep taking that on, I'd be grateful."

"What's wrong with social media?" Casey Joe asked.

"Nothing *wrong* with it," I said.

"Well, there's a shit ton wrong with it if we're being honest," Casey offered. "I pretty much hate it, but maybe just because I hate a lot of shit."

"True that." I huffed out a laugh. "I spent a lot of time on socials chasing the likes, follows, comments when I was out in California. It got pretty bad. Like I couldn't even function some days because I was so focused and dependent on that next dopamine hit. I'd find myself lost in this haze and several hours would have disappeared while I just kept scrolling, posting, and checking my likes."

Casey cocked his head with a frown. "Damn, man. That sucks. Yeah, I can see it. Don't sweat it; I've got the socials covered—I don't *like* them, but I don't have an issue with them. Hell, it's kinda refreshin' that there's somethin' I *don't* have to worry about bein' a problem for me."

"Thanks." It felt like more needed to be said, but the words weren't flowing, and Casey had already moved on.

He hefted the hammer and put it under the table before letting the cloth fall to obscure the hiding spot. "Don't need any kids whackin' each other with that damn thing before we're back here to keep an eye on shit." He gestured toward the other booths setting up at the festival. "Let's go see what they've got."

The sun glowed in the sky, the perfect contrast to the cool breeze, and Casey introduced me to a few folks I didn't know between saying hi to a lot of people I'd come to think of as friendly acquaintances in town.

By the time we'd made one whole loop, I couldn't hold off any longer. "Your toe okay?"

Casey's eyes shot to mine. After a moment, he grunted. "Yeah. Still sore, but I'll live."

"Listen, about—"

"We need to get to the table. I'll have one of the guys bring us some food later. Once the crowd dies down, we can head to the Roadhouse for drinks." Something must have shown on my face because Casey cleared his throat. "Not that kind of drinkin'. Not for me anyway. You can drink whatever the fuck you want."

I was so damn proud of him for the effort he was putting in to getting himself back to being healthy. I knew it wasn't easy, but he was working hard. If I was honest, though, I worried he was heading toward a break. Like he was so focused on the drinking, smoking, and healthier eating that he was missing something else.

All I could do was be there to support him if things went south. I knew damn well, from personal experience with myself and others, he wasn't going to make any real changes until it was his choice. If he wasn't willing to look at issues outside of the obvious, I'd have to be patient until he figured it out.

The next few hours were a blur of people, food, and laughs in the very best way possible. If I hadn't already been aware the Riggs family was highly respected in Haven Grove, the Fall Fest would have proven it.

Folks from all over town dropped by our table to chat, ask about the gym, bring us goodies, play the strongman game, and basically just be around Casey Joe from what I could tell.

It was a strange phenomenon that the man could be so brusque yet pretty much loved by all in town. Well, the preacher, Larry Holmes, didn't seem too pleased with the piss and vinegar personality, but I had a strong suspicion the leader of the local flock took issue with Casey Joe and his boys for more than just Casey's attitude. Casey mumbling something about Brother Larry needing punched in the face again cemented my suspicions. I had a feeling *that* was an interesting story.

When Brother Larry referred to himself as *the good shepherd* of Haven Grove and hinted perhaps he could work out at Armstrong Health & Fitness for free, I stepped in front of a growling Casey with what I hoped was a winning smile. "We'd love to offer you a discount, Preacher Holmes."

Casey pinched my side, and I smothered my laugh with a cough.

"How about we give you the first month completely free, and I'll even throw in some free personal training. After that first month, you can work out an unlimited amount at..." I tapped my chin, pretending to be deep in thought. "For you, let's do twenty percent off for six months." I leaned in, my words low. "But let's keep that just between us, ya know?"

Larry puffed up, his saggy jowls and ruddy cheeks making me think of a blushing basset hound. "Well, now," he drawled. "I don't want it looking like you're playing favorites—my flock are good people, and they deserve God's will—but doing the Lord's work is often thankless and tiring, so I humbly accept your offer." He placed a hand on his heaving chest. "Living as I do on such a limited income, the savings will be much appreciated."

"Always willing to help those in need," I said, handing him a clipboard. "Go ahead and put your information down there. We'll make a note of your special discount and get in touch to finalize membership before the grand opening."

Brother Larry all but frothed at the mouth as he scribbled down his information before shoving the clipboard at Casey and walking away from the table.

"Those in need?" Casey Joe hissed, his finger jabbing into my flank. "That asshole don't live on a limited income," Casey continued, anger lacing his words. "If anything, he's probably fuckin' stealin' from his damn *flock*."

I turned, grabbed the finger he'd been using to poke me, and leaned in close to Casey's ear, knowing full-well I was playing with fire. "The special discount I gave him is the exact same I'm offering to everyone who signs up today. Same one I'm giving to anyone who signs up before we open." I paused to appreciate the heaving of Casey's chest and the clean, citrusy scent of him. "He's not getting anything more than everyone else. And I know folks like him. He'll likely come a few days and then never come again. Probably keep his membership for a while at least, but he's too wrapped up in leading his flock to work in exercise. We'll make a decent amount from his membership and likely never have to see him."

Casey's eyes flickered to my mouth before he snorted

and backed away. "Leadin' his flock, my ass. He's never done a damn thing that wasn't self-servin' in his life."

I swallowed thickly and forced myself to add more distance between us. "No harm at this point letting him think he's getting something when he's not. Probably no different than the way he's treated some of his *good people* for years."

Casey harumphed, but he seemed content to let the topic go for the time being.

Chapter 15
Casey Joe

"HOW THE HELL IS A FRIED PIECE OF FLATTENED pork so damn good?" Bryce asked around a huge bite of tenderloin.

For a moment, I allowed my eyes to linger on his lips, but I pulled myself out of wondering what they'd feel like on mine and chuckled before taking another bite of my own sandwich.

Hudson and Jack had brought us food earlier—a huge tenderloin sandwich to split, peach shakeups...although, Jack had been sipping a lemon one...and a basket of spiral fried potatoes. I appreciated they'd brought us items we could share so I wasn't loaded down with unhealthy food.

Something I'd caught on to with Bryce cooking was to plan for healthy meals, pick good-for-you foods when possible, and not get too down on yourself if you had mess ups now and then.

I'd loaded up with eggs, oatmeal, and fruit for breakfast, so splitting the tenderloin and potatoes with

Bryce wasn't going to derail me completely—the exercise Bryce had us doing every day made it a lot easier to splurge on tasty snacks like festival food.

Jack would serve us up slivers of cake at the Roadhouse. While I didn't *like* the smaller portions, I appreciated Jack's way of watching out for me. And a sliver of cake was better than no cake at all. Jack and Henry had also been working on a complete menu of fun non-alcoholic drinks.

When I'd groused they didn't have to fuckin' baby me —I was perfectly god damn able to pick water or tea sweetened with monk fruit or some shit—Henry had pulled Jack to his side, kissed the top of his blond head, and said, "Not everything is about you, Dad, if you can believe it."

Jack had giggled into Henry's armpit before gathering himself and turning to me. "The new drinks have been a huge hit. Something I should have thought of a long time ago. Honestly, most nights, the mocktails outsell the alcohol in quantity about two-to-one."

That had stopped me short. I hadn't thought about so many folks wanting fun drinks without the alcohol. Whatever the reason people were choosing not to drink wasn't my business, but getting more people to order the mocktails definitely was. I'd set up some social media posts about the new drinks and sat back with a triumphant smile when sales had skyrocketed.

Jack had even had several requests for the mocktails to be available at his Lemon Drop Social Club gatherings. He'd only had two get togethers so far, but the second one had been even better attended than the first.

He was an honorary Riggs just like Lance, so it wasn't surprising the town flocked to him, respected him, and wanted to take part in pretty much anything he did. Just like Hudson's orchard and store, Henry's bar, and Lance's ice cream shop, Jack's endeavors continued to be a hit.

And I had every intention of making sure Bryce's business was just as successful. Armstrong Health & Fitness was already highly anticipated, but I wanted it to absolutely blow Bryce's goals out of the fuckin' water. I might have had a bunch of fuckups in my past, but I was damn well going to make sure my family and friends were successful. For the longest time, just barely surviving was the best I could do, but these days, I was determined my family would get the best of me for however much longer I could give it.

What about you? Are you getting the best of you?

Shoving aside the niggling voice at the back of my head, I took a final bite of my tenderloin, finished the peachy drink, and offered the last potato spiral to Bryce. Once we'd thrown our trash away, gathered up all the swag and shit from the table, and packed everything up, Lance came up the hill to help us get the strongman game to my truck.

Damn thing was awkward as hell to move, but it had been a huge hit. Had me wondering if purchasing our own would be a better investment than renting.

By the time we'd wrapped everything up at the Fall Fest, the setting sun cast golden shadows between the leaves, and the breeze had more of a bite. Quite a few folks would stay for the church service Brother Larry liked to have at the end of the festivities, but I was damn ready to chill out at the Roadhouse.

"Did you try that apple cinnamon tea yet?" Lance asked as we headed toward Henry's place.

Before I could answer, Bryce piped up. "I did. It's really good. Will be absolutely perfect on a cold autumn night by the fire."

And fuck if I didn't want that.

Right then and there.

Bryce and me.

Sitting by the fire at my place, sipping fuckin' apple cinnamon tea.

Who the fuck was I, and where the actual fuck was Casey Joe Riggs?

I trundled ahead, trying my damn best to push the image from my head.

Instead, I ended up imagining us pulling the swing over by the fire and cuddling up together under a blanket. I could almost smell the sweet and spicy apple cinnamon mixed with Bryce's citrus and cedar scent.

"Damn, man, where's the fire?" Lance called after me.

"Fuck off. I gotta piss." I yanked open the door to the Roadhouse and stomped to the damn bathroom. With the door locked, I leaned over the sink taking ragged gulps of air.

I wanted something with Bryce.

Holy fuck, *I wanted something with Bryce.*

Truth be told, I'd probably wanted something with him since the first time I laid eyes on him. But what I wanted went way beyond whatever he'd offered the other day.

But what did his offer actually mean? Distract me, get

us off, and then go back to whatever we'd been building? Just a friends with benefits thing? Would I be able to make do with that? Was it enough?

The icy cold water I splashed on my face did nothing to calm my pulse or the thoughts racing through my head. I needed a drink or a smoke, preferably both.

No.

I needed to get my damn self under control, go out there, enjoy time with my family. Bryce and I would talk. We had to. No doubt, he'd been trying to talk to me ever since he made his offer.

The thought of acknowledging his offer—let alone taking him up on it—terrified me. But more than that? The idea of *not* doing anything was worse.

Fifty more years of wondering? Longing? Pushing everything down deep and pretending it wasn't part of me?

That was the real terror.

But was I what Bryce wanted? Was what we had as friends too good to risk?

And…

And.

That fuckin' word teased and prodded.

Such a heavy word. So many years buried in one tiny syllable.

So much I needed to admit to myself. So much needed fixing.

Instead, I splashed my face with cold water again, dried myself the best I could, and unlocked the door. For now, I'd hide behind mocktails and family.

When I swung open the door, Hudson and Jack stood

on the other side. Jack's eyes flew wide as I stepped out of the restroom, but Hudson cocked his head and studied me.

"Sorry, didn't mean to make you wait." I gestured toward the restroom.

"What's going on?" Hudson stepped between me and my escape to the dining room.

"Nothin'." The way Jack flinched sent guilt straight to my gut. "Nothin' is wrong." I did my best to keep my voice less snappy.

"Don't lie to us." Jack's words were soft and pleading, a tiny frown between his brows, and regret washed over me.

Lies.

All the lies.

A lifetime of lies.

Henry stepped around the corner, menacing vibes radiating from him.

I'd never been afraid of my sons, and I hoped they'd never feared me, but at that moment, my gut knew for sure not to mess with my boys. I wasn't getting out of this one.

Like they'd choreographed it and practiced a million times, my three boys somehow herded me to the back office. Henry leaned against his desk and pointed at the chair like I was a damn fuckin' dog he thought was going to sit on command.

I turned to leave, but Hudson stood blocking the door.

Then Jack—that damn sweetheart with the damaged heart and so much love to give—took my arm and led me to the chair. He pulled a stool to sit at an angle to me with our knees touching.

Fuck.

This wasn't good.

"What the hell is this?" I clenched my fists, focusing on my nails biting into my flesh and doing my damn best to ignore the lump in my throat. My heart pounded like a jack rabbit, and sweat prickled on my forehead. "Fuck." I pinched the bridge of my nose and took a deep breath to quell the nausea. "Must've gotten bad pork or some shit."

Hudson snorted behind me.

"Fuck off."

"Dad, you didn't get bad pork," Henry said, always the quieter one, the peacemaker. "Something's going on with you, and we want to help."

For a moment as long as eternity, the room was silent except for the pounding in my ears. When the roaring eased, Jack had my hand in his.

"Everyone here loves you. We want you to be healthy and happy."

Hudson cleared his throat. "You don't have to come to any conclusions tonight. We just wanted you to know we see you and we love you."

Henry crossed his thick arms over his chest, but his eyes were soft as he watched Jack. "You always loved us just as we were and we love you the same."

All I could do was nod and blow out a long, slow breath.

"Let's get some cake," Hudson suggested.

I huffed out a weak laugh. "Yeah, just give me a fuckin' second."

The door creaked, and heavy footfalls sounded as Henry and Hudson exited the office.

Jack remained.

I glanced up to see him watching me, his hand on the doorknob. "I'll be there in a minute."

He nodded.

But he didn't leave.

Fuckin' kid.

"When I got to Haven Grove, it was the first time in my life I felt truly safe to be myself. This is a safe place."

And then he was gone.

Alone, I sat there with my head in my hands. My eyes stung, my head throbbed, and a vice squeezed tightly around my chest. But my boys had just confirmed for me what I'd known deep down. They loved me for *me* just as I loved each of them and Lance just as they were.

Whatever I decided was fine.

I'd be okay.

But if I wanted to have the life I'd never even let myself dream of having, I knew in the depths of my soul I had some heavy lifting of the emotional kind to do.

And I was getting closer and closer to acknowledging I wasn't getting through this without some help.

By the time I made it out to the dining room, Jack had a small piece of chocolate cake with orange pistachio frosting paired with a lemon peach sparkling mocktail at my seat.

Which happened to be next to Bryce.

Right where I belonged.

My heart was willing to die on that hill even if my head wasn't completely on board just yet.

Chapter 16
Bryce

"IT'S NOT THE SAME AS SITTING BY A FIRE UNDER the stars in your backyard," I said, gesturing toward the little firepit on the tiny back patio area outside the gym, "but the tea is perfect for a fall night."

After what I'd call a successful Fall Fest—the first of what I hoped would be many more to come—we'd spent the early part of the evening at the Roadhouse eating cake, drinking mocktails, and laughing with friends. My body and heart had thrilled with each brush of Casey's shoulder against mine, every press of our thighs together. Was it purposeful or just because the table was crowded?

Was I reading too much into it?

Or was the contact his way of letting me know he forgave me for my out-of-line suggestion?

Not that I was going to allow him to let me off the hook that easily. Sure, it would be nice to pretend like it hadn't happened, but our friendship meant more to me than that. I owed it to Casey to...well, I wasn't exactly sure what I owed him. An apology? An explanation? A promise it would never happen again? All of the above?

Yes.

But, no?

I wasn't completely sure I was sorry, and I wasn't positive I could promise it wouldn't happen again. If Casey told me he'd been uncomfortable or offended, then I'd for sure tamp down my attraction to him and keep my comments to myself. I damn sure didn't want to put him in an awkward position.

But if we talked, and Casey said it hadn't bothered him —or if a miracle happened, and he indicated he reciprocated the feelings or wanted to explore my offer— well, if that happened, I definitely wasn't sorry for what I said or for putting the idea in his mind.

Yeah, I knew I needed to stop the wishful thinking, but a guy could dream.

Casey grunted and took the mug of tea I held out for him. "Thanks."

We'd visited with Dizzy and Barb along with the guys that evening at the bar. My aunt beamed at Casey and me about twenty times, and I was torn between feeling guilty for letting her think we were together and elation over the fact people naturally thought we were an item.

When we'd gotten back to the apartment, Casey had said he was going to sit outside for a while. I'd opted to boil water and fill the tea pot with the apple cinnamon tea he'd brought home the day he and Lance went to pick up the strongman game. I'd found him sprawled in the folding lawn chair, the flames in the firepit casting orange shadows on his face, and his arms crossed over his chest as a brisk breeze scattered the smoke.

Once we both had our tea, we sat in silence for several moments. That was one thing I appreciated most about what Casey and I had, how easy it was to just exist with each other without feeling awkward. Despite meeting not so long ago, our friendship had clicked from the get-go as if we'd known each other for decades. Nights like that one always made something deep in my soul wonder about past lives. If people could live lifetime after lifetime, it made complete sense to me that Casey Joe and I knew each other during a different time, and our souls kept finding their ways to each other with each new lifetime.

Or maybe we'd just been the right people at the right time and place for each other.

Or maybe a combination.

Either way, sitting by the crackling fire, sipping tea, and enjoying the cool fall night was one of the simple pleasures I'd missed being out in California, and I hoped I'd never take it for granted now that I was back where I belonged.

Surprisingly, it was Casey Joe whose words broke into the quiet night. "I let my boys grow up thinkin' I'd lost the great love of my life."

Unsure of how to respond to that, I breathed in deeply, savoring the fragrant steam rising from my mug as I waited for him to go on.

"Told them some fucked up fairytale about how me and Missy's song was 'It Must Have Been Love' by Roxette." He scoffed at his words and took a long sip of tea. "That song ain't even close to bein' a love song."

Casey dropped his head back and stared up at the stars for so long I wondered if he'd dozed off. "But what we had wasn't even close to a love story, so I guess it was fittin'."

I cleared my throat. "I'm sorry you went through all that. You didn't deserve to hurt the way you did."

"Didn't I?" Casey snapped back. "Who the fuck am I? Why should I suffer less than anyone else?"

For the rest of my life, apple cinnamon tea would remind me of real talk with a man who had quickly become a friend the likes of which I'd never had in my life. I shifted in the camp chair.

"You're a good guy," I started. "Maybe you don't deserve to suffer *less* than anyone else, but does anyone *deserve* to suffer? I hate what your relationship with Missy did to you—what she took from you—and I wish things had turned out better for you and Billy."

Casey grunted and took another swallow of his tea.

"But you've built something really good here," I said, gesturing with my mug toward Haven Grove as a whole. "I'm glad to be here and be a part of it all."

"My boys made the Riggs family what we are today, no help from me."

I made a non-committal noise. "Maybe, maybe not. I can't say I know how involved or not you were back then, but I know both those boys have stories they recall fondly. And they learned their work ethic and manners from somewhere."

"Lance—" he started.

"Case," I interrupted. "You have a lot of shit to work through, you'll never get an argument from me on that. Hell, we all have shit to work through. But you have a good heart, you love your family and friends, and your boys are who they are today at least in part because of *you*. I'm not arguing with you on it. You want to feel sorry for yourself about a shitty love song? Your shitty wife leaving? Your brother drinking himself to death? Having a heart attack? Fine. But stop with the *I was a bad dad* routine." My words were louder and angrier than I'd meant for them to be, but I felt them in my soul.

Casey eyed me over his tea mug for a long moment. I could see he wanted to argue. Wanted to snap back. Instead, he finished his tea with one long swallow and thunked the mug down on the concrete. When his eyes met mine again, a smirk played at his lips. "Fuck you," he muttered, leaning back and closing his eyes.

I couldn't help the smile.

After several moments, he spoke again. "I just wish I had been a better role model. Hate they saw me drinkin' so much to dull the pain. I numbed myself with the alcohol, wallowed in the shit life handed me because it was easier. Just wish they could have seen me at my best."

Humming in reply, I waited a beat before going on. "I wish I hadn't ended up a shadow of the guy I used to be all because I got caught up in the dopamine rush of the in crowd and social media."

"Is that still a problem for you?" Casey asked.

"Not here, not right now. But it probably could be again. I maybe wasn't my best back then, but I've got the chance to be my best now, and that's what matters."

Casey's boot tapped on the concrete and his words were soft. "I really do want to be my best self. They deserve that."

"*You* deserve that," I murmured.

He stared up at the night sky. It wasn't quite cold enough for us to see our breath, but his chest rose and fell slowly with a long, deep breath in. "You ever feel like life's a five-thousand-piece puzzle?"

Not exactly sure where he was headed, I kept quiet.

I was rewarded when he went on.

"Like you've got these five thousand different pieces all supposed to fit together—and you know they *will*, eventually, but that might not happen until long after you're gone." He sat up, leaning his elbows on his knees, his gaze trained on the ground. "And you *know* you need to dive in and get started on the mess if you're ever gonna get anywhere, but just the thought of wading through all those shit pieces makes your gut sour and your chest squeeze a little too tight. So, you let it sit there, a scattered mess on the card table of life, gatherin' dust and lookin' like shit. But then somethin' happens and somehow, you've got two pieces together over here, a corner section over there, and bit by bit it may just start lookin' like somethin' real."

Barely daring to breathe, I waited for the rest of Casey's analogy to work itself out.

He sighed. "And some days, it feels like you could put together the whole fuckin' thing. Like all you wanna do is sit there until it's finished and beautiful. But other days, the corner pieces fall off the table. The section of four pieces you worked forever on seem to have no match no matter how many of those damn fuckin' pieces you try to shove in there." His boots tapped an unsteady rhythm. "You wanna just flip the whole damn table and walk away for good. Ain't nobody got time for shit-ass puzzles anyway."

Casey shifted and held his head in his hands, and I took the last cold swallow of apple cinnamon tea.

"But then," his soft words competed with the hissing and popping of the fire. "You have more good days than bad, and some of the pieces fit together like magic. You start to see what the big picture is supposed to look like. You hate that you wasted so much time lettin' the puzzle just sit there when you could have been workin' on bringin' the picture to life." He sighed. "Fuckin' hell, don't listen to a damn word I'm sayin'…"

"It makes sense."

He didn't speak.

Several minutes passed.

And then…

"Like you're sittin' there, workin' on the puzzle day after day, some days thinkin' you don't even fuckin' like puzzles, thinkin' you might as well just say fuck it and play a fuckin' card game instead, but somethin' keeps you glued to that puzzle, and now it's all you can think of, but that damn fuckin' naggin' in the back of your head keeps pokin' and proddin', remindin' you that you could have put all these pieces together years ago."

"Sometimes the puzzle pieces aren't ready to be put together," I offered.

"Do you think sometimes the person doin' the puzzle just ain't ready?" He scoffed. "Fuck, that was dumb. Never mind."

"It wasn't dumb. Yeah, we all work at different paces. Sometimes it's the puzzle, sometimes it's the person, and maybe sometimes it's a combination of the two." I nudged his foot with mine. "That's the beauty of it. We all get to work on our puzzles in the way that seems best for us."

Casey grunted. "Yeah, well, I've been draggin' ass on mine. For the longest time, I thought I'd never finish it—hell, didn't think I'd be around to even try—but now, it's like I've got all these pieces I'm tryin' to put together, but it's sometimes too much too fast. Like I want to see the whole picture, but some of the pieces are shitty and some are scary."

"But I think a lot of the pieces are beautiful."

Casey cleared his throat. "Let me guess. Sometimes you have to work through the shitty parts of the puzzle to get to see the beautiful pieces?"

I smiled into the cool, dark night. "Something like that."

He grunted, and I could almost see the way his hard mouth fought against pulling into a grin.

We sat in our easy silence with the fire popping for several moments. When Casey didn't elaborate any further, I took it as the conversation was closed for the time being.

"What time you wanna get started tomorrow?" I asked. The gym was coming along nicely. We had a lot of the big projects done, and I was thrilled with the way everything had come together. Having Casey leading the renovation had been an absolute god-send.

Casey yawned. "Right now, I want a shower and to sleep in." He stretched. "But let's grab coffee and breakfast at Glazed Buns, then we can get started."

"Coffee and breakfast *after* a run, *then* we can get started."

He grunted. "No run, just coffee."

Chuckling, I bumped my knee against his. "Absolutely not. We can't work all day on only coffee."

"Fuckin' hell. Yeah, fine. Run first, then breakfast. And *two* cups of coffee."

"Deal."

"Go ahead and grab a shower," Casey said, his head resting on the back of his chair. "Gonna enjoy the night a little longer." He played with the rubber band on his wrist.

"You good?"

"Yeah."

A long pause.

He sighed. "Perfect night for a smoke."

I raised a brow, not keen on leaving him outside on his own if the urge to light up was too much. I knew there was no alcohol in the apartment, but I wasn't quite as sure about cigarettes.

"Been workin' too damn hard to quit," Casey grumbled. "Can't say I miss my mouth tastin' like an ashtray and the cost, but not gonna lie, fuckin' miss the way a nice long drag washed over me like the perfect calm. I *want* a smoke, but it's not the same *need* as it used to be."

I must not have looked convinced because Casey huffed.

"Seriously, I don't even have any on me, so it's all good. Go take a damn shower. I'm a big boy, I can sit by the fire all by myself." He cracked an eye as he spoke. "Just don't use all the fuckin' hot water."

Chapter 17
Casey Joe

FUCK.

I wanted a smoke.

I wanted a beer.

I wanted that numbness from the chemicals taking over.

And that right there was ninety-nine percent of what made me know without a doubt I needed to take a step I was scared to fuckin' death of taking.

Just wasn't sure when I'd finally talk myself into jumping.

I was damn proud of being sober and smoke-free for so long, but I wasn't gonna lie and say it was easy. Some days I fought against the shakes and nausea with only that damn rubber band and Bryce distracting me with a run. Some days the headaches almost took me down. If I stayed busy, it was easier. But that didn't mean I didn't fight it every day.

I wasn't naïve enough to think I'd beaten these

demons completely. It was like I was waiting for that one moment to send me running back to the bottle.

Let's face it, it was just a matter of time. No one thought I'd stay sober this long, least of all me. But I was willing to keep fighting.

I at least knew it wasn't going to be that night.

No, right then, I'd gotten myself all up in my feels, and I needed a bit of time. Sending Bryce in to take a shower was the perfect plan.

Just when I thought he was headed inside and leaving me with the chaos of my thoughts, the fucker went on a sneak attack.

"Hey." His words were soft on the cool breeze. "What I said the other day—"

"Don't worry about it..." I *really* didn't want to talk about it. I mean, I was pretty sure I didn't want to talk about it. Because in reality—no, it was best to not let my mind go there.

Well, not let my mind go there any more than it already had.

Which was every damn minute of every day since that fucker had opened his god damn mouth.

"No, Case, let me get this out. Please."

Not like I could give him permission or stop him or any fuckin' shit.

I grunted, hoping the noise didn't sound as anxious and wheezy as it felt.

"If I made you uncomfortable, I'm sorry," Bryce said. "If I read things wrong, gave it too much wishful thinking, anything like that, I really am sorry, and that wasn't my intention." He huffed. "But my intentions don't mean shit if I put you in a bad position."

I didn't say anything. How the fuck was I supposed to say anything to that?

Fuck, maybe a pack of smokes and a case of beer was better than this shit.

Bryce moved a bit farther from the fire.

Part of me prayed he'd just drop it and go inside.

The other part of me was on my damn knees, whimpering for him to keep at it until he finally wore me down and made me admit how badly I wanted to act on what he'd suggested.

Instead, I found myself flailing smack dab in the middle layer of purgatory when he just kept babbling.

"I mean, the offer was sincere." His sigh was a leaking balloon dying a slow death, and I imagined him rubbing a hand over his face. "I like you. I like what we've got going here. And I don't ever want to fuck it up." His chuckle was a bit too high pitched. "But I also don't want to miss out on something good between us if you're maybe feeling the same as me."

Again, I had no words.

No.

I had words. I just wasn't sure how to string them together in a way that even came close to making sense.

Bryce was quiet for several moments.

"Can you say something?" The plaintive tinge to his words hurt something deep inside me.

"Don't know what you want me to say," I muttered, refusing to look at him.

He chuckled with absolutely no humor. "I don't know.

Say I didn't fuck things up. Say we're fine." When I took a long breath in through my nose and let it out slowly, Bryce went on, but this time his words were softer and laced with hope. "Say you've been thinking about what I offered. Say I haven't misread things." And then the final nail in my coffin. "Say you want me the way I want you."

My brain pleaded with me to just keep my mouth shut, but my heart couldn't let my friend stand there and suffer. I cleared my throat, but my words were still gravel against sandpaper. "It's all those damn puzzle pieces." I swallowed the lump of fear. "I want to put them together, but somedays it just seems like too much. Like I waited too long."

I wasn't sure how long the silence hung between us, but I swore neither of us breathed.

"So..." Bryce hedged.

"Good god, man," I grumbled.

Bryce made a noise somewhere between a laugh and a groan.

"You didn't fuck anything up," I bit out. "And I sure as fuck don't know what book it is, but you damn well didn't misread shit." Rolling my head toward him and cracking an eye, I nodded toward the apartment and tried to keep my breathing steady. "Now go take a fuckin' shower and leave me some hot water."

Bryce studied me for a moment before grinning. With a quick nod, he headed inside.

What the fuck had I just done?

The next morning, I was still asking that same question when I woke to the scent of coffee and Bryce's shampoo.

My dick was immediately ready to start the day, and I couldn't help but think of the way I'd imagined Bryce's mouth on me when I'd jerked off in the shower the night before.

Fuck.

On one hand, it felt really good to let go and give in to something I'd been fighting for so many years. On the other hand, it was scary as fuck, and I wanted to gather up all my thoughts, words, and actions in a slop bucket, slam the lid onto it, and throw it out back to be ignored forever.

But the images I'd allowed to run through my head—Bryce on his knees for me, bent over whichever piece of furniture we reached first, spread open on my cock...hell, I'd even let myself imagine what it would be like to give myself over to him—those pictures ran on a wild loop, and I wasn't sure I'd ever be able to rein them all in.

Recalling how good that orgasm had been when I let myself pretend my soapy, slick hand was Bryce's mouth, a shiver ran through me, and I was damn fuckin' sure I didn't want to ever give up on that feeling.

And why should I have to? I'd been burying the real me my entire life. Hiding behind the anger, the booze, feeling sorry for my damn self. I didn't have to hide any more if I didn't want to.

Did I want to?

Everything was fine until Bryce came to town. I had my boys, my best friend, and…well, that was pretty much all I had, but it was enough.

Really, it was.

But then Bryce showed up and…

No, I couldn't put it all on Bryce.

The health scare was the catalyst.

Facing death forced me to look at my life and what I wanted for the future.

Cutting out the smoking and drinking cleared away a curtain I'd been hiding behind.

And *then* Bryce came to town.

Having him in my life gave me something I hadn't known I was missing.

Actually, that wasn't true.

I'd known something was missing, but I'd pretended not to notice and just kept drinking everything away.

And what the hell was I going to do about all this shit now?

I ran my hand down my chest, scratched my short nails through the hair on my stomach, cupped my dick, and gave myself a squeeze as I contemplated giving myself another go.

Which was the exact moment Bryce chose to pop his head through the bathroom door into my room. "Get your ass out of bed. We've got a run to take."

Getting caught with your dick in your hand was one of the best ways to deal with morning wood, and I could only fuckin' hope Bryce hadn't noticed.

But I'd definitely noticed him completely naked after

his shower, covered only with the towel he held loosely, swaying tantalizingly in front of his crotch.

Fuck.

That was *not* the way to turn my dick off.

Luckily, Bryce was already gone. Which meant he missed me flipping him the bird, but it also meant I could roll the fuck out of bed without worrying my dick had a fuckin' audience.

After a long, satisfying piss—which was only slightly awkward thanks to the fuckin' thoughts my dick definitely shouldn't have been having—I hopped into the shower. I'd showered the night before, but I always felt better when I started the day with a quick wash and rinse. Once I'd climbed out and grabbed a towel, I was at least slightly more ready to function.

With a towel around my waist, I went to my dresser. "Mother fucker," I muttered as I recalled my laundry in the dryer.

I made my way into the kitchen, took a long swallow of the coffee Bryce had left for me on the counter, and moved toward the door. With slides on my feet, I headed down the stairs. "Damn sure ain't gonna miss this shit once I'm back in my own place," I mumbled.

But in truth, I had a feeling I'd miss Bryce like hell once I was back in my house.

As I rounded the corner to the washer and dryer, my brain registered Bryce's cup of coffee had still been on the counter next to mine, and he wasn't already in the gym as evidenced by the lights still being off.

And then I came mother fuckin' face-to—

Well, fuck.

Face-to-*ass*?

Bryce, dressed only in a fuckin' jockstrap, was bent at the waist pulling clothes from the dryer.

"God damn, mother fucker," I muttered. "What the actual fuck are you doin'?"

"Fuck, man!" Bryce jerked upright so quick I worried for a moment he'd slipped a disk. The basket of clothes lay forgotten on the floor, and he held a hand to his chest. When his eyes caught where my eyes had landed, his hand shot to his crotch.

As if he could hide anything.

Did he seriously think his hand would cover the fact his package fit very nicely in the snug little pouch of the jock?

"What the fuck?" I repeated, my brain synapses misfiring left and right. The question was all I could manage while I tried to get my cognitive function to reboot.

"Sorry!" Bryce didn't get flustered very easily, but I saw it flash in his eyes at that moment.

Then I lost the battle to keep my eyes from scanning his body, and his demeanor changed. He shifted his hands to hips, obviously no longer caring I could see his nearly naked body. "I was getting clothes. I didn't realize you'd tossed yours in on top of mine." His words softened as he shrugged. "I needed a pair of shorts."

I was suddenly very aware of being covered only by a damp towel wrapped around my waist. "Looks like you need a fuckin' pair of underwear too." I gestured vaguely.

Bryce grinned and glanced down at himself. "What? These are new. You like?"

Holy.

Mother.

Of.

God.

This fuckin' fucker.

"What the hell you need new jockstraps for?" Shit. Was he going on a date? Had I messed things up by focusing only on my own damn self while Bryce was out there looking for his person?

And did I care I maybe wasn't his person?

Fuck.

He chuckled, crossed his arms over his chest, and lifted his chin. A wicked gleam in his eyes. "Maybe I wanted to feel sexy today. They make my ass look good." He turned and cupped his bare ass cheeks. "Right?"

A literal growl rumbled through my chest. "Shut the fuck up," I grumbled, knocking my shoulder against his as I reached down to grab my clothes.

Whichever clothes I got my hands on were fine.

Anything was good enough as long as I got away from Bryce.

Quickly.

As if you really want to get away from him.

His skin was soft and warm against mine, and he smelled fresh and ready to start our day—like soap and coffee—and I should have walked away as quickly as I did the one and only time I caught my parents having sex.

Instead, I stood there like an idiot, breathing him in and recalling how damn good his ass looked in that damn jockstrap.

All those years of pushing it all aside.

The disgust I'd held so deep inside.

The chokehold of fear, loathing, and desperation gripping me every damn day.

All the lies I fed myself, half convinced it didn't mean anything, the other half of me begging and pleading with any deity that would listen to please make me stop having the fuckin' feelings I knew deep down were as impossible to stop as the sunrise.

The pieces had all been there from the very beginning.

All I had to do was give the puzzle a big fuck off.

Ignore.

Avoid.

Lie.

Until fuckin' Bryce Armstrong came to town and ran his stupid, perfect ass right across my property.

All the puzzle pieces I'd worked so hard to ignore slowly began clicking into place, and now I had no clue how to work the puzzle or if I even wanted to.

No.

I knew.

I wanted to.

But fuck if I had any idea how to be with a man.

"Sorry," Bryce murmured, his coffee-laced breath soft against my shoulder. "I'll just—"

As he shifted to move away from me, my arm shot out and caught him around the waist. Bryce's arm pressed against mine from shoulder to forearm, he faced the door, and I faced the dryer.

I could have let go.

Should have let go.

It would have been easy. Let go. Laugh it off. Go back to pretending.

But the ripple of emotion flowing through me, the zing of awareness zapping every single nerve ending from my head to my toes...how could I go back? How could I finally let myself *feel* what my heart and soul had been begging to feel for decades and then just shrug it off like it didn't matter?

It mattered.

This mattered.

He mattered.

And the potential sparking between us mattered.

I'd faced death, embraced the fear, and took hold of my health.

I'd recognized my addictions, owned them, and accepted I would never *not* be an addict. Recovery was something I'd forever be dealing with—and to be honest, deep down, I knew I needed to commit myself to it more than I had. Being in recovery was a scary place to be, but shining light on the dark corners of my life had been as healing as it was terrifying even if I was well-aware there were a lot more dark corners to shine that healing light into.

But I'd be fuckin' god damned if I was going to work my ass off through two of the hardest, shittiest parts of my life only to turn my back on the potential of something I'd desperately longed for as long as I could remember.

"Case..." Bryce whispered, his words heavy with the same desperate hope and smoldering desire burning inside me.

In one smooth motion, I hauled him against me,

bringing his chest flush to mine, and pressed his ass into the dryer.

Bryce grunted in surprise, but he shut up quickly when I covered his mouth with mine.

The kiss started slow and exploratory.

A kiss was a kiss.

But also, no kiss had ever been like that kiss.

New, unknown, and thrilling. I tested the hard press of our lips together, the rough drag of his stubble against mine. The simmering heat of our mouths together answered that long-unspoken question fermenting deep inside for all those years.

Even if I'd never allowed the question to be voiced, the kiss provided me with the answer.

The truth.

My truth.

With a gentle flick of my tongue, Bryce groaned and opened for me.

And then the kiss took on a life of its own. Hungry and deep. Tasting, demanding, savoring the flavor of his mouth on mine. Bryce's hands trailed from my waist to my shoulders and back down to my towel-clad ass. Gripping tightly, he pulled me hard against him, our stiff cocks pressing together.

The desperate moan was embarrassing as hell, but there was no damn way I could experience the kiss and the connection of our bodies and not react. I may have sounded like a fuckin' heifer in heat, but I didn't give a flyin' fuck. Bryce tasted too good. The fiery heat, the hard press of our bodies, that feeling of *yes*, this…this *is right*…

this *is what I've longed for* stole my breath and set fire to my blood.

Bryce tore his mouth away and rested his forehead against mine. Our chests heaved, our hard cocks pressed together, longing for more friction.

"Fuck." I sucked in a deep breath. "Why'd you fuckin' stop?"

Bryce chuckled. "I needed a minute. Didn't want to bust a nut two minutes in."

My dick begged for me to tell Bryce to get on his knees and give me what he'd offered.

My brain pushed back, saying to play it safe.

And my heart?

Well, my damn heart was already doodling *Casey Joe + Bryce* on the edges of my Biology notebook.

Mother.

Fuckin'.

Fuck.

"What do you want?" Bryce asked. "It's your call."

"The fuck it is," I growled. "You don't get to offer to suck me off—or whatever the fuck that was—and then make me do the damn decidin'."

Bryce groaned, burying his face in my neck. "It would be a lot easier to make good choices if my dick wasn't about to explode."

Knowing I had him just as hard as he had me shot a surge of pride racing through my veins. Fuckin' Bryce Armstrong wanted me, and damn if that wasn't a total ego boost. "If you don't want to take this any further, we need to get dressed and start workin' on shit."

Fuckin' hell.

Don't say you want to stop.

Please don't say you want to stop.

"What shit?" Bryce murmured against the sensitive skin under my ear, the soft whisper of his lips lighting my senses on fire. Senses I didn't know I had. Senses I wanted Bryce to explore all over my fuckin' body.

"Fuck if I know," I muttered. "Work shit. Any shit."

Bryce chuckled. "What if I want to take it further?"

My groan of indecision turned into a hiss of pleasure when Bryce traced his finger over my rock-hard cock, the textured material of my towel heightening the sensation. "Fuckin' hell."

I yanked Bryce out of the laundry room and toward the stairs.

Before I got us up five steps, Bryce gripped my hips and spun me around. With a gentle shove, he maneuvered me into a sitting position and knelt between my knees. His hand on the towel tucked tightly around my waist, eyes locked with mine, Bryce leaned in and feathered his lips over mine. "Are we doing this?"

The kiss flamed the inferno, but more than the molten desire it sent coursing through my blood, his lips against mine were a promise of more. I feasted on his mouth, savoring the rough burn of our stubble and the hard press of our lips. Kissing him may have been new and exciting, but it was also somehow surprisingly familiar and right—a staccato beat of *yes, yes, yes* thundered in my chest.

This kiss.

This moment.

This man.

I wanted more.

With Bryce.

I wanted *everything*.

With Bryce.

This man who had somehow become someone I turned to, someone I relied on, someone I enjoyed spending time with.

He had become my everything.

In the farthest recesses of my mind, a tiny *danger-danger* alarm wailed, but the heat of Bryce's tongue against mine, the sensual comfort of his hands caressing up and down my torso, and the throbbing of my dick thoroughly drowned out any rational thought.

"What do you want?" Bryce asked, nipping at my bottom lip.

"Fuckin' everythin'." The gruff words, whispered into his open mouth, coaxed a delicious moan from him.

"Gotta be a bit more specific." Bryce pressed a trail of kisses along my jawline, to my neck, and down to my chest. When he dragged his teeth over my nipple before sucking it between his lips with a soothing swipe of his tongue, I knew I'd died and gone to heaven. "You want me to suck you? Wanna suck me? Fuck me?" He panted through the options. His words hitched on the next ones. "Me fuck you? Fingers, mouths, full-on penetration?" He listed a menu of choices like we were at the most enticing all-you-can-eat buffet.

The way the word *yes* quivered out of me wasn't my finest moment, but who the fuck even cared? I cleared my throat and tried again. "Yeah, that."

"Which part?"

"All of it."

Bryce chuckled. "All of it? Of course, you'd tackle your first homosexual experience with gusto."

"Who says it's my first homosexual experience?" I managed to ask in words just above a damn whimper while Bryce sucked my other nipple and watched me with fire in his eyes.

He quirked a brow. "Is it not?"

I shrugged. "First one not just in my fuckin' head. Go big or go home."

Bryce gave me a wicked grin and moved down my body. Dragging his chin over the towel doing very little to hide my raging boner, he nuzzled his nose into my groin as his hands slipped under the cloth.

The air around us hung heavy with lust and potential. Like we both knew what happened in the next few moments would change things, we stared at each other— taking in heaving chests, dilated pupils, and rapid pulses just under the surface of bare skin—letting the tension build and maybe offering each other the chance to back out.

But backing out, hiding, and ignoring was what I'd been doing my whole damn life.

Pretending, covering up, burying myself in all the shit. The drama with Missy was real and intense, but it was also the perfect distraction. Being there for my boys— yeah, I knew I hadn't been the perfect dad, but my life truly did revolve around them—was a responsibility I never would have turned my back on, but it was another easy out that allowed me to push aside anything beyond surface-level survival.

I wallowed for years, numbing myself with alcohol,

keeping people away, and creating a whole damn personality out of being a jilted single dad who lost his wife. Losing Billy was just one more reason to close myself off.

Being faced with my own mortality opened my eyes.

Removing the numbness brought on by the alcohol forced me to acknowledge some things I'd been hiding from most of my life.

Fuck. Who knows? Maybe I would have kept on hiding if Bryce hadn't come to town. Maybe I would have gone to my grave with unanswered questions and secrets that used to scare the ever-loving shit out of me.

But Bryce *did* come to town.

And I didn't want to hide anymore.

Didn't want the easy way out.

I sure as shit wasn't *ready* to make whatever this next big step was, but I couldn't keep ignoring it.

Without taking my eyes from his, I nodded and spread my legs to loosen the towel. Bryce licked his lips and lifted his hands from my thighs to push the material away. I would forever crave that hungry fire in Bryce's gaze. I shifted, my cock bobbing against my stomach and dripping a bead of pre-cum onto the hair running from my navel to the base of my shaft.

Bryce leaned in and licked a hot, wet trail from my balls to the leaking tip of my cock, and I immediately knew two things.

One, this was going to be over a lot quicker than I wanted it to be.

Two, having a man's mouth on my dick maybe wasn't

the answer to all my problems, but I damn sure was going to enjoy the fuck out of it.

He swirled his tongue around my cock head before sliding me deep to the back of his throat. Was this the best blow job of all time because it was a man or because it was Bryce?

Yes.

Fuckin', yes.

"Spread your legs," Bryce demanded, pushing my feet up a stair and shoving my knees farther apart. He cupped my balls and ran a thumb between my ass cheeks before locking eyes with me and sinking his mouth down, down, down over my dick. He bobbed up and down, swallowing around me, never breaking eye contact. With one hand on each ass cheek, he exposed me just enough that each movement sent a cool woosh of air against my hole, and he massaged that sensitive area right under my balls with his thumbs the whole time he sucked me.

When he shifted and brought a thumb to my mouth, I sucked on it without thinking. But then the fucker pressed his spit-slick thumb against my hole, and I bucked wildly. The vibrations of Bryce's chuckles sent wicked sensations through me. Reaching out to grip his hair, I guided his head up and down as I pumped my hips, his mouth hot and wet around my cock. My damn back was going to have a hell of a bruise, but at that point, I didn't even care.

"Fuckin' hell," I bit out, thrusting too hard and only having a moment to think about how much I liked watching Bryce choke on my dick. "Holy fuck, I'm gonna come."

Bryce moaned, his hazel eyes locked with mine as he

feasted on my cock. His eyes begged for my load, pleading with me to come down his throat. I loved the wild, desperate longing painted over his face.

"You want that?" I asked. "Want my cum?" How I was able to string together a sentence, I had no clue, but the flame of desire in Bryce's eyes when he nodded spurred me on. "Gonna come so fuckin' hard. Gonna take every last fuckin' drop." My hands fisted harder in his hair, and Bryce gagged when I went too deep.

That sound and the press of his thumb into my hole sent me over the edge. With a low groan, I gave into the pleasure, pulsing my cum deep in the back of his throat. Bryce didn't miss a drop, swallowing everything I gave him as he milked me dry.

Eventually, he let my spent cock slip from his lips, and he slotted himself between my legs, cuddling into my chest. "You good?" he asked.

The only thing I could do was grunt some sort of affirmative.

Bryce chuckled.

We sat wrapped in each other's arms on the back stairs of our gym apartment for a moment that belonged only to us.

When my brain came back online, I sat there with only one thought on repeat and an overwhelming need to get Bryce off the same way he'd just drained my soul through my cock.

"I wanna do that," I mumbled into his neck.

He huffed. "Don't have to." When he shifted, I felt the rock-hard press of his cock against my thigh. "That's not why I—"

"Fuck off, I wanna suck you." Fighting against the boneless pleasure that insisted I just sleep off my orgasm on the stairs, I pushed up to a standing position. Grabbing Bryce's upper arm, I hauled him up to his feet. With me one stair higher, he was a full head shorter than me. I tipped his chin and brought our mouths together.

Bryce groaned in surprise, opening his mouth to my seeking tongue.

Fuck.

I liked kissing him.

Fuckin' *really* liked kissing him.

I'd decided earlier I'd never get tired of the taste of him on my tongue, but my release on his lips made for a unique flavor I wanted to feast on forever. And I knew tasting his cock, savoring his load, and kissing him with his cum still coating my tongue was an experience I'd been waiting for my entire life.

Maybe I'd made it this far in life without sucking dick, but that sure as shit didn't mean I had to live the rest of my years without it.

"Get upstairs."

Chapter 18
Bryce

"GET UPSTAIRS."

Casey's sex-roughened command sent a shiver of longing through me.

I made my way up the rest of the steps, knowing Casey Joe had the perfect view of my ass in the jock strap.

I hadn't worn it to entice him. Honestly, I'd just slipped it on because my clothes were in the dryer. But I wasn't going to complain about what had come of him finding me in nothing but a jock.

In all honesty, I didn't suck him off with the thought he'd return the favor. I hadn't thought he'd want to. I'd experienced enough guys throughout life who weren't picky when it came to who was blowing them but got real offended if they were expected to reciprocate.

But Casey's hands on my hips, his lips against my neck, and his chest pressed to my back as we reached the apartment door told me all I needed to know.

Casey was on board, and this was fucking happening.

A small part of me said we should probably slow things down, talk things through. He was a recovering addict diving headfirst into his first sexual experience with a man. It would make sense to talk and make sure we were on the same page.

My dick disagreed. It was on the same page as my libido which said we were consenting adults, and any fall out could be discussed later.

Shit.

I wanted this.

Casey's reawakening cock against my ass was proof enough he wanted this.

Would there be fall out?

Maybe.

Could we work through it if there was?

I guessed we'd find out.

"Never done this," Casey said, standing awkwardly in the doorway to his bedroom.

"You don't have to," I started.

"Shut the fuck up. Didn't say I'd never *wanted* to do this. Just that I never had." He gave his cock a quick stroke. "Fuckin' hell, I've wanted to. For so fuckin' long."

There was so much in those words.

A heavy longing.

Pain, regret, and wishes for what could have been.

But also a hint at something more. Pride, anticipation, and pure bliss. Casey was taking control and allowing himself to embrace his truth.

It didn't matter if it was a truth he'd known for decades or one he'd only recently discovered, he was living it, and I was damn proud of him.

Taking mercy on him, I sat down on the edge of the bed. "Then get on your knees and suck me."

Desire flamed to life in those cornflower blue eyes as Casey dropped to his knees in front of me. My cock ached, and the material of my jock was damp with pre-cum. And fuck if I'd ever wanted a blow job as badly as I did right then.

Being Casey's first meant something.

Knowing he'd kept this part of himself hidden for so long sent a pang straight to my heart. Sadness overwhelmed me that he'd felt he had no choice but to bury his true self, while at the same time, something like honor washed over me knowing I was the man he chose to break his silence with.

How do you know he'll break his silence? Maybe he'll get off and then pretend like nothing ever happened. What if he's just using you as an experiment?

Valid questions for sure.

I'd been through that in the past, and I wasn't looking to be someone's experiment at this point in my life.

But at that moment, Casey hooked his thumbs in the elastic of my jock and tugged. The underwear came down until my ass was in the way. With a huff of what appeared to be anticipation and impatience, Casey put a hand to my chest and shoved.

I let myself be pushed to my back on the mattress if only to see what he was going to do.

And fuck me.

Casey stood between my spread legs, shimmied the jock down my thighs, lifted my knees, and yanked the underwear the rest of the way off. Then he dropped to his elbows, pressing his chest to mine, and kissed me.

Heat and longing exploded on my tongue, and I begged the universe to let this be the beginning of something amazing and not a one and done.

When he broke the kiss, panting, with his forehead pressed to mine, Casey closed his eyes and took a long deep breath.

This was the moment.

Would he say he couldn't go through with it?

Say he—

"I wanna suck you so damn bad, but I also wanna jack you off and fuck you." His desperate words washed over me. "Like a kid with a damn bag of Halloween candy and I can't decide which one to eat first." He dragged his lips over mine in a hard, wet kiss. "Fuckin' want it all."

"Suck me," I begged. "We've got time for all the rest."

A harsh sound escaped him. "Fuck if we do. Wasted so much of my life."

Hooking my legs over the backs of his thighs, I gripped his ass and rocked our hips together. Then I trailed my hands up his back before cupping the sides of his face. "Case, look at me," I demanded softly. His eyes, brimming with unspoken emotion, locked with mine. "I'm here. We're going to live our lives and take advantage of the time we've been given."

Maybe I was speaking bullshit.

Maybe Casey didn't even want that.

But the words came from my heart.

He nodded. "Yeah, that's good. Fuckin' good," he

murmured against my lips. "But I'm not fuckin' waitin' long. We're usin' the whole damn day."

I chuckled. "I'm good with that."

And then, like I was in a damn dream, Casey Joe Riggs reached between us, grabbed my dick, and kissed a trail from my jaw to my pecs to my stomach. "Not even gonna say sorry if this sucks because it's gonna fuckin' suck," he said with a crooked grin, "but I'm damn sure willin' to practice until I'm better."

His mouth was hot, wet, and curious on my cock. He took his time, tasting me, swirling his tongue, stroking with his fist.

I kept my hands fisted in the sheets. Anyone sucking dick for the first time didn't need me gripping his hair and thrusting until he gagged.

Later.

Fucking hell, I hoped there'd be time for that later.

Casey cupped my balls while bobbing his head up and down.

I'd been near to blowing my load on the stairs earlier, so it was no surprise I was so close the moment his lips closed around my cock. "Fuck, Case, I'm close."

He hummed.

"No, like—" I gritted my teeth to keep from exploding as I watched Casey pop off my dick and swirl his tongue around my cock head, his eyes never leaving mine as he continued to fondle my balls. "Fucking hell."

Casey grinned. "Ain't as fuckin' hard as I thought," he said. "Just do what you like yourself and you're gold."

I couldn't help but laugh. "You get one dick in your mouth, and now you're a damn expert, huh?"

He shrugged, stroked me with one hand and teased a finger over my taint with the other. "Got you fuckin' close to comin' don't I?"

Before I could argue with the arrogant bastard, he took me back between his lips and as far back as his gag reflex would allow. With his fist stroking me and a thumb massaging just under my balls, I gave up any pretense of controlling my orgasm.

"If you don't want me to come in your mouth, pull off," I warned.

Casey hummed and sucked harder, his fist gripping tighter.

"Fuck, Case, I'm serious. I'm gonna—" The finger he teased between my ass cheeks and pressed against my hole sent me over the edge before I could get the warning out. My load exploded, my cock pulsing between his lips.

He swallowed once, twice, and then pulled off to stroke me and watch two more long ropes spurt across my stomach. Casey proudly swiped a finger through my cum, smeared it on my lips, and then brought his hot mouth to mine in a searing kiss.

When he finally pulled away, he grinned. "That wasn't half bad for my first time, right?"

I gently slapped his ass. "Not half bad at all."

Just when I thought he'd stand up, Casey shifted to the mattress and rolled us to our sides, playing big spoon to my little spoon. "Probably oughta shower, but this feels too good right now. Nap first, then shower. Then I'm fuckin' your brains out."

An orgasm-induced exhaustion took over before I could even finish laughing.

I woke later—we hadn't slept the *entire* day away, but it was definitely late afternoon—and took a long moment to savor the heavy warmth of Casey's arm slung over me.

My heart fluttered at the thought of there being something real between Casey and me, not just fake dating to pacify Dizzy. Would Casey want to actually date? Was he planning on coming out? I wasn't the type to take to the closet at nearly fifty, but I could give him time if that's what he needed.

What if he wakes up and panics?

Maybe you're making this into something it's not.

He's probably freaking out right now.

How much time are you willing to give being his dirty little secret?

Casey shifted behind me with a low groan. "What's it called when you jerk two dicks off at once?"

After I almost choked on a snort of laughter, I said, "Frotting?"

"Yeah," Casey said, his lips tickling against my neck. "Frotting. That's what I want to do."

Jesus.

He was maybe gonna kill me.

But damn, what a fucking fine way to go.

Casey rolled me to face him and pressed his hips into mine. "Get off like this, take a shower, then I'm fuckin' this ass." He gripped my ass cheeks but pulled back slightly. "If you're okay with that. Ain't some jerk who doesn't know consent is important. Been teachin' my boys about it since they were knee-high."

The rough and soft, harsh and sweet of this man turned my heart into a squishy pile of goo. "Consent is sexy," I murmured against his lips, "and I'm totally okay with you fucking me."

Casey gave my nose the sweetest little nuzzle with his own. "You think one day maybe I could try lettin' you fuck me?"

Holy.

Shit.

"I mean," he went on, "I know some guys don't like to bottom, and some guys don't like to top. The boys have told me everyone is different, and some guys don't want any type of penetrative sex."

The fact Casey was rocking his hard cock against mine while babbling about preferences when it came to sex was possibly the most surreal experience I'd ever had.

"So, if you only like it one way, I'm cool with that," he continued.

I cupped his cheek and kissed him softly. "I lean toward bottom, but I'm verse, so we can try whatever you want."

Casey quirked a grin and captured my lips as he reached between us and took both our cocks in his big hand. With the sun streaming into the room, and tiny dust motes dancing in the sunbeams, a completely mesmerized Casey watched as he fisted our cocks, thumbing through the pre-cum leaking from our slits.

I had to admit it was a gorgeous sight.

Casey stroked harder and took my mouth in a hungry kiss.

"Get on your back," he demanded, pressing my shoulder to the mattress.

His warm weight spread over me, and I opened my legs for him.

"This okay?" he asked.

I nodded and ran my fingers down his back to grip his ass. Pulling Casey's hips into me, I threw my head back in a moan as our hot cocks rubbed together. His hot lips against my neck sent electricity zinging through me, and the smooth glide of our dicks pressed together had my body begging for another release.

What I really wanted was to find the lube, prep myself, and plead with Casey to just fuck me into the mattress right then and there. But I was the one trying to convince him we had all the time in the world, so I needed to take my own advice.

We found an absolutely perfect rhythm of rocking hips and thrusting cocks, work-roughened hands digging into strong, broad shoulders, and unintelligible words whispering gruffly into the stillness of the room.

"Fuck," Casey bit out. "Fuckin' hell. I didn't know." He buried his head in my neck with a groan—a mix of pleasure and frustration—and thrust his hips harder. "Fuck. Wish I'd known."

With only a brief moment to worry regret would hold Casey Joe back from living the life he was meant to live—whether that was with me as a friend or something more... and I truly wanted to believe I meant that—I dug my fingers into his ass and held tight as an orgasm ripped through me.

The moment I let loose, Casey tumbled right over the edge after me with a long, low moan. We made another mess on my stomach, but the resulting press of his sticky belly to mine was a price I was willing to pay just to have Casey in my arms.

"You good?" I asked. Respect and genuine concern meant I had to ask my friend if he was okay after his first —okay, technically, second—sexual experience with a man. Life lessons, selfishness, and abject fear of losing someone I'd grown to care about meant I was terrified of what he might answer.

Casey huffed a warm breath into my sweaty neck. "So. Good."

Relief and joy tumbled through me like kittens in a field of wildflowers.

Part of me warned endorphins were likely keeping Casey from any sort of freak out. But it also seemed more and more likely he was handling these new experiences okay with each passing moment and every additional interaction we had.

"Sex with a guy or not, I know how crusty dried cum can get," Casey murmured against my shoulder. "Fuckin' bitch to get out of pubes. We should shower."

Who could argue?

So, we ended up sharing a shower. When Casey climbed out and dried off, I told him to make us something to eat while I finished up. By the time I took a brief moment to myself and exited the bathroom in just a towel, Casey had a little picnic feast arranged on a tray I'd never actually used.

"This looks good," I said as I surveyed the spread.

"Looks like a damn rabbit buffet," he grumbled. "But it'll do."

I chuckled. "Rabbit buffet? The bunnies should be so lucky."

We settled onto his bed, propped up on pillows, and demolished the snacks he'd put together.

Casey popped a dried peach slice in his mouth. "Before my stupid heart attack and you came along, I would have filled this tray with chips, donuts, some cold pizza, and beer." He chomped into an apple slice. "Now I'm sittin' here eatin' like a damn health nut."

I snagged a carrot and dipped it into the little bowl of garden pesto dip. "No one is forcing you to give up the unhealthy snacks," I said.

Casey snorted.

"What? You disagree?"

He was quiet for a bit while he chewed on a grape. "No. I miss the shitty snacks, but they just don't hold the same appeal. I know this food is better for my body. I feel better without all the chemicals. Plus, if I'm gonna put in the work with the exercise, it feels dumb to shovel all the shit into my mouth." He swiped a carrot through the pesto dip and crunched down on it loudly. "The snacks were probably the easiest because it wasn't too hard to replace them with healthier foods that tasted good."

We ate silently for a bit.

"The smokes and the beer were harder." He took a deep breath, and for a moment, I thought he'd elaborate. But he popped another dried peach in his mouth and kept quiet.

I knew Casey still struggled with addiction—especially with alcohol.

I was so damn proud of all the changes he'd made for

his long-term health, but it was no secret addiction could be a lifelong battle, and the struggles that came with recovery ebbed and flowed.

The unhealthy food had been more of a bad habit to break—much like me with the dopamine highs I found myself constantly seeking on social media. The cigarettes were a nasty, unhealthy habit Casey pushed through until he figured out replacement activities for when he was feeling stressed. Exercise had become his number one outlet for times when he would have reached for a pack of cigarettes in the past.

But alcohol was a different beast.

And I wasn't one hundred percent sure where Casey was in regard to his recovery journey. He spoke of his therapist. He acknowledged he was an addict. He'd insinuated he was well-aware addiction was a lifelong challenge.

Would he fight tooth and nail through relapses for the rest of his life?

Would the tiniest stressor send him back to the bottle?

Would he be the type who could drink socially without falling back into the desperate cycle of burying his pain with alcohol?

No matter what, I was prepared to stand by Casey's side.

I just hoped he wanted me there.

Chapter 19
Casey Joe

SITTING NAKED IN BED WITH A MAN WHILE WE laughed and ate a picnic of heathy snacks wasn't on my bingo card, but fuck if I didn't like it.

As a horny teen getting off to images of my baseball coach's son, I couldn't even fathom one day I might be in a position where any of this was even possible.

Is it possible?

Does Bryce know what he'd be getting into with you?

What the hell could you even bring to a relationship?

As I'd gotten pretty good at doing recently, I quickly swept up the negative thoughts under the rug by cleaning up our little picnic and returning the tray to the kitchen. I was one hundred percent aware I had a lot to work through still—hell, I'd probably be working through my shit for the rest of my life—and I very much knew I wouldn't be able to tamp down reality forever.

But that didn't mean I had to turn the crank on my own emotional jack-in-the-box at that exact moment. I could at least enjoy whatever came next in our steamy little day at home before I allowed my mind to send me into a spiral.

It was coming.

I knew it was.

I just wasn't ready to face it.

No, that wasn't accurate.

Actually, *facing* it wasn't the hard part. I'd been looking that shit in the face since it all tried to kill me.

Taking action on my reality was the part I didn't want to deal with.

Don't get me wrong, I was proud of the progress I'd made since my heart attack. Honestly, almost dying was probably the very best thing that ever happened to me. As fucked up as that sounded, it was the kick in the ass I'd been so desperate for all those years. Deep down, though, I knew I had barely scratched the surface of the true fixes I needed.

But it was easier to throw myself into helping my boys run their businesses, keeping the Riggs family name in good standing, and restoring the gym with Bryce than dealing with reality.

And really, in addition to exercising, taking some college classes, and supporting my boys, what better way to avoid reality than by burying myself in my first homosexual experience?

"What are you laughing about?" Bryce asked as I walked back into the bedroom.

I shook my head and crawled into bed, not bothering to turn on the bedside lamp despite the room darkening as the sun inched lower on the horizon. Had it really been just that morning I found Bryce in his jock and my whole life changed? Nah, my life had been changing by bits and pieces since Bryce trespassed on my property, and probably even before that. "Just that words are funny sometimes. You want to watch a movie or something?"

We ended up turning the television to a streaming channel of nineties movies, but cuddling with Bryce after a warm shower, food, and two toe-curling orgasms made the perfect recipe for sleep.

The windows were lit by moonlight when I opened my eyes sometime later. The television screen had switched to power-saving mode and cast only a dim glow into the room.

Bryce slept soundly in my arms.

He smelled clean and warm, and I breathed him in deeply as I nuzzled my nose into the base of his neck. I'd worked a bit in therapy about mindfulness, and I took the quiet moment to do a body scan. From head to toe and back again, I felt no pain, no stress, no tension. Only the comfortable soft press of our bodies together, the heat where our skin met, the nip of coolness in the air because we'd both refused to turn on the heat just yet.

Damn, if teenage Casey Joe could have seen me now.

That damn, stupid kid truly did love Missy the best he knew how—which sadly, for all involved was very, very little. He was hiding, pretending to be the only thing his family would have accepted—truth be told, he didn't even grasp that anything else was even an option back then, because, in all actuality, it wasn't—and he and Missy were drawn to each other like toxic magnets. If the magnets had been wrapped up in barbed wire and coated in the serum of poison-dart frogs.

Toxic.

As.

Hell.

With Bryce in my arms, the pain of the past was just that, the past. I'd held on to it for so long, like a security blanket—a shield—because it was easier to deal with the pain and betrayal than it was to acknowledge the real me. But with Bryce by my side, everything was softer, gentler, and simpler.

More real.

"Got some heavy-duty thinking going on back there?" Bryce's sleep-roughened words pulled me from my thoughts.

"Fuckin' mind never wants to stop these days." It was the damn truth. Without the haze of alcohol, my brain ran a million miles a minute. I trailed my nose from his neck to his ear. "Think there's only one way to make it shut up."

Bryce chuckled and pressed his ass backwards. "Yeah? Anything I can do to help?"

We'd eaten and fallen asleep naked, so my quickly thickening cock nestled perfectly between his ass cheeks. "Pretty sure I can figure something out."

Bryce turned his head over his shoulder, his lips seeking mine, and I crashed our mouths together. I'd only been kissing him for a day, but it had quickly become my favorite thing to do.

How damn lucky was I to have this beautiful man *want* to kiss me back?

My right arm was snaked under his neck, my hand holding his, and my left arm ran up and down his torso trying to touch every millimeter of his body. Our searing kiss sent heat pooling in my belly, and the gentle rocking of his ass provided just the right amount of friction to have my dick pleading for more.

When I tangled my fingers in the coarse hair of his lower belly, Bryce moaned into my mouth. I took the heavy weight of his cock in my hand and stroked him gently, thumbing through a bead of pre-cum. In all of my fantasies, I'd dreamed of touching a man in such an intimate way but never given any thought to the potential of it really happening.

But there I was, holding Bryce, stroking him, bringing him pleasure.

Was this seriously my life? It was the most surreal and precious moment of my life since my boys were born and placed on my bare chest.

And just like the overwhelm of emotions way back then, feelings and thoughts lodged in my head and heart even now as I held Bryce in my arms.

My body screamed for me to move things along, but my head held back like a dog braced against being pulled along on its leash.

"Hey," Bryce said after breaking the kiss and rolling in my arms to take my face in his hands. "What's up?" I liked that he knew me that well, but I also hated it.

Pressing my forehead to his, I took a deep breath. "I don't know what the fuck I'm doin'," I admitted.

Bryce nuzzled my nose and kissed my cheek. "You did great with your first blow job."

I huffed out a laugh. "Yeah, but most blow jobs are still pretty good even when they're not." I paused. "As long as we keep teeth out of the equation," I amended and grinned at his shudder. "But I've never had this type of sex with a guy. I want it to be good for you, and it can be really bad if I do it wrong."

Bryce put a finger to my lips. "Did you ever have anal with a woman?"

I nodded.

"So, I'm assuming you took your time and made it good for her, right?"

"I mean, she didn't have any complaints, and we both got off."

Bryce kissed me then, gently teasing his tongue against mine while our dicks rubbed together. When he broke the kiss, I groaned, chasing his lips for more. But he went on, "How did you get her ready for you?"

I blinked slowly, trying to reset my brain to comprehend the question. "Um." I cleared my throat, glad the room was dark. "I ate her ass and used a lot of lube."

Bryce's grin was barely visible in the moonlight. "Then eat my ass and use a lot of lube."

Fuckin' hell.

I rolled him to his back, my mouth devouring him. How the hell was I supposed to keep my damn dick under control when he said shit like that?

We rocked together, our breaths heavy as our hard cocks built up enough friction to light a campfire. When I realized I could have easily gotten off just like that *again*, I shifted to my knees between his legs and took a long, steadying breath.

Bryce grumbled. "What's wrong?"

I ran a hand over my face and reached to turn on the lamp. "Gotta make sure we're both thinkin' straight."

"Um, I haven't been thinking straight for most my life," Bryce teased.

I snorted. "Yeah, well, my dick is a lost cause these days, at least around you it seems."

"So, what's the problem?"

I reached into the bedside table. "We've got lube."

Bryce bit his lip, and I had a hard time remembering why I wasn't already balls deep in him. "I can get myself ready if that's—"

"I can eat ass just fine, thanks," I grumbled.

Heat flared in Bryce's eyes. "Then what the hell is it?"

"Condoms."

Realization dawned on his face. "Oh," he said on a sigh. "I have some."

When he made to get out of bed, I pushed him back to the mattress and swallowed thickly. "Do we need them? I'm on board with whatever you decide."

Bryce's brows shot up and his Adam's apple bobbed.

Like I couldn't stop my damn mouth, I just kept talking. "It's been a long dry spell for me—like don't ask me who was president because I'm not gonna fuckin' say —but I've had a shit ton of bloodwork and shit recently, and I purposely had them run shit for STIs and shit."

Casey Joe Riggs, folks. So eloquent with words.

Bryce ran a hand over his stomach, and I tried to focus on his words rather than how good his dick looked against his skin. "I haven't been with anyone since my last bloodwork, and it was all clear. But I'm one hundred percent okay with whatever makes you more comfortable."

I slammed the bedside drawer shut. "I don't wanna use them." If Bryce had leaned toward using condoms, I would have rolled one on and gone to town. But hearing him say he was comfortable either way was exactly what my questioning head had needed.

I lowered myself to my elbows, bringing my chest to his, and feathered my lips over the corner of his mouth. "Not like I'm plannin' on downloadin' ClickC*ck and hookin' up with other guys. If I'm fuckin' you, you're the only one until we decide we're through."

Bryce tangled his legs with mine. "And what if we never decide we're through?" he asked, his words heavy with emotion.

"Fuckin' fine by me," I answered truthfully. "Lookin' for someone to spend what's left of my life with sounds pretty damn stupid when I already found the only fuckin' person who can put up with my shit in a thousand-mile radius."

Bryce chuckled. "Such a sweet talker."

He wasn't laughing when I flipped him to his stomach and lowered myself between his legs. Burying my face in a sexy ass wasn't anything new to me. Having that ass attached to someone with a dick who happened to be a person I could easily see spending the rest of my life with was the part I was unaccustomed to.

But the noises Bryce made as I swiped my tongue over his hole assured me it was something I'd have no problem getting used to.

And definitely no problem loving.

None at all.

"Oh, shit, Case," Bryce whimpered into the mattress when I flattened my tongue and pressed it over the sensitive flesh. "I'm ready. Seriously," he panted, thrusting his hips, "I'm good. Fuck, so good."

I chuckled, purposely directing a puff of air over Bryce's entrance. "So greedy. Why ain't I surprised you're impatient as hell?" I swirled my tongue around his hole before pressing a kiss to one cheek then the other. "Not yet."

Bryce whined. "Fucking hell." He squirmed under my feasting mouth. "Please, Case," he begged.

Ignoring his pleading, I coated my finger with spit and pressed it to his hole. "This okay?" I didn't move until Bryce answered.

"Oh god, fuck, yeah it's good. Fuck, Case," Bryce rambled.

When my finger breached him, Bryce hissed, and I paused. "You good?"

He took a deep breath and rocked his hips. "Yeah." A deep groan. "Give me more."

With more spit and more tongue, I slicked the way for a second finger and wondered if it would be possible to make a mix tape of Bryce's bedroom sounds to listen to as I fell asleep at night.

Or you could just fuck him and listen to his sweet noises every night, dumbass.

Yeah. That sounded like the best fuckin' plan ever.

"Please, Casey." Bryce's desperate words, muffled by the mattress, spurred me one.

"You wanna get off like this? Come with my fingers

and tongue?" I asked, knowing I'd gladly get him off just like this even if my own dick was screaming to be inside him.

"Yes," Bryce moaned. "But not tonight. Fucking hell, CJ."

I froze. I'd never heard that name on his lips.

I liked it.

"What do you want?"

"Inside me. Fuck me. Make me come." Bryce lifted himself to his hands and knees, but I slapped his ass.

"Get on your back. I wanna see your face when you take my cock." Pumping lube into my palm, I slicked myself and worked the rest into Bryce. "Fuckin' hell, look at you."

Bryce lay before me, his legs spread just for me. His hard dick bobbing against his stomach just for me. His eyes full of heat and desire.

Just for me.

I moved closer and lifted his legs over my thighs. With the slick head of my dick pressed to his hole, I inched in slowly, my eyes never leaving his.

Watching for hesitation.

Discomfort.

Regret.

But all I saw was longing.

Passion.

Pleasure.

Moving my gaze to where his body opened for me, my breath hitched. "Fuck, Bryce, look how good you look on me. That hole openin' for me." I shifted forward, my hands connecting with the mattress above Bryce's shoulders, my cock sliding the rest of the way into him until my balls met his ass.

Looking between us, I had to stop and get myself under control. His ass was hot and tight, but it was more than that. This was Bryce. A man, yes, but my *person*. The missing piece of my heart. More than anything, that was what took my breath away.

"You okay?" Bryce croaked out.

With hot tears stinging my eyes, I nodded as I slowly pulled out of his tight body. When Bryce whimpered, I caught his fiery gaze and thrust back in, making him cry out.

Dropping to my elbows, I anchored my arms under his shoulders. What I'd planned to be a hard and fast fuck morphed into something slow, sensual, and completely unexpected. But as we moved together in an unhurried, gentle rhythm, I couldn't help but think about his earlier words.

All the time in the world.

We didn't have that.

Deep down, we both knew our time together wasn't guaranteed.

But whatever time we did have was perfect.

And beautiful.

And ours.

Bryce wrapped his legs around me, and his arms snaked around my neck as he pulled me into a kiss. Our tongues thrust together in the same deep, slow rhythm of my cock in and out of his ass.

"Case," he whimpered. "So close."

"Come for me," I whispered at his ear. "Let me feel

that pretty ass around my cock." Three more thrusts and Bryce threw his head back with a cry of ecstasy.

I lifted up to watch his orgasm splash across his belly. The tight ring of muscle clenching rhythmically around my cock and Bryce whispering, "CJ, CJ, CJ," with each glide of my dick into his spasming body was enough to send me over the edge.

Gripping his hips, I held him tightly and buried myself balls deep inside him as the first pulses of my release shot from my cock. Needing to be closer to him, wanting to meld every inch of our bodies together, I returned to my elbows and wrapped him tightly against me as I emptied my load into him. "Fuckin' hell, Bryce. Fuck." Something like a sob escaped me. "Bryce," I whispered like a god damn prayer. "Fuck." The word escaped me on a ragged breath, partly from the exertion, but mainly from emotion clogging every cell of my being.

I collapsed on top of him, certain I'd never be able to move again. The boys or Lance would eventually come looking, and they'd just find me there, covered in cum, overdosed on the best sex of my life.

When my brain waves finally booted back up, I shifted just enough to slip from his ass and curl onto my side with Bryce cuddled against me.

"That was..." he started, looking up at me. "It was good, right?"

I hated that he looked worried. Kissing him, I sealed everything amazing from the day with my lips. "Best ever."

"Would it ruin things if I told you I love you?" Bryce asked. "If it's too—"

I shut him up with a kiss. "Say it for real."

Bryce chuckled. "What?"

"You didn't say it for real. You asked if it would ruin things *if* you said it." I nuzzled my nose against his. "I wanna hear it for real."

He kissed me. "I love you."

Gathering him close, I pressed a kiss to his temple. "Fuckin' hell," I tried to say without my words catching. "I love you too."

Three orgasms had wiped us out, and the thought of trying for a fourth was enticing but not realistic. We eventually dragged ourselves out of bed, showered, downed two water bottles each, and climbed back into bed after putting new sheets on.

"We could just use my bed," Bryce said.

I grunted and hauled him close. "I like having you in my bed."

It was ridiculous, and probably very caveman-ish of me, but fuck it.

After several quiet moments, Bryce traced a finger over my lips. "You're okay? Not regretting anything or freaking out?"

I gave his question consideration. "I have a lot of regrets, but never about anything involving you and me— unless we decide to never do this again." Kissing the corner of his smile, I went on. "We should probably sleep."

Sleeping with Bryce in my arms was the most satisfying and deep rest I'd gotten in decades. Who knew all I needed was a queer relationship to make it happen?

Of course, the me of several years ago wasn't anywhere

close to being ready for something real with anyone, queer or straight.

And as much as my heart wished we could have avoided all the pain, I would never change the timeline if it meant losing the chance to have my boys. I'd go through Missy leaving, Billy dying, and three more heart attacks to keep my boys in my life.

The last thing that danced through my mind as I drifted off to sleep was what would a future with Bryce look like and a deep, nagging fear.

Several hours later, I woke with a start just as the sun was blinking itself awake on the horizon.

Stark reality glared brightly in my mind.

Not a dream, but crystal-clear clarity like I'd never known before.

My stomach plummeted as complete recognition cascaded over me.

I slipped out of bed and left Bryce sound asleep, and hoped it wasn't the last time.

Chapter 20
Bryce

I WOKE TO THUNDER.

No.

Not thunder.

What the hell was that?

Pounding.

Someone was about to break down the outside door to my apartment.

"What the fuck?" I asked as I sat up.

Then I realized Casey wasn't in bed with me.

Well, shit.

As I rolled from bed and yanked on an old pair of Casey's sweats I found on the floor, I did my very best to calm the terrified thoughts rushing through my head.

Where was Casey?

Drinking?

An accident.

A medical emergency.

Casey getting in his truck and driving off, running from his past. Trying to escape his reality.

Throwing a t-shirt on, I swallowed thickly and took a deep breath as I hurried down the stairs.

By the time I reached for the door handle, I was fully prepared to see the county sheriff, Brother Larry, or even my dad come to break bad news to me.

Finding Henry Riggs with his hand raised like he was preparing to knock the door down like my very own big bad wolf was *not* what I was expecting.

"Henry?" My scrambled brain tried to make sense of what I was seeing. "What's wrong?" Despite it being a friend at my door, I knew he could still be the bearer of bad news.

Henry ran his hand over his face. "Hudson texted me and Jack asking why Dad is at his old place, sitting in the cold in pajama pants."

Knowing Casey was just up the hill calmed me a bit. Worry still coursed through me, but at least I knew where he was. I stepped back to let Henry enter. "Come up while I make coffee."

It was clear Casey's son would have rather just gotten a quick answer, but he made his way upstairs behind me. "What happened?" he asked as we entered the kitchen.

The heat in my cheeks might as well have been Rudolph's nose. I busied myself preparing the coffee and did my best to avoid making eye contact. Henry was my friend, but I wasn't comfortable telling him his dad was maybe having a major freakout because he fucked my brains out a few hours ago.

Honestly, I wanted to tell the whole world Casey was

mine and we'd spend whatever time we had left loving each other, but it wasn't really my place to share that information with his sons or anyone else.

Henry must have caught my red cheeks because his brows shot up and he snapped his mouth shut. "Oh." He blinked slowly. "Oh, shit. Okay. It's okay. We all figured this was coming…"

Guilt washed over me. "I—"

"It's fine," Henry assured me. "I won't tell him I know anything. It's not like you told me, I'm just pretty good at reading people."

"What if it's not fine?" I scooped ground coffee into the machine and poured in water.

"What do you mean?" Henry crossed his arms over his chest. "Did you guys have a fight?"

Pulling the thermos from the cabinet, I shook my head. "No, no, nothing like that." The comforting scent of coffee filled the air. "Things are good. Well, things *were* good," I amended. "But he's there, and I'm here, and maybe things aren't as okay as I'd let myself believe."

Henry leaned against the counter as I fought the urge to add cream and sugar to the thermos. "Dad needs time to himself sometimes. You're the best damn thing that's happened to him outside of a near-death experience kicking his ass into gear. Everyone in town can see it. Hell, even *he* sees it. But Dad is Dad. He's probably doing some big time thinking about life and what he wants going forward."

"Or he's freaking out." I tried unsuccessfully to tamp down the worry.

Henry started to protest but clamped his mouth shut

with a shrug. "Not gonna lie, he might be. He's dealt with a lot of shit in life. He's been dealing with a lot of changes lately—not saying the changes have been *bad*, just that Dad isn't the most flexible."

A fond smile teased my lips. "I should go over there." It was a simple statement, but it hung in the air like an uncertain question.

"Lance was heading that way when I came over here." Henry nodded toward the cabinet. "Let's have some coffee and give those two some time to talk," he suggested.

I wanted to fill the thermos, push past him, and run all the way to Casey's house to see for myself the man I loved was okay.

And if he told me he'd made a mistake?

Told me he misspoke and didn't really love me?

Sneered in disgust at what we'd shared?

Blamed me for coercing him into a situation he hadn't wanted?

No.

Casey Joe might have been freaking out, but it wasn't because of what we did or because he loved me.

Well, no, that wasn't accurate.

It was very likely exactly because of what we did and because he loved me.

But it wasn't a freakout about being with a man or falling for a man.

Casey was so sure he'd wasted his life away. Convinced he'd spent his fifty-some years being a rotten father and wallowing in heartache instead of living life. He dug his hole deep, deep, deeper, and filled it with anger, alcohol, and self-loathing.

Yeah, Casey was maybe freaking out, but I didn't think it was in a negative way about me or us.

Did I know that for sure?

No.

Was he very possibly sitting outside his house trying to figure out how to tell me he couldn't truly love me? Didn't want to live with me? Needed some space?

Yes. It was possible.

Hell, anything was possible.

If I walked my ass to Casey's house on the hill and he told me he couldn't be with me in a romantic or sexual way...well, I wasn't sure I wanted to think about that.

Would I be crushed, but understanding? Let him know I still wanted to be friends?

Or would I get angry and demand he be true to himself? Push back at him and force him to see how good we were together?

Instead of answering those questions—in all honesty, I had no clue what the answer would be—I sat at my kitchen table and drank coffee with Henry while my stomach churned in anticipation of what was to come.

Things were up in the air.

Tension buzzed through me.

Change was inevitable—sometimes good, sometimes bad, but always unavoidable.

I wanted more than anything to promise myself Casey and I would be okay, even if we returned to our simple friendship.

But my heart was camped out in my throat, and worry trickled through my soul.

Things between Casey Joe and me had been going so

well. There was no guarantee we were off track, but also no promise everything was copacetic.

The unknown was scary as hell.

Casey loves Bryce

When Henry turned down a third cup of coffee, I did my best to hide my relief. The smirk, only slightly hidden by his beard, told me he knew I was about to go insane waiting for him to leave.

I knew Lance was with Casey Joe, and the friends needed time to chat, but that didn't make me want to run up the hill any less.

"Jack wants you and Dad to come try his sugar-free dark chocolate raspberry cake with the warm peach bourbon drink we've got for the fall." He must have caught the look on my face. "We've got a mocktail version too."

I walked him to the door. "Sounds amazing." I loved the fact Henry and Jack had so easily adapted to making healthier food and drink options for Casey. "Tell Jack hi for us."

Henry paused in the hallway. "You're really good for him," he said.

There was no reason to pretend like I didn't know who he was talking about. "He's good for me too," I said. "But we're no better off together if we can't be good for ourselves."

Henry smiled and nodded. "I rest my case."

With Henry gone, I washed my face, brushed my teeth, and pulled on socks and boots before shoving my phone in my pocket. After putting on a zip-up hoodie, grabbing the thermos, and deciding at the last minute to take a flannel shirt for Case, I locked the door behind me and headed down the stairs.

Crossing the street, I absently noted four cars in the Glazed Buns drive-thru line. Good for them. I was glad their decision to add the drive-thru option had proven successful.

The door to the bakery and coffee shop swung open, and my brain did a record skip when I saw Dizzy walking toward me.

"There's my Brycey," she called out with a wave.

I buried the groan deep inside and offered my aunt a smile. "What are you doing here so early?" Clearly, the Universe was making sure Lance and Casey got their discussion time.

After a quick hug, my aunt and I moved away from the street to stand off the corner of the sidewalk.

"Barb and I have breakfast or lunch at least once a week. It's a breakfast week and my turn to visit her." Dizzy held up a bag and drink carrier. "Glazed Buns is my absolute favorite. I'll deny it if you tell anyone back home, but this place is hands down better."

"You better make the trip over here once my gym opens," I teased.

"You better believe it." She patted my cheek. "It's only a fifteen-minute drive."

I raised a brow. "Damn, woman. How fast are you driving?"

She waved me off, ignoring my question. "My living arrangement is perfect, but I have to say, I really like it here in Haven Grove. Coming here is never a problem, and now that you and Barb are both here, I'll be visiting all the time." She shook the bag. "Have to work off these breakfast sammies and cinnamon rolls." Dizzy took in the flannel and thermos. "Where you headed this early?"

I glanced toward the hill. "Up to Casey's place."

My aunt narrowed her eyes. "Thought he was staying with you? You two have a spat or something?"

Guilt coursed through me. "Um, I gotta be honest with you about that." I hoped Casey wouldn't be mad, but I couldn't keep up with the lie.

Dizzy put her breakfast and drinks on the nearby bench and faced me with her arms crossed. "Go on."

I swallowed thickly. "Um, Casey and I were never really dating."

She eyed me suspiciously. "You seemed pretty date-y."

Shaking my head, I smiled. "Case felt bad for me when you were trying to set me up with guys, so he opened his mouth and said something stupid." Stupid, overprotective, and rash, but damn if I didn't love the fact he'd stood up for me. And the farce had been enough to push us together, so I couldn't be *too* upset about it.

Regret washed over Dizzy's face. "Well, damn. I sure didn't mean to put you in a bad spot. I'm sorry if I caused you any trouble."

"No, you're fine. Just probably better if I find my own dates."

She cocked her head to the side. "Wait, so you don't have a thing for Casey Joe?"

I huffed a laugh. "Oh, I definitely have a thing for him. I just felt bad lying to you."

She nodded. "I don't like being lied to, but I can see how I put you both in a pickle." Dizzy paused and let her gaze travel toward Casey's house. "So, *he* doesn't have a thing for you? Damn sure coulda fooled me," she muttered.

Graphic images of our time together splashed through my head, and I was grateful for the cool air against my fiery cheeks.

I cleared my throat. "We might have something going on *now*," I admitted. "But I didn't want to keep the lie going." I glanced up the hill again. "And the ball is kinda in Casey's court now."

Dizzy nodded sagely. "If it's not right, it's just not right."

For a moment, those words hurt, but then I realized they didn't describe Casey and me. "I don't think it's as much about things not being right between us," I mused as I pictured Casey on his hill. "Pretty sure I've never felt anything so good and right." When Dizzy gave me a questioning look, I went on. "It's one of those things where it's more about the timing. Things are very, *very* right, but maybe it's just not the right time."

For a moment, sadness washed over me.

Maybe Casey was right about wasting so much time or not having much time left.

Did we still have so much to work on with ourselves that we'd need to accept things between us just couldn't happen the way we wanted them to?

Dizzy hummed softly and picked up her bag and

drinks. "Back when you were in your twenties, I would have told you something completely different than what I'm about to say. But different advice for different phases of life sometimes. If you two have found something right together, I say fight for it. We don't have forever—just ask me how many friends I've lost and how many are knocking on heaven's door these days—so, maybe you need to accept the timing for what it is and realize nothing will ever be perfect." She tucked the bag under her arm, balanced the drink carrier in one hand, and reached up to pat my cheek. "If we keep waiting for everything to be perfect, we'll find ourselves at the end of it all wishing we'd just lived our lives instead of looking for perfection."

I smiled sadly. "You're preaching to the choir."

Dizzy gave me one last pat. "Well then, don't you two get hung up on some myth of perfect timing. Spend your time livin' and lovin'," she said with a wink. "Pretty sure your parents expect you at dinner sometime soon." And then she headed off in the opposite direction towards Barb's place over the Dairy Palace.

Dizzy's words rolled around in my head.

I didn't know what to expect when I got up to Casey's place, but I had a gut-deep longing to be near him and talk through whatever was bothering him. Maybe it was corny and cliché, but the idea we could get through anything as long as we were together had sprouted roots and taken hold in my head.

Pushing aside the doubt and worry, I opted to focus on how amazing things had been between Casey and me over the last twenty-four hours—and long before things had taken a turn toward the hot and steamy.

Yeah, we had to build this thing on more than just sex, but we'd already set a strong foundation with our friendship.

Every cell in my being was confident Casey and I had something real and worth fighting for.

I was ready and willing to fight.

Was he?

I started toward the hill.

Chapter 21
Casey Joe

"You always did like watching the sun come up at the ass-crack of dawn," my best friend said as he shuffled his boot-clad feet through the dewy grass.

Summer hadn't completely given up yet, but she'd been sharing the day with crisp, cold mornings for a week or so now. It wouldn't be long before she was gone completely, replaced by frosted grass and the need for a sweatshirt all day long.

"Not my fault the sun wants to rise at the ass-crack of dawn." I gestured toward the ombre colors just beginning to paint the sky. "At least it's later now than in the middle of summer."

Lance eyed the beer bottle in my hand, but he said nothing as he took the seat next to me. With our boots stretched out on the fire pit, our pajama pants, and sweatshirts, I was sure we made quite an early morning image.

"You wanna tell me why you're drinking at sunrise?"

Lance asked, somehow managing to make the question completely non-judgmental.

"You wanna tell me why you're railin' my kid so damn hard the whole fuckin' town can hear it?" I shot back.

Lance snorted. "Who says I was the one doing the railin?"

I tipped the beer bottle his way. "Touchy," I quipped, doing my best to bite back the grin.

Lance snorted at the joke.

Way back when we were teens, we'd seen the word *touché* in a book we had to read for homework. We'd pronounced it *touchy*, and it wasn't until class the next day that we heard the teacher pronounce it correctly. Lance and I had nearly pissed ourselves laughing over our mispronunciation, but we'd kept using it for years after. The word was always sure to bring a bit of levity to a moment.

And fuck if that moment didn't need some levity.

"Been a while since I seen you with a beer," Lance tried again.

"Been a while since I had one." I held it out to him. "I've got plenty."

Lance shook his head. "Nah, Hudson was fixing breakfast when I left."

We sat in silence for a moment.

"What's going on?" Lance asked.

"Not a damn thing," I drawled, rolling the beer bottle from one hand to the next.

"What's got you thinking about drinking?"

"Who the fuck says I'm thinkin' about drinkin'?"

"You gonna drink that?" Lance didn't look at me, just

stared straight ahead at his breath crystalizing on the cold, still air.

"Maybe." God, I wanted to. Wanted to slice open a vein and just pour the whole damn six-pack right in. Lose myself to the numbness.

"You want me to go buy you a pack of smokes too? Fuck it all in one fell swoop?"

"Fuck off." Truth was, the smokes had been the hardest to break, but they were the ones I wanted to turn to the least. The constant fullness in my chest, the congestion, the low throbbing in my head, all of that had cleared up without the smokes. Taking a run didn't send pain screaming through my lungs anymore. My clothes didn't smell like smoke. Even my damn teeth looked better.

"Maybe you hand that over and go home." Lance still wasn't looking my way, but I knew he was there one hundred percent. My rock, my friend, my support even after all these years.

"This is my fuckin' home," I bit out, but I handed the bottle to him.

Lance twisted the cap and poured the amber liquid into a frothy mess in the grass.

I snorted. "Damn mother fucker, wastin' my beer." Grabbing another from the six-pack, I twisted it open and held it under my nose. Breathing in deeply, I let it transport me back to all the times I'd lost myself to drinking.

"What's up, Case?" Lance's words were quiet on the crisp air.

"Used to be so easy," I said, my eyes trained on the gorgeous colors filling the horizon beyond the orchard.

Lance took the bottle from me and poured it out.

With a third beer rolling from hand to hand, I recalled the wash of nothingness that would take over when I'd worked my way through a six-pack—sometimes even nine or ten. No more hurt, no more shame, no more anger, just oblivion.

When the bottle slipped from my hands and thunked in the frosty grass, Lance picked it up and emptied that one too.

"I've got more," I said, grabbing the fourth bottle. I hadn't had a drink in a while. I could probably bury it all with just three beers.

"Where's Bryce?" Lance asked.

"Fuck off."

Lance just hummed in response.

"What the fuck's that supposed to mean?" I asked, chucking the beer bottle at his head.

The fucker caught it.

Fuck.

Lance smiled. "You know it doesn't matter to any of us."

I didn't answer.

"We don't care if you find someone or stay perpetually single, bemoaning the one who got away for the rest of your life," Lance said like he didn't have a care in the world.

"Fuck off. Missy wasn't the one who got away."

Lance cocked a brow my way. "Who said I was talking about Missy?"

I spit and picked up the fifth bottle of beer.

"Stay single, date women, date men, fall in love with

Bryce...none of it matters to us," Lance continued. "We love you just the way you are. The only thing we care about is that you're happy and healthy. We want you here with us for the long haul."

My chest ached like a fist squeezed my heart in a tight grip.

I twisted the cap off the beer and sniffed it again. "Bryce is in bed," I said. "My bed."

Lance hummed again.

We sat silently.

"Is that what has you wanting to drink?"

"I don't want to drink," I answered as I poured the beer to the ground.

"Then what's going on?" Lance asked.

"Sometimes feelin' all this shit is a bunch of shit."

Lance chuckled. "Agreed. But what's the alternative? Numbing yourself to within an inch of your life and missing out on truly living?"

"Being numb is a lot easier."

"Is it?"

I picked up the sixth and final beer bottle. "Do you know how many years I missed?"

"Do you know how many years you still have left?" Lance asked. He held his hand out for the beer, but I didn't give it up.

"I think there's somethin' I need to do," I said. "Don't wanna fuckin' do it. Don't even wanna fuckin' talk about it."

"Sometimes we have to do shit we don't want to do if it means making things better." Lance knocked his boot against mine. "You didn't want to give up smoking and drinking, but you did it because it was for the best. Didn't want to start exercising, but you did it because your health was on the line."

He let those words sink in.

"Hell, I think there were some times way back then you didn't even want to keep on keepin' on, but you did it for your boys no matter how bad it hurt."

The noise I made was supposed to be more of a scoff and less of a sob, but I figured Lance got the idea all the same.

I opened the beer and took another long, deep breath. One beer wouldn't hurt. Hell, even my doctor had said I didn't have to cut out alcohol completely. I could just take a few swigs.

But it wasn't about the beer.

It was the longing for the numbness.

The desperation to avoid everything and just bury it all.

It was about not having the right tools to deal with the feelings bombarding me.

Not knowing how to come to terms with what I'd missed all these years.

Knowing what I wanted but not knowing how to handle the influx of emotions without masking the pain with chemicals.

Not everything was raw and painful. I had my boys, Jack, Lance, and Bryce. Everything with the most important people in my life was good.

Really good.

But I'd quickly learned it was nearly impossible to let

the good shit in without having to deal with the bad shit too.

I wanted nothing more than to look forward to all the good that came next, but I knew deep down I couldn't take that step if I didn't fix myself first.

I had to learn how to deal with the bad if I ever wanted to be free to live the good.

"You okay?" Lance asked.

"I will be."

It was maybe the scariest truth I'd ever spoken.

After the sun cleared the horizon, Lance stood and stretched. With a hand on my shoulder—I guess he figured I wouldn't get in too much trouble with just one beer left—he said, "Do what you have to do, bud. Your family? We're here, not going anywhere." He made it a few paces back toward his and Hudson's place before he paused and turned back to me. "I'm counting Bryce in that too. Pretty sure he isn't going anywhere either. Whatever you two decide you've got going, I think he's here for the long haul."

The sun was higher in the sky when the beer bottle being taken from my hands jerked me awake. Bryce smirked but didn't say a word as he tossed the bottle to the grass on the other side of the fire pit and handed me a flannel shirt.

We still hadn't spoken when he moved the second chair closer and took a seat next to me. He reached over, spread the flannel over me like I was damn fuckin' toddler, and then took my hand in his under the material.

And still we sat quietly.

Finally, I couldn't stand it.

"Hey," I mumbled.

"Hey," Bryce said. I didn't need to look at him to see his soft smile.

"Sorry I left."

He shrugged. "It's okay. Probably still be sleeping if Henry hadn't tried to knock my damn door down."

Then I did look at him. "What? Why? What's wrong?"

"Lance and Hudson saw you over here and woke up Henry and Jack to see if they knew what was going on. When they didn't have an answer, Lance headed over here and Henry came to my place."

I winced. "Sorry about that."

"It's all good."

Silence fell over us again.

It wasn't uncomfortable. Sitting with Bryce had always been easy whether we talked until we ran out of words or we just took up space.

"I told Dizzy we weren't really dating." Bryce rolled his head on the back of his chair to look my way.

"Why?" Did I want to know the answer?

He shrugged again. "Just always felt wrong to lie. Wanted to clear the air." He gave my hand a squeeze. "So, I guess we aren't fake dating anymore."

And there it was.

My opening.

I took too long, and Bryce breathed in deeply. "This is the part of the day after amazing sex with your friend and roommate where you say you're glad we aren't fake dating anymore because you want us to date for real."

I chuckled. "Oh, really? Is that what I'm fuckin' supposed to say?" I returned the squeeze.

"Only if it's what you want," he whispered. "If not, I'm being one hundred percent honest that I can make do with just being friends. I love you, I love your family, I love this town. If you don't feel the same about me, I'll take you in whatever way I can get you."

I leaned over the arm of my chair and hooked my hand around the back of his neck to pull him close. With my forehead resting against his, I rubbed my nose to his. "That's a fuckin' nice sentiment, but it's a bunch of bullshit and no way to live. You should either have every single part of the man you love or tell him to fuck right off. None of this *we can just be friends* shit." I pressed a hard kiss to Bryce's mouth. "'Cause I gotta tell you, I feel a whole fuckin' lot different toward you than I feel toward Lance. He's my best friend, but you're my—" I took a deep shuddering breath to cover the way my voice cracked. "I don't think I can be just friends with you, and I sure as fuck don't wanna try it."

Bryce's lips opened on a whimper as I took his mouth. The warm, comforting kiss full of promise, but laced with the unknown.

When we broke for air, Bryce's eyes met mine. "Okay, so what pulled you from bed? What has you up here with a six-pack?" He closed his eyes for a long moment. "What does all of it mean for us?"

Chapter 22
Bryce

MY HEART SANK WHEN I FOUND CASEY JOE WITH an empty six-pack of beer overlooking the orchard. A slip wasn't the end of the world. Even a full-blown relapse didn't mean he'd failed.

Casey and I had spoken at length about his addiction. He and I both knew it was a lifelong thing; there would be ups and downs. Celebrations and setbacks.

Slipping up wasn't the problem.

The problem was whatever had driven Casey to grab the case of beer in the first place.

But when I'd taken the beer, his eyes had flown open, clear and bright.

When I'd covered him up and took his hand, there was no sign of drunkenness.

And when Casey's mouth had come down on mine, I'd tasted only *him*, no lingering trace of beer.

I'd meant what I said about taking whatever I could

get. If friendship was what Casey could offer, I'd find my peace with it.

But I wasn't going to lie. Hearing him say he wasn't willing to do just friends stirred up a mess of hope in my heart and butterflies in my belly.

"What does all of it mean for us?" I asked.

After a long moment, I worried Casey wasn't going to answer.

Maybe he didn't have an answer.

Then he cleared his throat.

"Pour me some of that coffee if it's the good kind."

I made quick work of passing him the thermos cup full of steaming black coffee.

He took a long sip, cursed because it was so hot, and reached for my hand. Holding tightly like I was his lifeline, Casey said, "I need help, and it's not something I can do on my own."

My heart simultaneously sank and cheered. "Whatever you need. You know we're all here for you."

Casey didn't speak, but I felt his nod.

The right words sometimes took him a bit to put together, so I waited.

"I have people who love me," Casey said. "I know that's a lot more than some people have, and I feel damn guilty acting like it's not enough."

"Hey," I interrupted. "Us being here and loving you is real, but that doesn't mean it's the only answer. It's okay if we're not what you need."

Casey took a deep breath and blew it out. "Sometimes, the smokes, the alcohol, everything from the past, it all just blinds me to the good in my life. It's like deep down I know I have friends and family—those boys mean the world to me," he gave my hand a squeeze, "and I'll be damned if I'm not lookin' forward to whatever fuckery you and I might get up to—but all the shit in my brain is too loud for me to hear the truth. Sometimes it feels like I'm all alone and the only thing I'm good enough for is drowning all the pain with whatever chemicals I can get my hands on."

A cool breeze blew across the hill, and Casey shifted to put an arm around me. I cuddled up to him the best I could with the arms of the chair between us. "I think it's important to remember whatever you're feeling is valid and real. Sometimes though, we have to question those feelings because they aren't always true."

Casey scoffed.

I huffed out a laugh. "Sorry, didn't mean to sound like a therapist."

"Never stopped you before," Casey teased.

"I just want you to know we're here." I took a long, cleansing breath. "Before I came back home, I knew all too well what it was like to be surrounded by people and feel completely alone. So, even if your brain is telling you you're on your own, don't believe it. You have all of us here loving you and ready to support you in whatever you need."

Casey pressed a kiss to the side of my head before shifting in his chair to put the cup on the ground and lean his elbows on his knees. With his head in his hands, he sat there for several long, quiet moments.

"I think I need to leave."

"What?" I'd just told him we'd support him in

whatever he needed. I couldn't let on that my heart was now at my knees.

"Leave this place. Get some perspective."

I swallowed thickly. "Where would you go?" Maybe he meant a solo camping trip or a long hike through the state park.

He couldn't mean leaving for good.

Right?

Casey laughed with no real humor. "If my damn dumb ass from way back then could just see me now." He shook his head. "There's this retreat thing my fuckin' therapist keeps tellin' me about."

I allowed myself a tiny breath, just enough to clear the spots floating in my vision. A retreat was usually short, maybe he wasn't talking about leaving permanently. "How are you feeling about it?"

"Like fuckin' shit," Casey grumbled to his feet. "A retreat? What the actual fuck am I even thinkin?"

I chuckled and rubbed my hand up and down his back. That was my Casey. Quick with the gruff and snappy, slower and more hesitant to get to the deeper emotions.

But he'd eventually get there.

"Scared," he mumbled. "Feelin' fuckin' scared."

And there it was.

I let my hand continue tracing lines up and down his back. "I think that's pretty normal. New stuff is scary. Being vulnerable is scary. Not knowing people is scary. Add all that together plus the unknown, and it makes complete sense to feel that way."

Casey slowly turned his head to drill me with a serious look. "Are you fuckin' kiddin' me right now?"

I bit my bottom lip to hide a smile. He was so sure people thought he was an asshole, but I saw right through him. "What?" I let my lashes flutter slightly.

"Well, let's start with the fact if I wasn't already scared shitless of goin' to some *let's all vomit our emotions around a campfire* retreat, I sure as hell am now." He slapped a hand to my thigh and squeezed. "Fuckin' hell, man."

I yelped in surprise. "Sorry, I was just saying it's normal to feel what you're feeling. If you and your therapist think the retreat would be a good thing, then you know we'll support you through it."

Casey pulled me close and kissed my cheek. "I just hate the thought of missing everything here."

A little warning siren sounded in my head.

How long was a retreat? A weekend? A week? Maybe ten days?

I swallowed thickly. "We'll cover for you and make it work." Pressing a kiss to his lips, I did my best to sound casual. "How long does the retreat last?"

Casey took a deep, shuddering breath, and I knew I wasn't going to like the answer. But I also knew it wasn't about me. Casey didn't need my whiney ass making him feel bad for leaving. He needed his family backing him up and supporting him as he took steps to make sure he had a future to look forward to.

Chapter 23
Casey Joe

A WEEK AFTER I MADE THE DECISION TO ATTEND the stupid retreat, I was ready to strangle my therapist and cancel the whole damn thing.

To be fair, she had done nothing wrong. My childish ass was just mad because she was the one encouraging the retreat.

The night before I left, Henry and Jack closed the bar an hour early so our little group could gather in private. I didn't need the whole damn town knowing I was leaving for six weeks.

Six.

Fuckin'.

Weeks.

Fuck.

In the grand scheme of things, it was nothing.

In my head, it was long enough for the town, my boys, and Bryce to all figure out they were better off without me.

Realize they didn't really need me.

"This peach shit is so good," Hudson said as we all sat around the fire pit at the Roadhouse. "Perfect for a cool night."

I knew damn well the original recipe for the peach cider had bourbon in it, but Jack had made the mocktail version and heated it up with cinnamon sticks and warm cream. It really was delicious, and I didn't think I was the only one not missing the alcohol at all.

"Anyone want more bread and dip?" Jack asked.

The kid lived to feed people. It wasn't an exaggeration to say every time someone enjoyed his drinks, his food, or his desserts, Jack's heart doubled in size.

That night, he'd made the garden pesto dip slightly thicker and served it with tiny little knives for spreading it on homemade cheddar bread. Knowing I wasn't supposed to eat a bunch of sugary, chemically-laden, processed snack-type foods, I took one bite of the bread and knew two things.

One, at least it was all homemade.

Two, I was possibly going to die by carbs.

But at least it wasn't sugary snacks, right?

Determined to at least *try* to be healthier, I stuffed myself on healthy veggies before filling my plate with pesto bread.

By the time the warm peach cider and Jack's new recipe of sugar-free dark chocolate raspberry cake made an appearance, I was barely able to eat my sliver of cake and sip the cider.

Luckily, the damn retreat had a gym, and my therapist

assured me we'd be outside getting plenty of physical activity every day.

Yippee-fuckin'-skippee.

I was having a real hard time picturing my ass at a retreat in general, let alone having activity time outside with a bunch of fuckin' strangers.

My therapist kept telling me I was making it out to be a lot more like fictional movies I'd seen than reality.

Didn't stop my imagination from going wild.

All too soon, it was time to leave.

Henry was quieter than usual, but he gave me a big hug. My gentle giant.

Then he was pulling a teary Jack from my arms.

Hudson was all smiles, but I recognized the mask. Damn. Wonder where my little boy got that from.

When Lance gave me a hug and slapped my back, I whispered in his ear, "Take care of him. Don't let this get him down."

Lance had smiled and given me a nod. "You get yourself all retreated up, we've got things covered here."

And then Bryce and I were back at the apartment, showered, and ready for bed.

But I wasn't sure I'd sleep a wink.

"When I can get mail, you'll have to let me know how the gym opening goes," I said as we settled into bed.

Bryce's silence was a little too heavy.

"Bryce?"

He cleared his throat and pulled the blankets up to cover our naked bodies from the cool bite in the apartment air.

"Fuckin' hell," I muttered. "Do *not* tell me you think

you're holdin' off on openin' the damn gym because I'm gone."

He winced. "We're at least three weeks from being ready to open as it is. What will it hurt to wait three more so you can be here for it? The only reason this damn place will be ready to open is because of you, and I want you here."

His words deflated me slightly, and I pulled him into my arms. "I get it," I paused to press a kiss to his temple, "but I don't want to know you're missing out on turning a profit while you wait for me to get home."

Bryce pulled back slightly and kissed me. "I love you, and I love that you put others first, but I'm not destitute. The gym can wait—"

"Fuck if it can. I swear to god, Bryce. If you don't open when it's ready, I will break out and come back here to fuck shit up."

Bryce laughed.

The fucker laughed.

"Shut up," I grumbled.

"Break out? It's not prison," he said on a chuckle. "And what good would coming here to *fuck things up* do? Huh?" He tickled me, and I yelped before howling in laughter.

"Stop, stop," I groused.

The man figured out I was ticklish and used it against me damn near every day.

"I will open the gym when I decide it's ready." Bryce feathered his lips over mine. "And not a moment before. If that means we don't open until the man I love is there to celebrate with us, then so be it."

"Fuckin' hell," I muttered. "Who knew lovin' you would be such a pain in my ass?"

Bryce snorted against my mouth. "Pretty sure it's *my* ass dealing with any pain." Before I could respond, he patted my cheek. "It doesn't hurt, I'm just joking."

I rolled my eyes. "Told ya, I'm willin' to switch things up."

He groaned and rocked his hips into me. "And I'm one hundred percent going to take you up on that."

"Tonight?" Excitement and anxiety skittered through me.

"Definitely not," Bryce said as he ran his fingers through my hair. "You're leaving tomorrow, and that's not the type of thing I want you experiencing for the first time the night before you leave. It can be something we both look forward to when you get back."

"Gonna miss you," I murmured against Bryce's lips.

"Absence makes the heart grow fonder," he quipped.

"I don't know about *fonder*, but somethin' is fuckin' growin' for sure."

Bryce groaned. "Oh god, not the dad jokes."

"Damn sure not talkin' about growin' dicks with my kids, so it don't count as a dad joke."

The teasing stopped when our kisses morphed into something more.

Heated and heavy.

Slow and sensual.

Warm, bare skin.

Arms and legs tangled.

When I slid into his tight body, we gasped as one.

We'd found some way to get each other off every day of

the past week. Mouths, fingers, and jerking off, but every time I'd entered him—each time he let me in, spread open on my dick, crying out with every thrust—I knew two things as truth.

One, I was one hundred percent in love with this man. Crazy for him.

Meant to be with him.

Never giving him up.

Two, I would possibly lose my mind or cry myself to sleep every night I was away from him.

Maybe both.

"Fuck, Bryce," I whispered at his ear as his tight body welcome me home. "Love you so fuckin' much."

"Case," he whined. "Oh god, that's good. Case," he panted. "Fuck. Do that again."

"Jerk yourself," I demanded, shifting to my knees and pulling his hips up on my thighs. "Fuck, I love how good your hole looks spread open for my cock." It was truly the most gorgeous thing I'd ever seen. "Come for me." Filling Bryce with my release, his ass clenching around me as he painted his stomach, had quickly become one of my favorite pastimes.

Bryce jacked himself in the same rhythm as my cock slid in and out of him. "Oh, fuck, Case. Fuck." Then he groaned low and deep as he shot his load, thick ropes splattering his belly.

The grip of his tight ring around my dick sent me over the edge. With my hands clutching his hips, I slammed into him and grunted, my cock pulsing cum deep into him.

I collapsed on top of him, and we both groaned as my

softening cock slipped from his ass. Rolling to the mattress, I pulled Bryce close, our legs tangling together. He snuggled close, and I pressed my lips to his head.

Damn stupid tears stung my fuckin' stupid eyes.

My breath caught as I tried to steady myself enough to speak.

"Gonna miss this so fuckin' much," I managed to get out.

Bryce shuddered in my arms. "I know." He pulled back and looked up at me. "But we can send letters, and six weeks will fly by. You'll be home before you know it."

Heavy emotions kept us quiet, only the sounds of our soft breaths filling the air around us, until we drifted off to sleep.

We woke once during the night. I gathered Bryce in my arms, making love to him, my heart convinced I'd never hold him again.

When morning dawned, we spent a few extra moments holding each other, savoring our time together, and forming memories to get us through the next six weeks.

At least I hoped we'd get through.

Bryce would likely be fine.

Me on the other hand? I was already convinced I was fucked.

No longer able to compete with the clock, we dragged ourselves from bed and showered.

Just as I pulled the coffee from the cabinet to start a pot, a knock sounded at the door. Bryce closed the fridge, where he'd been looking for ingredients for omelets if I had to guess, and made his way toward the door.

"Case."

I turned to see Lance in the doorway.

Bryce kissed my cheek and moved toward the back of the apartment.

Lance held out a bag and a drink carrier. "Hudson and I wanted to make sure you got a good breakfast before you left."

My jaw hurt as I held back the tears, and I could only nod. "Thanks," was all I managed to get out.

Lance placed the bag and carrier on the table and grabbed me up in a hug. "I'm damn proud of you, Case."

I scoffed. "What the hell for?"

"Swear to god, I'll let you get one good punch in for the Hudson thing, but if we ever go a few rounds, I'm gonna knock your lights out just for being so damn stubborn and stupid," he muttered over my shoulder. "What the hell for? How about for those two beautiful boys you've got? Two of the best people on the planet, and *you* made them who they are."

I started to protest, but Lance steam rolled right over me.

"Surviving the shit with Missy. It's for the best you two didn't work out, but that doesn't make it any less painful. Not letting everything with Billy get you down."

This time I snorted and elbowed him in the gut. "You got a damn fuckin' interestin' definition of not lettin' somethin' get a person down, man. I damn near lost everythin', almost drank myself to death—hell, if my heart hadn't turned on me, I probably woulda followed Billy right to the damn grave."

Lance gave me an affectionate shove. "That's exactly what I'm talking about, Ceej. *All* that shit, and you made it through for your boys. Kept going even when you wanted to give up." He patted my face with a bit too much force, and I wondered if Bryce would frown upon best friends sparring in his kitchen. Probably wouldn't look good to show up at the retreat with a black eye or split lip, so I didn't punch him right in the damn mouth.

"The boys deserved—"

"Those boys deserved a dad who loved them, and they got that in spades. They never wanted for anything. You kept them safe." Lance poked a finger at my chest. "Not a damn parent on this planet is perfect. You and I fuckin' know it."

Crossing my arms, I nodded. "I know. I just can't stop thinkin' about how much better I could have been for them if I hadn't been so buried in my own shit."

Lance shook his head. "I get what you're saying, and it's a conversation we've had a million times. We can't change the past. Sometimes, I think being able to would be the worst thing ever. We're here—you, the three boys, me and Hudson, *Bryce*—all because of who we are thanks to our pasts. Changing that would maybe take all this away."

An icy fist gripped my heart.

Fuck.

I hated when Lance was right, but he was damn smart, so he was right more often than not.

Wasn't gonna tell him that, though.

"I hear what you're sayin'," I admitted. "Doesn't mean I want to leave the only home I've ever known and work through feelings and shit for six damn weeks."

Lance patted my cheek again in the taunting way only a

lifelong best friend can do. "When you get back, you can teach us campfire songs, maybe show us how to weave baskets."

"Fuck off," I grumbled around a grin.

"Do you think there will be a talent show?" he asked with a smirk. "Just don't sing, you'd probably drive them all to start drinking again."

"Fuck. Off." My words were rough with humor and emotion.

Lance hugged me again. "Love you, Case. We'll hold things down here. Just focus on getting yourself healthy so you can come back here and be the grumpy, pain in the ass we all love."

Lance laughed when I flipped him off. He called out a goodbye to Bryce and then he was gone.

Bryce appeared and wrapped me in a hug. "You good?"

I grunted.

Could have meant yes or no.

"Want to eat?"

At that, my stomach grumbled. "Might as well. No need to let food go to waste."

I dug into the bag.

Oatmeal with berries.

Spinach, mushrooms, and egg white breakfast burritos.

Yogurt parfait with fruit and granola.

"Those damn mother fuckers," I muttered.

"What?" Bryce asked, looking over my shoulder.

"Did you do this?"

"Do what?"

I gestured toward the food. "Tell them to get all this healthy shit. Damn. A guy can't even head off for six weeks with an ooey, gooey cinnamon roll? Or a donut? Not even a bit of fuckin' cheese on the burrito?"

Bryce laughed and slapped my ass. "The fruit and yogurt will be just right for the sweet tooth."

I glared at him. "I swear to god, if there's herbal tea in those cups, I'm gonna chase him down and kick his ass."

Bryce was still laughing when I took my first long, fortifying sip of coffee.

Strong and black, just the way I liked it. At least my best friend and son didn't let me down with the drinks.

We stood against the kitchen sink, our bodies pressed together from shoulder to hip to thigh. The food was the most delicious last meal I'd ever had, but it also tasted like sawdust. I would have eaten damn egg white burritos for the rest of my life if it meant never having to leave.

But time was not our friend that morning.

"You sure you don't want me to drive you?" Bryce asked as we stood wrapped in each other's arms by the door.

"No." My whisper was rough. "Easier to say goodbye here. Plus, you can't come into the retreat center, so we might as well get it over with here."

Bryce ran his lips over my jaw. "I love you."

"Why?"

He choked on a laugh. "What kind of question is that?"

I cleared my throat. I wasn't fishing for compliments, and I didn't want to be dramatic, but anxiety and guilt competed heavily over the fact Bryce had come to town and ended up saddled with me. "I'm just sayin', you're worth more than my fucked up small town ass. You could—"

Bryce shut me up with a kiss. "I'm a grown ass man, and I can make that choice on my own."

Holding him tightly, trying to soak up every bit of him before walking out the door, I breathed him in deeply. "I know it ain't fair to ask you to wait on me—"

"Good god, man. Would you stop?"

I chuckled, my lips feathering over his ear. "What I was sayin'," I said, "is it ain't fair to ask you to wait on me, but I'll beg if I have to. I love you more than I thought I was capable of, but I owe it to us both to get my shit straightened out before we build a future together. You deserve better than the fucked-up version of me."

Bryce cupped the side of my face and pressed our foreheads together. "Well, I'm pretty far gone for the fucked-up version, so don't go changing too much."

I closed my eyes and savored the way our bodies fit so perfectly. "Not gonna change the real me. Just gotta work through my shit and come home healthy. For you, the boys, for *us*."

He traced a thumb over my lips. "Don't do it just for the boys and me."

Shaking my head, I let the truth wash over me. "Nah, it's for the kid who was scared to death his parents would figure out he watched the boys in tight baseball pants a little too long. That kid who begged any god who would listen to take away the way he felt about the coach's son. The kid who convinced himself it was better to only live half a life as long as no one ever figured out his secret."

Bryce wiped the tear from my cheek. "That kid is lucky to have you."

With a deep, shuddering breath, I whispered, "I'm fuckin' scared. I don't know if I can do this."

He tipped my chin. "You know I believe in you, right?" His soft kiss sent shivers through me. "I'll believe in you enough for the both of us until you can believe in you too." He pressed his cheek to mine. "I'm not going anywhere, Case. I'll be here waiting on you, believing in you, and loving you until the end of time." He pulled back and met my eyes. "Just don't make me actually wait that long."

"Fuck. Six weeks is gonna do me in." Every fiber of my being begged for me to stay. Pleaded for me to keep holding onto him. I didn't *have* to go to the retreat. Even my therapist had admitted I could work through my shit with her or someone else without attending the retreat.

But no.

I'd made the decision.

My family was supporting me.

I'd go to the fuckin' retreat.

For my health.

For my future.

Fuck it.

At this point, it kinda felt like I had to go just to prove to myself I could do it.

Chapter 24
Bryce

I SMILED SOFTLY AND RAN MY HAND OVER THE black three-ring binder. As had become my routine with the mail over the last six weeks, I made a cup of apple cinnamon tea and settled in to read the newest letter from Casey Joe.

In the beginning, about a week into his stay at the retreat, I'd bundled up and enjoyed the crisp fall weather by the fire pit as I read the newest sheets Casey had sent to add to the binder. But the air felt a lot more like winter these days, so I'd taken to cuddling up on the couch with my tea while I read the new additions.

The first mail Casey had been allowed to send was the binder, and I loved I could revisit each and every note we'd shared while he'd been gone. The binder had arrived first with only one sheet of lined paper held by the three rings, but Casey had written me nearly daily, so getting the mail and adding his letters to the binder had become the highlight of my day.

For now, the binder held the pages Casey had sent me and most of the letters I'd sent him. He'd kept a few of my letters and sent some back to me. It was a hodgepodge, but it was ours, and I looked forward to organizing it with Casey by my side once he was home.

With my socked feet stretched out on the couch, I sipped my apple cinnamon tea and re-read words I already knew by heart.

Our letters were silly and heartfelt.

Sometimes filled with funny stories, sometimes with words of longing and love.

Some pages were blunt and poignant, while others required reading between the lines.

Some pages were covered in colorful doodles.

One whole section of pages was devoted to little notes about songs we heard and wanted to share. I'd become a complete sap and cried over multiple songs we'd sent to each other.

More than anything, I wanted Casey home for good, but the handwritten correspondence we'd shared these last six weeks had eased my aching heart. Working my ass off with Lance, Henry, Hudson, and Jack had played a big part in keeping me busy enough to avoid some of the hardest parts of Casey being gone.

The newest letter would likely be the last I'd receive because Casey was due home that evening. The guys and I had spent all day finalizing everything for his homecoming, and I now had too many hours to get through before he finally got home.

The pages blurred and time ceased to exist as I sat there reading. The words connected me to Casey. The time he'd been gone had been long and hard, but I'd witnessed his healing through the words he penned to me over the six weeks, and I was so damn proud of him.

When the room grew too dark to see the letters, I stood, stretched, and turned on a lamp. Lighting a candle first, I made a trip to the bathroom and then started more water for another cup of tea.

The apple cinnamon stuff Casey bought a while back was really good. He'd told me the retreat center purchased some at his request, and I loved knowing we were sipping the same tea even when we were apart.

With my mug refilled, I clicked through my phone and pulled up the playlist Casey and I had been building since he'd been gone. The list was an eclectic mess, but most of the songs had a reason for being there. Many of the titles spoke to us in some way, and sharing the songs back and forth was a way to stay connected and communicate how we felt about each other. Some were on the list just because we liked them. A few were there because Hudson called them old people songs, so we added them out of spite.

With a burning lump in my throat, I leafed through the pages.

Dear Bryce,
 Listen to "Survive" by Lewis Capaldi.
Fuck if those lyrics don't speak to me. For
real, give it a listen. Talk about a fucking

punch to the gut, but also a damn wake up call.

Some days I really don't feel like I'll survive but knowing I'm coming home to you gives me the strength to go on.

Love,

Case

P.S. I just reread that and realized it screamed codependency. Not the vibe I was going for ;) Just know I love you and I can't wait to see you.

Dear Case,

I've been crying over "Grow as We Go" by Ben Platt and "With You Til the End" by Tommee Profitt and Sam Tinnesz. It's like they were written specifically for me to tell you how I feel. Like the universe knew we'd need the words to get us through the hard parts.

Not going to lie, I'm looking forward to standing by your side and growing with you. The easy days, the hard days, and every day in between.

Love you,

B.

Dear B.,

I used to feel like "Somebody Save Me" by Eminem and Jelly Roll was my theme song, but these days it's more like "It's My Life" by Bon Jovi. Now or never really speaks to me. It's true, I ain't living forever, but that line about living while I'm alive? Damn, that one really hits.

And how about another oldie? "Love of a Lifetime" by Firehouse. I think it should be "our song", whatcha think? Have you ever really listened to that song? It's a gut wrencher for sure. Does claiming that one as our song make us old? Fuck 'em.

Do you know how damn much I love you?

Always yours,

LJ

Some of the letters were short and sweet. Quick notes about songs. Me telling Casey about Brother Larry asking for the retreat address so he could visit and pray for one of his flock. Casey replying he better not see that damn hypocritical preacher anywhere near the retreat center and how glad he was that no visitors were allowed.

Casey writing to let me know the food was pretty decent—not as good as what I cooked, but he wasn't going to starve. He questioned if I'd gotten word to the staff to let them know he wasn't supposed to be eating snacks. When I replied, I assured him that, even if I had tried to foil his plan to snack his way through the retreat, I had not been successful in that endeavor.

Casey doodling two cute little jockstraps on the paper with a heart in between them and our names. I'd been sure to let him know I'd ordered us both jockstraps, and I was excited for him to get home so we could wear them out for a night on the town.

Casey's doodle response was an obscene peach and eggplant along with a short note saying if we put on jockstraps within five feet of each other, we wouldn't be going out on the town, we'd be naked in bed in under ten seconds.

Casey asking about his house and if any correspondence from the insurance had come through. I put that one off by telling him I'd check with the boys and hoped like hell he wouldn't ask again. Shitty? Maybe. But I wasn't the greatest at keeping secrets, so the less I had to talk about it, the better.

Me hinting maybe it would be best to hold off on opening the gym and doing my best to convince him there were small bits and pieces that needed to be done before we could open. Casey threatening me to within an inch of my life if I delayed the opening of the gym.

Spoiler alert: the gym opened on a soft launch which Casey assumed was the big opening. He was unaware we had a big grand opening planned for once he got home. Would he be mad? Probably. But we all figured we could ask for forgiveness once he figured it out.

P.S. Armstrong Health & Fitness had opened three weeks ago, and it was already turning a profit. The guys had helped as much as they could, and I was beyond ready to get Casey into his position. The grand opening was as much a celebration of Casey being home and healthy as it was of my gym functioning successfully.

Several of Casey's letters were clearly written after therapy sessions or on days when he was struggling more than usual. Those were hard to read, but it felt like Casey had truly embraced the chance to work through his shit. I figured the retreat staff letting clients write letters instead of having access to electronics or digital media was probably a great way to encourage them to get their feelings out while avoiding online distractions.

Dear Bryce,

Good thing you got me used to all this exercise and health shit. There's this trainer here who is ten times worse than you. She's one of those cheery people who makes you think she'll be nice, but then she makes you cry when she forces you to run twenty miles or bench press a thousand pounds. At least you mostly prepared me. And you don't make me cry. But she's like you—she really actually likes exercise.

I try to be outside a lot. In the

beginning, it was easier because the weather was amazing. But now it's colder, so I'd rather be inside by the fire with my hot tea. Why does that make me sound like an eighty-year-old hermit? I still go outside as much as possible. The sunshine and fresh air make me feel better. I guess I always knew that, but now I'm living it.

At first, I thought all the group activity shit would be the worst. But it's not. The worst is when we have time to ourselves. I figured that part would be great, but it sucks to be alone with my shit. I mean, I do it because they make us and because I know it helps me get through shit, but I actually prefer the group shit. Makes me realize I'm not the only one with shit going on.

Never would have thought it, but I've actually made some friends. Makes things not feel so lonely and hard. And I've figured out people here, and people everywhere, are all dealing with shit. Maybe different shit. Maybe dealing with it in different ways. But we're all going through it.

For some reason, that helps.

How many times can I use the word shit in one letter? Maybe that's the theme of this retreat for me. Shit.

Sorry this is so long and rambly, just had a lot to get out today.

Love you,

CJ

Dear Casey Joe,

The gym is packed today. We've already sold a bunch of merch. The place looks great with the sunshine coming through the window. Dizzy and Barb are here right now using the elliptical machines. Your nametag and staff shirt are ready and waiting for you to get home.

Hudson and Jack came in today and made fun of me for having old people music on the speakers. But members have commented on how much they love the playlists we're using, so I told the boys to shove it. Hudson told me he'd give me a senior discount next time I came to the Juicy Peach.

We all miss you like crazy.

Love you, always and forever,

Bryce

. . .

Dear Bryce,

So, my parents were kind of pieces of shit. Not sure this is a new realization, but I worked through some shit today and it's pretty fresh. My parents weren't abusive—not like hitting and screaming type shit. But they raised Billy and me to know exactly what they did and didn't approve of. We couldn't make the family look bad. Couldn't make the family seem like "less." Couldn't fail at anything.

Being different in any way was not allowed.

I knew it from the beginning. I hid anything about me that wouldn't be approved. Got angrier and more buried in shit as the years went by.

Wish I could have stood up to them back then.

But proud of myself for being there for my boys, letting them be their true selves, and learning from them how to be the real me.

Feels good to know I stopped the cycle

of shit my parents put me through. I wasn't the best parent to my boys, but I never wanted them to think they couldn't be true to themselves because of me.

Damn, word vomit again. Therapy is a bunch of shit. But I guess it does its job.

Fuck, I miss you.

Love,

Case

Dear Bryce,

It's almost time to leave here. I haven't loved it, but I think it's been good for me to learn shit about myself. I think a part of me thought I'd leave here "cured" or some shit like that, but it's not like that.

One thing I know is I've never had to do so much damn talking as they make you do here. I hate it. Well, mostly. I hate it while it's happening, but after it's done, it's like everything in me settles down and says, "See, that wasn't so hard was it? Don't you feel better?" And fuck if I don't.

Some people came here with this big goal of healing. I guess I kinda had the same goal. But we learned there's no specific endpoint you reach that says okay now you're healed, everything is good. It's more about taking all your shit out, examining it, sitting with it, talking about it, sitting with it some more, figuring out which shit you can throw out and which you need to keep working on, and then working on yourself until you know you can walk through life with your shit because you have the tools to cope with it. Like, nothing I do here is going to change the shit I carry, but I understand it all better now. I can't go back and change anything—and I've come to the sincere realization I wouldn't want to because all of it made me who I am... without all of it, I wouldn't have my boys, the family businesses, or you. So, it's all still there, but I'm able to see it for what it is now.

Like, I know I'll always be an addict, that's not something I'll ever be able to say isn't who I am. Weird as it sounds though, I've also learned addiction maybe isn't my biggest problem. Anger, shame, and fear have always held me back, kept me from being the real me, speaking my truth. The addiction made it worse, but I probably would have always had problems even if I never started using the alcohol to numb everything. If I hadn't turned to alcohol, it would have been something else.

Figuring all that shit out, knowing I can put aside the anger, shame, and fear was like a weight lifting from my shoulders. Those things aren't the real me. Those things were forced on me because of shitty parents and not being allowed to be my true self. Would I have come out as gay or bi? Hell, who knows. But the fact I didn't have the option back then shaped me into someone who wasn't living their truth.

Okay, that's enough shit for now. Hell, I hope you don't fall asleep reading through all my rambling. Sorry this is so long, but it felt good to get it all down on paper.

I think they save some of the hardest sessions for last. Maybe they figure they've worn us down by this time and it's easier to get us to work through the worst of it.

Whatever it is, I'm really glad I'm leaving here soon. Not because it's been the worst, but because I don't know how much longer my heart can survive without being near you.

Yep, six weeks was all it took to turn me into a fucking sap.

I love you so damn much.

Love,

CJ

A text buzzed across my phone screen. It was Jack telling me Henry and Casey Joe were about half an hour out.

I blew out the candle, threw any perishables into a garbage bag to drop at the dumpster out back, tucked the binder under my arm, and picked up the suitcase I'd placed by the door.

It was showtime.

Chapter 25
Casey Joe

"WHY WE GOIN' UP HERE?" I ASKED AS HENRY steered the truck up toward the hill. I didn't want to seem ungrateful, but I honestly just wanted to get home and see Bryce.

"Jack's up at Hudson's. They all wanted to see you."

I gritted my teeth and tried not to scream. Of course, I wanted to see my boys and best friend. But I also wanted to see my boyfriend. Plus, Henry had Jack, Hudson had Lance. Not like I thought Bryce couldn't survive without me, and I knew the guys had kept him company, but if he'd been missing me even a fraction of how much I'd missed him...

Yeah, I just wanted to see him.

Henry slapped my shoulder. "It's all good. Bryce is up there too."

I tried not to let my son see my relief, but Henry just chuckled. I flipped him off. "Sorry, I'm just exhausted and ready to be home."

"Home is ready for you too," Henry said. He glanced over at me. "We're all real proud of the work you put in at that retreat."

I looked out the window. Comments like that did a weird mix of things in my gut. On one hand, I knew it was a compliment. On the other, I worried people at home were going to expect me to be different—like they'd be disappointed if I was still the same ol' grumpy Casey Joe.

And I was.

I mean, I knew I was better off than when I'd left— healthier physically, emotionally, and mentally—but I was still the same me I'd been six weeks ago. Still cussed too much, still hated going for a run, and still blunt as hell. Sure, I was in a lot better shape, didn't have a toxic relationship with alcohol, and liked myself a whole lot better than I ever had. I'd even done a pretty damn good job of breaking my addiction to processed junk food.

But what happened the first time I flipped someone the bird and told them to get the fuck out of the road if they were going to drive like a fuckin' idiot?

Or some meathead at the gym made a rude comment to a person just trying to live their best life and get some movement on the treadmill, and I had to tell the asshole where to shove the barbell?

Or when Brother Larry tried his bullshit on me and I told him to take a flyin' leap head first into his flock's dung pile?

Would everyone shake their heads and talk in whispers about how they'd had high hopes for me, but they'd never really thought I could change?

"I ain't a different person," I blurted.

Henry gave me a brief sideways glance with a raised brow.

"Just sayin'," I muttered. "I don't want people thinkin' I'm some completely different person. Still me. Still gonna screw up."

Henry slapped me on the shoulder. "No one else we'd rather you be. We don't want you to change. Just want you healthy and happy. Screw ups and all."

Henry pulled the truck into the driveway at Hudson's place. For a brief moment, I imagined us all gathered around a campfire, cracking open beers, frozen puffs of laughter lingering on the air as we caught up.

And now I was the party pooper.

Damn. I'd been feeling strong and confident leaving the retreat, but each mile away from the safety of that experience had piled on a pound of self-doubt and worry.

As I climbed from the truck, I caught sight of the guys standing on the porch, bathed in the warm glow of the fairy lights Hudson liked to keep burning year-round, and took in the steaming mugs in their hands.

Wasn't a requirement to be around me these days— and I didn't want them thinking it was—but a hot cup of coffee on the brisk evening sounded a lot better than a cold bottle of beer.

Who said Casey Joe Riggs couldn't change?

I snorted at the thought, but damn, how long was this back and forth between feeling ready to face the world and wanting to hide under my bed going to last?

Jack was the first to put his mug on the little side table next to the swing and throw himself into my arms. The kid was lithe and lean, nothing like the solid blocks of my boys, and the way he held me tight warmed something deep inside.

Jack wasn't mine by blood. He hadn't been raised by me. But that kid was a Riggs in every single way that counted.

Lance and Hudson both hugged me and welcomed me home.

"You look amazing," Hudson offered.

I knew from the before and after pictures the retreat staff took that I *did* look a damn sight better than when I'd left. I'd packed on some pounds and muscle, my skin glowed a much healthier shade than the former *sick bed* pallor, and there was a sparkle in my eyes I hadn't seen since maybe middle school.

"Thanks," I answered, trying my best not to seem ungrateful for the welcome home.

Lance slapped me on the back. "Might as well put him out of his misery."

Henry smirked, his arm around a grinning Jack.

Hudson nodded toward my old place. "Bryce ran up to the house for a bit. Said you could meet him up there if you want."

I was down the steps, grabbing my bag from the truck, and headed up to my house in under a minute.

"Come back for coffee if you want," Lance teased. "We can keep a pot warm."

With my middle finger raised, I shouted over my shoulder. "Y'all can fuck all the way off. I'll see you tomorrow. Maybe the day after that."

Their laughter followed me up the hill.

I didn't care if Bryce and I had to share the house

with...okay, I'd actually say fuck no if snakes or skunks were involved, but I could maybe deal with racoons, squirrels, and possibly an opossum.

I had every intention of grabbing Bryce up, holding him close, and not letting go for...well, forever if he'd have me.

The scent of the fire hit me first.

When I rounded the corner of the house, my breath caught.

Bryce.

Yellow-orange flames cast shadows on his face.

His eyes were closed, his head tipped back, and like a punch to the gut, all I could think was how absolutely beautiful he was.

Home.

The word washed over me, sinking all the way into my bones.

Not because we were at the house I'd grown up in.

Not because we were in the only town I'd ever lived in.

No.

Bryce was my home.

If he up and moved back to California, I'd have no choice but to follow.

If he said he wanted to build a new house in another county, I'd ask when he wanted to start.

Buy an RV and travel the country? Let's do it.

Tossing my bag to the ground, I crossed to the fire in five long strides.

And then he was in my arms, pressing his face to my neck, breathing me in.

Everything was right with the world.

When his mouth found mine, I knew he was my forever.

We kissed for eternity and even that would never be enough.

Eventually, the kiss ended, but he kept me wrapped in his arms.

"I missed you so much," Bryce whispered. "It wasn't all that long, but it felt like the longest, hardest thing I'd ever done."

"Longest and hardest, huh?"

He snorted and kissed me. "Did the guys tell you why I was up here?"

I pulled back to study his face in the fire light. "Uh, I was hopin' it was so we had some privacy and didn't risk early clients at the gym hearing us goin' at it." I cocked a brow. "Was I wrong?"

Bryce smiled. "Well, that's part of it. But there's more." He gestured toward the house. "If you want to see it?"

Up until that moment, I hadn't noticed the ever-present tarp on the corner of the house where the fire damage had been was no longer there.

"Well, I'll be damned." I took Bryce's hand and pulled him toward the repaired corner. "When did this get done? No one thought to tell me?"

Bryce beamed. "We wanted to surprise you with it when you got home."

"You win. I'm surprised." I couldn't tell with only the porch light and the fire, but it looked like the repair had been made almost seamlessly. "Does the inside look this good?"

"I think it looks better. Wanna see?"

I nodded and let Bryce lead me up the steps. When he opened the door and made a sweeping gesture with his arm to usher me inside, I couldn't stop myself from cupping the sides of his face and kissing him.

He tasted of coffee and promises.

"This is amazing. I love you." My words hitched slightly. "Thank you."

Bryce rested his forehead against mine. "Welcome home."

Somehow, the warmth and love in my chest blossomed into a fuckin' inferno of emotions. How was I this person? How did I come out on the other side of a bunch of shit and get to fall in love? Get to call this gorgeous man *mine*? Get to build a home—

Just as Bryce flipped on the light switch, a realization hit me like a damn bag of bricks.

This was *my* home, but Bryce had his apartment.

Before he could show me the fixed portion of the house, I grabbed his hands and held tight. "You can say no. It's probably stupid. So, fuckin' stupid," I muttered. "But this isn't my home unless you're here. I'd rather live in an apartment over the gym forever if it means living with you."

Bryce blinked slowly.

Once.

Twice.

"What are you saying?"

"Move in here with me. Rent out your apartment. Live with me."

Tear glistened in his eyes, and he nodded. "I brought my bag thinking I'd stay the weekend."

"Fuck that shit." I sealed it with a kiss. "Your commute just got longer."

"Yeah, but I got a sexy as sin roommate in the deal. It's a good trade."

I let him give me the briefest tour of the newly remodeled portion of the house, the two new recliners and sectional couch, and the new appliances in the kitchen.

"What the hell? Didn't need any new shit."

Bryce slapped a hand over my mouth. "Shut up and accept it. The boys wanted to redo a few things. Lance got you something too."

I narrowed my eyes. "What did that fucker do?"

He laughed and led me to the bedroom. "Brand new mattress and box springs."

My phone buzzed.

> Lance: You gotta get some blinds. I can see right into your damn bedroom.

> Me: You got me a fuckin' bed?

> Lance: No, I got you a mattress. It's good quality. It can take a real pounding. Put a towel down.

> Me: Fuck off

He sent me a fuck ton of rolling laughing faces.

I flipped the switch on the wall and tossed my phone on the bedside table. "Start the shower. Gonna grab my bag from outside. Then we're spendin' the next forty-eight hours in bed."

Something crossed Bryce's face, but he covered it quickly.

"What?"

He shook his head. "Nothing. Go get your bag."

I narrowed my eyes again. "The house is the only surprise, right?"

Bryce wrapped his arms around my neck and kissed me until I didn't care one fuckin' bit about the answer to that question.

An hour later, after blow jobs in the shower to take the edge off, we tumbled to the mattress in a tangle of damp limbs, exploring hands, and slow, wet kisses.

My brain comprehended there was no hurry. Intellectually, I knew we were together and had as many years as fate saw fit to give us.

But the horny fucker living in my dick pounded his fists on the table chanting, "Now, now, now!"

"I want you to fuck me," I blurted.

Bryce froze. "What?"

"I want to bottom. Been thinking about it for weeks. Went through my fair share of Vaseline at the retreat. Porn makes you think fingering yourself is a lot easier than it really is."

Bryce laughed, his mouth wide open while he tried to kiss me. "You're sure?"

With my hands gripping his ass cheeks, I pulled him

close, letting our cocks rub together. "Never been more sure of anything." I rested my forehead to his temple. "Might find out I hate it. Might decide it's only something I like to do from time to time." Then something hit me. "Wait, would you rather not top?"

Bryce snorted. "I'm one hundred percent down with topping. If you love it, we can swap whenever the mood strikes. If you hate it, I'm completely fine with bottoming." He cupped my face. "Or we can get off together without either. As long as you're here to kiss me and hold me, I really don't care how I'm coming."

Fuckin' hell.

How did a stupid handful of words make me wanna preen and cry like a stupid fool?

"I love that, and I love you," I murmured against his lips. "And I want your dick in me like yesterday."

Bryce rolled from the mattress, rummaged in his suitcase, tossed a bottle of lube next to me, and climbed back into bed. "Put your head up by the pillows and turn on your side. Bend your knee."

I thought I followed directions just right.

Bryce pushed my knee into the mattress and made me bend it further.

"I ain't your own personal Gumby," I muttered.

He chuckled, hiked my knee up higher, and pressed a kiss to my ass cheek. "Careful, your age is showing with that reference."

"Fuck off."

"That's the plan," he said.

Once Bryce took my leaking cock in his fist and buried his face in my ass, I lost all track of time and place.

Everything ceased to matter except for Bryce stroking my dick and tonguing my hole.

"Fuck, fuck, fuck, stop, you gotta fuckin' stop," I said. "Too close."

Bryce stopped, and I immediately regretted everything I'd just said. "Wanna straddle me so you can control how deep I go?"

I shook my head. "No, I wanna watch you. Want you on top so I can see your face when you take me."

"Fuck, Case," Bryce whispered and squeezed his cock. "Gonna make me come just talking about it."

"Not yet. Wait until you're inside me. Wanna feel it."

Never in my life had I thought I'd want someone to take control of me, but letting Bryce be in charge was one of the headiest, most empowering, and relaxing moments of my life.

He moved with such care and patience. Spreading my legs, smearing lube over my hole and working me open with one finger and then two. The whole time murmuring how good I was doing, how pretty I looked opening for him.

Who knew I was such a slut for praise?

"Fuck, Bryce. Please," I begged.

And then he was between my knees, his slick cock head pressing into me.

He worked his way in so slowly, letting my body adjust inch by glorious inch. Taking his entire dick was a whole lot more intense than fingers, but it was so fuckin' good. My eyes traveled from his to where our bodies connected and back again, an overwhelming wash of emotions flooding through me with the perfection of the moment.

When he bottomed out, his balls pressed tightly against me, we both sighed. He dropped to his elbows and gathered me in his arms to feather soft kisses all over my face. "You good? It's okay?"

I nodded, my throat too thick with all sorts of lovey heart shit to speak.

"Can I move?" Bryce asked through gritted teeth, and I knew just how much effort he was putting into holding back while my body opened for him.

"Fuck, yes."

Bryce pulled out slowly and slid back in over and over, his balls pressing tight against my ass each time he thrust in hard and deep.

The noises I made were completely insane, but no one was around to hear them. And even if they were, fuck them. My boyfriend was railin' the fuck out of me, and I'd make whatever mother fuckin' noises I wanted to.

He pushed up on his hands and watched between us as he pumped in and out.

Suddenly, I wanted to see him under me as I rode him and shot my load over his chest. "Roll over, wanna ride your cock."

Bryce pulled out and moved to his back.

I straddled him—probably not my most graceful move, but the sooner I had his dick back in my ass, the better. Reaching behind me, I guided him back to my hole and lowered myself down.

The angle was different.

The stretch was insane.

And every single cell of my body rejoiced to know I got to spend the rest of my life with this man.

"Fuck, Case, look at that cock. Fuck, yeah, ride me." Bryce took hold of my hips and held tight as I ground my ass on his fuckin' magnificent dick, my own bouncing in rhythm and slapping against his treasure trail.

"Oh fuck," I groaned when his cock head teased over that sensitive spot deep inside. Sensations like warm honey being poured over my insides washed through me. "I'm close. Fuck."

Bryce sat up and helped me position my legs around him. He wrapped me in his arms, pressed our chests together, and buried his face in my neck. We rocked together as one to the rhythm of a song only we could hear.

My orgasm shattered through me, cum exploding between us and dripping down our stomachs. The pulsing clench of my tight ring was enough to send Bryce over the edge, and his cock unloaded, throbbing as he gave me every last drop.

"Holy. Fuckin'. Shit."

Bryce chuckled weakly and moved to lay back on the bed, taking me with him, and kissing me with so much gentle ferocity I wondered if it was possible to die from a kiss.

At some point, we shifted, Bryce pulling from my body and curling us into a spooning position. "You good?"

"Never gonna be the same, but never better. Fuckin' hell."

We dozed for a bit until something woke me.

"What the fuckin' hell?"

"What?" Bryce was instantly awake and concerned.

"That was fuckin' fantastic. But I ain't a fuckin' fan of

your cum drippin' out. Oh god, that's maybe the worst feelin' in the world."

Bryce laughed and pulled me into a kiss. "Sorry to be so drippy."

For some reason, my short-circuited brain thought that was hilarious and we spent several moments laughing into each other's warm skin. As soon as I'd think I had my giggles under control, one of us would start back up.

When we were finally laughed out, I tried my best to settle into Bryce's warm embrace and sleep, but the wetness oozing from my ass was too distracting.

Bryce was still amused when I headed to the bathroom for my second shower in as many hours. "It's not *oozing*," he teased. "You make my cum sound like some kind of Ghostbusters slime."

I popped my head out of the shower so I could see him lying in my bed.

Our bed.

"If it's ever green, I'm done."

I threw a washcloth at him so he could clean up while I finished in the bathroom.

By the time I was dried off, Bryce was sound asleep.

I climbed into bed and gathered him in my arms.

For the first time in my adult life, I fell asleep in my childhood home feeling safe, content, loved, and hopeful.

Casey loves Bryce

Waking up with Bryce in my arms was maybe one of the top five best feelings I'd ever experienced.

Waking up with my hard cock nestled between his perfect ass cheeks was also in the running for a trophy.

I knew the exact moment Bryce woke because he stretched like a cat and wiggled his ass against me. "You planning on doing something with that?" His sleep-rough words were sexy as hell.

"Fuck you into this mattress, sleep, eat, rinse and repeat," I whispered at his ear, nibbling on the fleshy lobe and loving the way he shivered. "Figure we don't have anywhere to be until tomorrow."

Bryce's hesitation was slight, but I noticed it.

"Bryce? What?"

"Nothing," he muttered into the pillow.

"Bryce," I growled.

"It's all good," he said a little too quickly. "We've got time this morning, the sun isn't even up yet. And tonight is all ours."

"What the fuck have you done?"

He buried his head in his pillow and rocked his ass into me. "Believe me, I'm one hundred percent regretting it at this moment."

"Whatever it is, we'll just skip out on it." Maybe Brother Larry had organized a potluck to take advantage of his flock. I swore he always filled his freezer with the casseroles and his pockets with whatever tithes he was able to guilt his parishioners into handing over.

Or maybe Henry and Jack had something planned at the Roadhouse. I mean, I could do with some cake, but

Bryce's ass was currently more tempting than even Jack's most decadent slice.

Bryce groaned. "We really can't. But we have a few hours. Don't let them go to waste."

I didn't have to be told twice. Grabbing the lube, I slicked up my throbbing cock, worked a generous amount of the viscous liquid into Bryce's ass, and positioned myself at his tight hole.

Never in the rest of my life would I ever tire of the gasps and whimpery groans Bryce made as my dick breached his body. With our bodies nestled together on our sides, Bryce's bent knee pressed into the mattress, and his thick cock in my fist as I fucked in and out of his tight ass, I vowed to forever appreciate the twists and turns our lives had taken in order to bring us together.

He was my person.

My soulmate.

My true love.

And facing the unknown of my future would always be a bit scary, but having Bryce by my side made it a little easier.

Burying my face in his neck, I whispered over and over how much I loved him.

And when his release spilled over my fingers, I gently bit his shoulder and shot my load deep into him as his body clenched around me. The heat of our sweat-slick bodies wrapped around us like the warmest, coziest blanket, and we collapsed into a haze of slumber.

Later, after sleeping off our amazing orgasms, we showered quickly before Bryce tossed something black in my direction.

"Put it on," Bryce demanded. "We'll both be wearing one, and all day long we can think about fuckin' each other's brains out tonight."

I pulled the jockstrap on and had to admit my ass did look good in it. Bryce's looked even better, and I had no idea how he thought I was going to keep my dick under control all day when I knew he was wearing nearly nothing under his sexy-as-hell jeans.

We made our way to Glazed Buns. When Bryce offered to split the egg white and spinach breakfast burrito with me if I wanted to share a cinnamon roll, I knew he was trying to butter me up.

"What the actual fuck have you done?" I asked around an ooey, gooey bite of sweet, yeasty goodness. "It has to be bad if you're plying me with sugar and carbs."

Bryce just eyed me over his coffee.

"Let's take a walk," he said as he ushered me out the door into the crisp, late morning sunshine.

Haven Grove was a gorgeous little town. I was biased —and didn't have much to go on—but I knew cozy and quaint when I saw it. The last of the leaves were barely hanging on, and winter was threatening with each passing day.

We needed to enjoy our chances to walk around town without freezing our asses off while we could. As much as I hated to admit it, I had a feeling I'd be longing for outdoor runs long before spring made her appearance.

When we arrived at the gym, I glanced at Bryce with a *you've got to be kidding me* glare. We were greeted with a huge grand opening banner, a golden ribbon—the kind made for cutting with those stupidly large scissors—and a crowd of people.

My boyfriend blushed and tried a *you love me so you can't possibly be mad at me* shrug. This was his fault, but I knew for sure he hadn't come up with it all on his own.

At least I knew how I would keep my dick under control for the rest of the day.

Being surrounded by my boys, my best friend, and half of the town at the fuckin' grand opening of a gym I was under the impression had already had a fuckin' grand opening was a definite boner killer.

Did I love being surrounded by people? Not really, but I'd always been decent at shootin' the shit.

And seeing how many people were already enjoying their memberships to a gym I helped to build wasn't exactly a hardship.

Didn't fuckin' love that the guys let me think they'd already done the whole grand opening thing, but I also didn't hate getting to be involved.

In fact, the logo on the window and all the merch gave me a little thrill to know I'd had a part in all of it.

The stupid staff t-shirt and name tag should *not* have made me feel so much shit, but I guess that was just who I was now. A guy who loved his boyfriend, loved his family, loved his life, and got stupid feelings over shit like name tags and staff shirts.

I did actually try to be pissed and shit, but I don't think I pulled it off very well. Hell, who could really be mad that their friends wanted to include them in something that was a pretty big deal?

In the grand scheme of things, as long as I was going

home with Bryce and had my boys, I didn't really care how many social gatherings and surprises they wanted to put me through.

I was damn lucky to be alive and loved by these people, the least I could do was endure a grand opening celebration.

Plus, later that night, Bryce made it up to me by teaching me exactly what he meant when he'd said jockstraps provided easy access.

Chapter 26
Bryce

CASEY JOE HAD BEEN HOME A COUPLE WEEKS, and I really didn't think my life could be more perfect. We'd made loose plans to meet up with my parents every other week—switching between Haven Grove and their place—and I kinda loved that my mom adored Casey, and my dad spent the better part of dinner the week before talking Casey's ear off about engine parts and vintage trucks.

And Dizzy had been a Casey Joe fan almost as long as I had.

We saw her more often since she came to town to see Barb and attend Jack's Lemon Drop Social Club meetings. I'd loved my aunt when I was a kid, but having her around in my adult life was proving to be something I hadn't known I needed.

Looking back on that kid who wanted nothing more than to escape small-town USA, I sure as shit had to smile at how comfy cozy I'd gone and let myself get right smack-dab back in a small town.

But it was all different these days.

Of course, I had my family—and I never wanted to take for granted that not everyone was in the same position. I knew how lucky I was that my family had always loved me exactly for who I was.

But I had true friends this time around. Yeah, I was part of an inner circle, but it wasn't just about being friends with the Riggs family or knowing the right people. Haven Grove was a place where a name or money only meant something if those behind it had the respect of folks in town in the first place.

The Riggs family had that in spades, and I'd be damned, but the Armstrong name was quickly coming to mean something around town too. The fact citizens in town knew I could be trusted, was well-educated and experienced in my line of work, and I'd give them a fair deal meant the world to me.

I no longer needed the ritzy, fake crowd of people who meant nothing to me and sucked me dry. Didn't need to be associated with certain names just to get business. Didn't need the endless scrolling for tiny hits of dopamine each time I got another like, another follow, or another comment.

I had a healthier relationship with social media now —partly because CJ took care of a lot of it for me, and partly because my business counted a lot more on word of mouth and me being present in town to drum up more memberships. Ever since our soft-launch opening— and even before that—folks in town had proven again and again they appreciated and valued a business owner who was out and about, working with them, catching lunch with them, willing to walk them through a workout, or asking about their latest doctor appointment.

That was exactly what I'd been missing all those years out in California, and I absolutely loved being a part of the Haven Grove community. Plus, I had a whole crew out there recruiting members for me.

Hudson had proven to be a damn good advertiser for Armstrong Health & Fitness. The guy saw so many people throughout the day at the Juicy Peach and through his odd jobs, and he sent folks our way all the time.

Henry was quieter with drumming up business, but he had a soft-sell way of suggesting the gym to people that had them committed to trying out a membership before they'd even finished their last bite of steak at dinner.

Lance and Jack were both enthusiastic in their word-of-mouth recommendation of Armstrong Health & Fitness. And honestly, all four of the guys used the gym so they were excellent ambassadors of what healthy exercise could do for a person.

Casey was a machine when it came to getting potential clients through the doors. No one would ever mistake Casey Joe Riggs for being anything but bluntly honest, but his experiences with health scares, addiction, mental health, and working his way back into exercise were ways he could easily connect with people. I think people saw CJ as a regular guy just like them, and if he could improve his health, they knew they could too.

"Come on," I said with a tap on the counter where

Casey was working. "We need to head out if we want to get there on time."

Casey tapped a few more things on the keyboard and then clicked the mouse. "Done. Just wanted to get that membership activated so she could start tomorrow. Told her I'd walk her through all the machines."

I smiled and took his hand as he walked out from behind the counter. I already had my coat on, but I handed Casey his. With a wave to the few clients still working out, we headed toward the door. Bon Jovi streamed through the speakers as we left the gym, and an icy cold blast of air hit us smack in the face.

"Fuckin' hell," Casey muttered, pulling his coat on quickly. "Is it fuckin' spring yet?"

My laugh hung in an icy puff in the air as we made our way to the Roadhouse. "You and I both know we've got several long months of this and worse before we get back to spring."

"Gonna put on five layers, start a fire, and not leave the house until at least April," Casey groused.

As I pulled open the door to the Roadhouse, warmth washed over us along with the scents of amazing food and laughter of friends and family. "Nah," I said with a hand on his lower back, "we'd miss this too much."

Casey just shrugged, but his eyes sparkled as he headed toward Jack and Hudson who ushered us toward the small area Jack used for his cakes where folks had gathered at any empty seat available.

Soon, Henry joined us.

"Sam's got it all under control," Henry said, gathering

Jack to his side and pressing a kiss to the blond's hair. "You ready?"

Jack took his place in the front, surrounded by at least twenty people other than our little crew. "Thank you all for getting out in the cold to come to another Lemon Drop Social Club. We should all be thinking about if we think a pause in gatherings would be for the best given that winter can be brutal."

"You keep serving that dip and cake, I'll be here," someone called from the back of the room, and several people agreed.

Jack's ears pinked, but he continued on. "We had a really nice collection last time, and I want to make a decision tonight on where to donate. We're already making those really nice knotted fleece blankets to give to the hospital, the county family services, and that soup kitchen." He gestured toward the tables. "You can all fill out the little ballots to vote on where we want the donated money to go."

"Sounds good," someone else piped up. "Tell us about the food so we can get started."

I couldn't help the silly grin on my face as I watched Casey Joe beam proudly at Jack. Case loved his boys to the moon and back about five times, but Jack walking into the Riggs family had been just what Casey needed. True, I hadn't known either of them before Jack arrived, but it was easy to see they were good for each other. It was so damn amazing to watch the mutual support and love between them.

Jack ran through the menu of a butternut squash soup, red pepper jelly spread with crackers, pumpkin spice cake, and an apple cinnamon crème brulee drink available warm or cold, with or without alcohol.

Just when I thought Jack would tell people to eat, drink, vote, and donate, Casey stepped close to him, said a few words, and then took the floor as Jack stepped aside.

Casey cleared his throat. "Wanted to say thanks to everyone who helped the boys while I was gone," he started. My heart warmed with the way *the boys* encompassed our entire little family group. "Thought I'd say a few words about why I was gone, not because anyone fuckin' needs to be in my damn business, but because I know I need to take responsibility." He glanced my way, his eyes searching. At my nod, I thought he'd go on, but he took two strides my way and gripped my hand. "The rumor mill in this damn town works better than anything, so I doubt any of what I'm gonna say is news to anyone."

Dizzy, front and center next to Barb, nearly wiggled out of her seat.

"Y'all know I had a heart attack," Casey went on. "If you've been in Haven Grove for any time at all, you probably know all the shit with my former wife, my brother, and my drinkin'—I'll be honest and say those three things are listed in no particular order when it came to all my shit. Suffice it to say, havin' a fuckin' heart attack sucks donkey dick and really opens your eyes to what's important in your life."

Surprised chuckles peppered the room, and I caught fond smiles on Hudson and Henry's faces. Those two were almost as big of fans of Casey Joe as Jack was.

"Thanks to my family and friends, I've been workin'

my ass off to get myself healthy again. If you've known me for any length of time, you know I had a long-ass way to go." He gave my hand a squeeze. "This guy has been a huge help on that journey. I guess I just wanted to say sorry to anyone I may have hurt with my drinkin' over the years and ask that you help me stay accountable." Casey leaned over and kissed me on the cheek. "And if any of you fuckers have an issue with me bein' in love with a man, you can see yourself out and fuck right off on your way."

The crowd laughed and applauded, but they were a lot more interested in getting their hands on Jack and Henry's food than worrying about who Casey wanted to kiss. Honestly, most were so accustomed to his grumpy persona, they likely didn't even think a thing about his grumbly little speech.

Casey steered me toward the counter where Jack had already placed a tray with our food and drinks—okay, being part of the inner circle *did* come with some perks. Just as we smeared some of the red pepper jelly spread onto crackers, a couple joined us.

"Well, I'll be damned," Casey said after a pause. He finished chewing his cracker and shook hands with both people. "I haven't seen the two of you for a damn few years. How are things? How's the campground? Guess it shows how long it's been since I went fishin' since I ain't been out there in so long." He turned to me. "Bryce, this is Pete and Wendy. They've been in Haven Grove forever. The campground and bait and tackle shop are theirs." I reached out to shake hands as Casey went on. "This is my boyfriend, Bryce. He owns Armstrong Health & Fitness."

"Nice to meet you," I said.

Pete and Wendy returned to the greeting.

Casey gestured toward a table off in the corner. "Sit on down, tell us what's been going on." He slapped Pete on the back. "Damn, man. It's been too long. You been hidin' out there?"

Pete and Wendy filled us in on the campground and bait and tackle shop. I also learned that Pete and Wendy had both been married to other people many years ago. The four of them had been friends. Between the four of them, they'd owned the campground and the bait and tackle shop. When Pete's wife died, and a couple years later, Wendy's husband died, Pete and Wendy had turned to each other for support.

"At first, we were just grieving friends," Wendy said. "But we figured out we had a thing for each other and hopefully a lot more years together, so we decided to give it a go."

"She's my Wendy," Pete said, taking her hand.

"He's my Peter Pan, he keeps me young," Wendy said.

"She takes me to Never Never Land." Pete gave a little wink-wink and we all laughed.

"Well, it's damn good to see you both. You need to make it a habit to come around more often. We'll get you set up with gym memberships," Casey said over his mug of hot apple cinnamon crème brulee cider.

"Well, we actually just came tonight to say our good byes," Pete said.

"The fuck you say. You're leavin'?" Casey asked.

"We are. We're getting too old for these cold Midwest winters. The Sunshine state is calling our names." Wendy rested her head on Pete's shoulder. "Shuffleboard, early buffets, and never having to deal with snow again. Sounds like a dream."

"We've got a place lined up," Pete said. "We're driving the RV down and setting up in a campground lot. We'll stay there for a few years until it's time to move into something with a bit more support." He patted Wendy's hand. "We're ready to be done with owning a business here, but we're not ready for assisted living just yet."

"That sounds like a damn good plan," Casey said around a bite of cake. I knew by the way he chewed it was absolutely delicious. He put his fork down, probably so he could savor each remaining bite a little later. "We're just hitting our strides with the businesses, but I can see getting to a point where you're ready to let it go."

"Are you selling or closing down?" I asked. I'd seen the campgrounds and the bait and tackle shop on the east side of Haven Grove. Both were close to each other on the other side of a large lake. I knew very little about either business, but the few bits I heard led me to believe they were lucrative set ups.

"Well," Pete started. "We've asked our grandsons to take over. God-willin', they'll be interested, and the family businesses will continue on."

Wendy shrugged. "We know we can't force them to do it, but they grew up here, so we're hoping they'll want to come home and keep things going."

Casey cocked his head. "Those boys of yours were a few years younger than Hudson if I'm remembering right. Fuckin' hell if I can remember their names."

Pete chuckled. "Travis Dean and JC."

Casey slapped the table. "That's right. Travis Dean because his dad was Travis too. JC...feels like I maybe didn't hear him called that much."

Wendy smiled. "I call him JC, he went by Joey a lot."

Casey nodded. "Damn, it's all comin' back. They were best friends, right? Feel like I used to hear stories about them plannin' to take over the businesses. I bet they'll love comin' home to do that."

A look of something, maybe guilt, passed between Pete and Wendy.

"Well, the boys didn't leave Haven Grove on the best of terms. We aren't even sure they've kept in touch. We each talk to our grandsons often, but they haven't kept us in the loop on whatever misunderstanding sent them off on their separate ways never looking back," Pete said.

"So, we're letting them know the businesses are theirs if they want them. If not, we'll sell them and live our life." Wendy took her final bite of cake. "We really need to visit with some of the others before we head home." She dabbed a napkin to her lips. "It was so good to see you both."

We said our goodbyes to Pete and Wendy, wishing them all the best on their new adventure down in Florida, and they went off to chat with others just as Jack had intended with his social club.

"This is the best cake that boy has ever made," Casey said, his eyes closed as he savored the last bite.

I elbowed him. "You say that about every cake Jack makes."

"Fuck off. I mean it this time."

"I'm going to the restroom, be right back," I said, pressing a kiss to Casey's cheek. "Give you some alone time with your cake."

Casey snorted. "Shut up. It's damn good cake."

When I returned from the restroom, Dizzy was talking to Casey. Her eyes lit up when she saw me, and she patted Casey's leg. "Barb and I are heading out. You boys will be over for dinner this week, right?"

We agreed, and I gave my aunt a hug. "Be careful driving home."

"Oh, I'm just going to sleep at Barb's. It's a lot easier to drive home in the daylight. And we're going to take some of the blankets to the hospital tomorrow anyway."

"Tell Cassie I said hi." I needed to take Casey out to meet my sister and her family soon.

By the time we'd done what Casey referred to as *shootin' the shit* with everyone else, helped Jack by gathering trash and dirty dishes—which he swore we didn't need to do—and given hugs to the guys, Casey was a bit twitchy.

"You good?" I asked as we headed toward the hill.

He jerked his gaze toward me. "Yeah, why?"

I raised a brow. "I don't know, you just seem jumpy or something."

"Yeah, I'm good. Just wanna get the fuck home. It's too damn cold and not even really winter yet."

Casey nearly ran up the hill.

It was cold and windy, sure. But he was acting weird all the same.

"Grab the mail," Casey said as we reached the house. "I gotta piss."

I carried the one piece of mail inside and tossed it on the counter before noticing Casey was lighting candles. "Whatcha do? Stink up the bathroom?" I teased.

Casey ignored me. "Anything in the mail?" he asked, his back turned to me as he took off his coat and hung it on the back of a chair.

"Just one thing. Probably a get well card for you." I placed my coat next to Casey's and stretched.

"Can you get it?" Casey asked as he rushed to the living room.

"What? Why?" Casey had never been one to be too concerned about the mail. *Always just some damn fuckin' bills or junk* he usually said.

"Just wanna read it," he said.

He was already in the living room, so I grabbed the card and followed him.

Holding it out to him, I studied his face. "Babe, I'm not tryin' to pry, but did you accidentally get the spiked drink tonight? You're all twitchy and weird."

He pushed the card back at me. "Open it, looks like it's for you."

I scowled and studied the name on the front. "How? Who even knows I'm living here? And who would send me a card?" I turned it over and then back again. "There's not even a stamp on it."

Casey shrugged.

When I opened the envelope and removed the card, I saw a gorgeous watercolor painting on the front. Inside, I found a folded-up piece of paper.

Glancing at Casey, I saw his eyes on me, watching intently.

"What is this?" I asked.

He nodded toward the paper. "Just read it."

Dear Bryce,

I needed to write one more letter, but this one isn't to help pass the time as we await homecoming from the retreat.

This letter is maybe the most important I'll ever write.

The days my boys were born were the two most important days of my life. They made me a father, and for that, I will forever be grateful. My life would be nothing without them. I plan to spend the rest of my life making sure they know they are loved and supported by their dad.

The day my wife left was one of the most instrumental in changing me into who I am today. When Billy died, it all felt like too much. From that moment on, all my life experiences up to that point worked together to shape me. Sometimes, it felt like they were trying to break me, like I couldn't keep on, but I came out stronger on the other side.

And then there's you.

So many points in my life seem like they can be broken down into before and after. Before Missy, after Missy. Before Billy died, after Billy died. Before my boys were born, after my boys were born.

Something wonderful and new and damn fucking important started the day you showed up here. Before Bryce and after Bryce, and nothing will ever be the same.

From the first time I saw you at the Roadhouse, I was drawn in. When Lance was talking to you, I wanted to be right there hearing your voice, just soaking you up. When Hudson called you a snack, I wanted to know more about you, even wanted to ask damn questions just to learn about who you were.

And then you ran your damn ass across my property, caught me at one of my lowest moments, and sat with me. That was the first time in a long time, maybe in my whole life, I felt comfortable and safe to just be me with someone. Probably one of the only times trespass turned out positive around these parts.

I didn't go to the retreat for the boys or Lance or you.

I went to the retreat for me.

But also for the boys and Lance.

And for you.

For us.

You are the only person on this planet who cheerfully and patiently puts up with my shit, and you have since day one.

You're the only person who calls me on my shit without hesitation.

No one else I'd rather live with, work with, or spend my time with.

I hope like fuckin' shit I'm not messing this up, if it's too much too soon, just tell me to fuck right off.

The letter ended.

No closing.

No *Love, Casey*.

Just cut right off.

I turned the paper over.

Nothing.

Then I looked at Casey.

In front of me.

On one knee.

With a matte-black ring held between his finger and thumb.

He took my hand and cleared his throat.

"You weren't the *only* reason I survived, but you're one of the reasons that made all that work worthwhile," he said. "I'm grateful to have a future to look forward to, and I want that future to be with you. If you'll have me." When Casey looked up at me, tears glinted in his eyes. "Bryce, will you marry me?"

The lump of emotion in my throat was too much to swallow down, so I nodded and pulled Casey to his feet. I was still nodding when our mouths met in a way too toothy kiss, and we both laughed.

"Is that a yes?" Casey asked.

"Yes," I finally managed as he slipped the ring onto my finger.

"This might be dumb, but..." He paused and reached into his pocket to reveal a second ring. "I thought—"

I snatched the ring away from him so fast and reached for his hand. "I love you, and I'd be honored to spend the rest of our years together." Slipping the matching wedding band onto his finger, I lifted his hand to my lips and kissed his knuckles. "Where'd you get the rings?" I asked as I studied our ring-adorned fingers in the dim light of the living room.

Casey smirked. "Dizzy was a dog with a bone the moment I mentioned it. She took care of everything. Just had to wait for you to go piss so she could make the drop. Honestly, thought she was goin' to explode from excitement." He glanced toward the dark window.

"Wouldn't shock me at all if she's out there right now."

I laughed and let Casey hug me close. "She'll tell folks for the rest of her life she got us together."

Casey shrugged. "Figure it don't hurt. That little fib I told maybe got us together a bit faster than my dumb ass would have figured shit out. But if it makes her happy to claim matchmaker, I don't mind." He touched the ring on my finger. "If you don't like—"

"Shut up," I blurted. "I love it. It's perfect." I savored the new weight, the warmth of the metal against my skin, the way the black band interrupted the usually bare skin of my finger. "I don't care if we go to the courthouse tomorrow, see Brother Larry on Sunday, or just exchange our own private vows together, this is all I'll ever need."

"Fuckin' hell," Casey groused. "We are *not* asking Brother Larry to marry us. He'd probably have a fuckin' stroke." He hugged me close. "I think a backyard wedding right here. Small, just us, the guys, and your family." Casey rocked me back and forth. "And maybe a cruise for our honeymoon? I've never been on a big ship. Maybe we make it a whole group thing?"

"I've never loved the sound of anything more," I murmured into his chest.

"You sure you want to be stuck here in Haven Grove with me for the rest of your life?" Casey asked.

"Do I want to run my business with the man I love, spend every day with friends who have become family, be close to my parents, sister, and her kids, and get to be part of whatever shenanigans the Riggs family gets up to in the years to come?" I asked with a cocked brow.

"When you put it like that, it does sound pretty fuckin' amazin'," Casey said. "Hell, sign me up."

"Sign me up too," I murmured against his lips. "I'm here to stay."

Casey sighed into the kiss. "Fuckin' hell. Best damn words I've ever heard."

Epilogue
Casey Joe

The Following Fall

"Keep your hands on the bar," I ordered. Looking over Bryce's shoulder, I watched in the mirror as his cock bobbed in front of him and dripped pre-cum on the towel we'd placed on the floor.

We enjoyed sex in the gym as often as possible. There was something about fucking in front of the mirrors, knowing anyone who thought to look through the window could *maybe* see us, and walking by the same machines later in the day just to catch each other's eyes and recall what we'd been up to that morning.

The weight benches and any equipment with an overhead bar had quickly become our favorites. And before you start in with your lectures on hygiene, fuckin' all over the gym meant we kept things spic and span, both for ourselves and our members.

"Fuck, Case, please," Bryce begged, his eyes meeting mine in the mirror. "Touch me, please."

I absolutely loved ordering Bryce to keep his hands up on the bar and fucking him from behind. Eating his ass as he straddled and sucked me on the weight bench was also in the running for best use of gym equipment. Riding him on the weight bench as a close third place.

"Only because we have a weddin' to get to," I whispered gruffly at his ear. "If we didn't, I'd let you beg a little more."

"Fuckin' hell," Bryce panted. "What did I ever do to you?"

I chuckled, letting my hot breath tickle over his soft earlobe. "How about last week when you edged me to within an inch of my life?"

It was Bryce's turn to chuckle. "Oh, right." He sighed and dropped his head back on my shoulder when I finally took his leaking cock in hand and stroked him firmly. "Fuck," he whimpered. "Please, Case. Fuck. Please let me come."

Honestly, I kinda wished we had a little more time before the wedding preparations because I would have loved to draw out his orgasm for a bit longer.

"Next time, I'm gonna make you beg for hours," I growled.

With one hand on Bryce's hip and one hand stroking his shaft, I pumped in and out of his tight heat, my eyes never leaving his in the mirror.

"Shit, Case, I'm close," Bryce said, heat and pleasure lighting up those gorgeous eyes while he watched me.

"Almost," I bit out. "Fuck." With a final slam into him,

I held an arm across his waist as my orgasm ripped through me, and I filled him with my hot release.

Bryce tensed in my arms and groaned, spilling over my fist in hard, fast pulses.

And then he turned, and his arms came around my neck, our mouths meeting in a slow, dirty kiss as our orgasms sent liquid pleasure oozing through every inch of our bodies.

"Fuck," I whispered into his mouth. "Do you know how damn much I love you?"

"Probably enough to fuck me in our gym and marry me on our hilltop."

"Yeah, definitely that much."

Bryce slapped my ass. "We need to clean up the mess and get ready. Jack will have a conniption if we're late to our own wedding."

Twenty minutes later, we'd started the laundry, sanitized the equipment, mopped the floor just in case the towel missed anything, and wiped down the mirror. It wasn't often we hit the mirror, but that one time was enough to make cleaning it a habit after we'd made use of the equipment for exercises that were much more for pleasure than physical training.

We made our way to the truck. Could we have walked? Sure. Did I want to do the walk of shame after fucking my fiancé in front of the gym mirror? No, I did not.

So, we'd brought the truck.

"Gonna be a nice day," Bryce said, taking my hand.

The weather looked to be a quintessentially fall day in the Midwest.

The leaves were absolutely perfect.

The air had a nip to it as we drove, but by the time we were all gathered in the backyard, it would be the exact right mix of warm sun and cool breeze.

"Just enough time to shower before they get here," I said when I parked the truck.

And I was right.

Bryce and I had showered and dressed in old jeans, flannels, and work boots when Hudson and Lance's heads appeared coming up from their place. Henry and Jack pulled in only a few moments later.

The whole crew spent the rest of the morning and into the afternoon cleaning up the yard, placing huge, gorgeous mums, setting up a wooden archway with autumn leaves and twinkle lights, and putting wooden benches out for the handful of guests who would arrive soon.

We laughed, we wrestled, we ate lunch, and we enjoyed every minute together.

And then it was late afternoon.

Bryce and I showered again while the guys went off to get themselves ready.

"Are we seriously wearing these?" I asked as I stared at the black and white jock strap made to look like a tuxedo.

Bryce snorted. "I guess she wouldn't know if we didn't, but they're kinda cute." He held up his jock and wiggled it around. The words *Casey's Husband* shimmered in gold font. He tipped his chin. "Come on, let's see."

With a long-suffering groan, I pulled on the custom jock Dizzy had purchased for us. *Bryce's Husband* was front and center on the waistband, and the pouch was adorned with a black bow tie. "At least it's not in 3D, I'd say fuck no to that."

"Eh, since we aren't doing the whole tux thing, I think it's nice if we wear them so we can say at least our underwear was dressy."

"Fine, but if she fuckin' asks to see them…"

Bryce cracked up. "No, we'll draw the line there."

"Alright, get your ass out of here," I said, slapping a hand against Bryce's perfect butt cheek.

He yelped and turned into my arms. "I'll see you out there." A kiss. "Love you." Another kiss.

"Love you," I whispered, nuzzling my nose against his. "Let's go get married."

Casey loves Bryce

"You ready?" Henry asked as he straightened the collar of my plaid flannel jacket.

I glanced down at my dark wash jeans and new work boots. "Ready to get out of these damn clothes," I grumbled.

Bryce and I had similar wedding attire. My flannel jacket was a brown and burgundy plaid, while his was mostly burgundy. Our jeans were a different fit—mostly because his ass was too perfect and hiding it in the jeans my flat ass needed was a sin—but both in the same dark wash. My boots leaned a bit more toward the *work* boots side while his were a slight bit more on the casual side of dressy casual.

"You look great," Hudson said. He patted my pocket. "Got the ring?"

I batted at his hand. "Got it. I seriously can't believe I let you talk me into this."

My youngest beamed. "What? I'm a jack of all trades, why not get ordained so I can officiate my dad's wedding?"

"Just make sure we end up married for real. I'll take you runnin' the show a thousand times over Brother fuckin' Larry, but I don't want to find out ten years down the road you forgot a part."

Hudson hugged me close. "I'm really proud of you," he whispered. "Bryce is amazing, and I can't wait to watch the two of you enter your geriatric years listening to your old people music."

"Hey," Lance said with a chuckle as he entered the room. "Be careful who you're calling geriatric."

Hudson popped a kiss to my cheek and turned to Lance grinning ear-to-ear. "Sorry, babe. You know I don't consider you old." He winked. "Our bedroom is like the fountain of youth."

Lance kissed Hudson, whispered something that made my son laugh, and they walked toward the backyard.

"He better hope his lube and arthritis cream never get mixed up," I muttered.

Henry snorted. "You got this," he said, pulling me into a back slapping hug. "We really are proud of you. All we've ever wanted was for you to be healthy and happy. Bonus points that we get to be here for it."

Jack showed up at the door. "It's about time."

Henry gave my back one last slap, kissed Jack and told him he'd save his seat, and then my oldest was gone.

Jack clasped his hands in front of him. He, of course, was dressed up a bit more than Hudson, Lance, and Henry in their nicer jeans and fitted sweaters. Jack's outfit was some sort of purplish gray with a large checker print in a very subtle, thin purple line. The pants were what I'd call too tight, but they fit him well. The jacket was fitted, and the plain black t-shirt underneath pulled it all together. The best part, according to Jack, were his boots. I had to admit, I probably wouldn't ever *wear* boots like that, but they did look good with his outfit.

"Ready?" he all but squealed.

"Damn, boy, tone it down." I rubbed at my ear.

"Sorry," he said, not looking the least bit sorry. "I'm just excited."

I took pity on the kid and put my arm around him. "Well, I guess we need to get me fuckin' married."

Right then, "With You Til the End" started playing through the speakers set up around the yard. Jack's eyes lit up and my heart nearly beat out of my chest. I took Jack's arm, and he led me to the side of the yard.

The kid nearly wiggled himself out of his boots as we waited for Bryce and Dizzy to take their place on the other side.

And then he was there.

The love of my life.

Smiling at me from across our backyard.

Dizzy beamed at *her Brycey* as they walked toward where Hudson stood.

I watched as Bryce hugged Dizzy and moved to hug his mom, dad, sister, brother-in-law, and their kids.

Then Jack tugged on my arm.

It was all a blur, but we ended up in front of Hudson, and Jack hugged me. "Thank you for being the dad I never had. Henry might be my true love, but I think I needed you just as much as I needed him. Love you."

I held onto the kid a few extra beats trying to gather myself.

Fuckin' hell.

"Love you too, kid."

And then I was facing Bryce, our hands joined between us, and Hudson going on about a love of a lifetime and soulmates. Luckily, someone was recording so I could watch it because my brain and heart were both crashin' the fuck out.

"I think Bryce was going to start with his vows," Hudson said with a smile and a wink. The little shit knew I was short-circuiting.

Bryce squeezed my hands and took a deep breath. "From the moment our eyes met across the room, I knew there was something different about you, and it wasn't just your cranky ass and foul mouth." He winked and everyone chuckled. My heart slowed to only a million beats per minute. "Everything about you breathed new life into me. You challenged every fiber of my being. Parts of my soul that had never been on fire were all of a sudden firing on all cylinders because of you. Then you gave me the greatest gift of all by feeling the same. I never really thought I had a chance, but the universe had different plans." He shuffled and laced our fingers. "When I decided I needed to leave everything behind and return to my roots, I never knew doing so would bring me home in more ways than one. Yes, I returned for myself—I needed my family, I needed the slower pace, and I needed a reset. But I know now I also returned because my heart knew where I needed to be so I could meet the most wonderful, crabby, genuine man I've ever known.

"I'm so damn proud of you for tackling your healing. I know you had to do that on your own, but don't ever forget I'm here. Forever. Even though I didn't come here looking for it, I know in the depths of my soul I've finally found the love of a lifetime."

"Niiice," Hudson whispered. Into his mic so everyone had a good laugh.

Luckily, they were laughing so they hopefully didn't see me about to lose my fuckin' shit. "Fuckin' hell, man." The sniffle was definitely heard on the mic, and there was no way I could go on without wiping my damn eyes. "Who the fuck decided to have a weddin' above a peach orchard? Damn allergies."

Henry, quiet and unassuming as always, stepped up next to me and handed me a white handkerchief. With a few quick swipes over my eyes and my nose, I figured I was as good as I was gonna get.

Fuck.

Really should have made notes.

"Had you told me when I was sixteen I'd one day fall in love with a man and marry him right here on Riggs family land, I would have flipped you off and cussed you out, but deep down I would have been scared to fuckin' death someone had figured out my secret.

"For the longest time, I punished myself—some for things I couldn't control and some for things I could—but it didn't help. Punishin' myself didn't ease the pain. Didn't heal the parts deep inside that needed healed. One thing I've learned over the years is that the sayin', *time heals all wounds* is a bunch of bullshit. I should know. I wasted a bunch of years wallowin' in self-pity hopin' to heal the broken pieces of me. In reality, it's what you *do* with your time that truly heals those wounds. And you sometimes have to fuckin' admit that even when you're feelin' healed, those old wounds might still hurt.

"There I was just learnin' I had to be the love of my own damn life when you waltzed into town and threw me for a loop. You brought somethin' to the surface I'd been hidin' from. It would have been easy to push it back down, keep wallowin' in the pit I'd let my life become, but bein' with you lit a flame deep inside me, and I didn't want to put it out. Don't know if I could've ignored it this time around."

I took a cleansing breath and closed my eyes, savoring the way Bryce's hands gripped mine.

"Thank you for standin' beside me as I worked through all my shit." Turning first to Hudson and then to Lance, Henry, and Jack, I said, "Thank you all for puttin' up with me while I took my damn sweet time fixin' my shit." Looking back at Bryce, I let myself get lost in his eyes. "You were there for me, and it would have been so easy to let *you* be the reason I was happy—and you are, don't misunderstand that —but I knew I had to be happy for myself. I couldn't rely on you or anyone else for my happiness, and it means the whole damn fuckin' world to me that you understood that.

"I'd written off ever being happy, let alone findin' my forever love. Then you fuckin' turned my world upside down. I used to feel like I wasted the first half of my life, but I know now I was just gearin' up to spend the rest of my life lovin' you. Good shit, bad shit, all the shit—as long as we're facin' it together, I have no doubt we'll be kickin' ass."

I started to pull Bryce in for a kiss, but my damn smartass son put out his hand. "Uh-uh, not just yet." He cleared his throat. "Well, now. I'm pretty sure we just set the record for the most cuss words in wedding vows *ever*. Good job, Dad. Proud of you."

I flipped him the bird.

Hudson just beamed. "If you two would like to put your rings back on, I'll finish things up all neat and tidy here."

Bryce pulled my ring from his pocket, and I pulled his from mine.

We slipped them back onto each other's fingers.

"Well, with the power vested in me from a very reputable and not at all questionable internet site—"

"Hudson," I growled.

"I'm joking," Hudson said with a chuckle. "Mostly. *Anyway*, Dad you can now kiss my new daddy."

"Fuckin' hell," I muttered, but that was all I had time for before Bryce had me in his arms kissing the ever-lovin' hell out of me.

"Friends, family, and folks," Hudson said, "may I present to you, Mr. and Mr."

Everyone clapped and whooped and hollered as we made our way down the tiny aisle. While Bryce and I took pictures with Cassie, Jack and Henry set up the cake and finger foods.

Cassie took one last picture with the sunset behind us.

"That's going to be my favorite one, I can tell." She checked her phone. "Okay, it's time for your dance."

"Love of a Lifetime" started floating across the yard on the cool, crisp breeze. Taking Bryce's hand, I led him to the middle of what we were calling the dance floor under the twinkly fairy lights.

It was an old song—fuck, an *older* song...couldn't call it *old* because it wasn't anywhere as close to as old as Bryce and me—but I sure as shit had never heard a song that fit like it did.

"Your vows were great," Bryce said.

"Thanks, figure I didn't fuck 'em up too bad." His lips were soft under mine. "Yours were beautiful." We swayed slowly to the music. "Dizzy's watchin' us."

Bryce snorted. "She asked if we were wearing our underwear."

"Fuckin' hell." Our lips melted into the warm kiss. "What did you tell her?"

"That we wouldn't be later."

My laughter had the guests casting glances our way, but I didn't give a flyin' fuck. I'd spend the rest of my damn life laughin' and lovin' with Bryce by my side.

~The End~

Also by A.D. Ellis

On Cravenwood Block- the complete four-book series in a box set. Or start with Jett & Leighton in book 1 HERE.

Adore (Remington Place 1) is a steamy, age-gap, bi-awakening, dad's best friend M/M romance with a sassy smartass and a sexy silver fox. It's the first book in the Remington Place series and can be read as a stand-alone.

Crave (Remington Place 2) is a steamy, friends-to-lovers, fake relationship M/M romance with a virgin nursing student and a gruff, grumbly construction worker.

Desire (Remington Place 3) is a steamy, age-gap, hurt/comfort M/M romance featuring a heart-of-gold mechanic and a twink who's a lot stronger than he realizes. *Please note: This story has mention of sex trafficking and sexual abuse.*

Yearn (Remington Place 4)- a steamy, enemies-to-lovers, forced proximity M/M romance between two EMS workers who have hated each other for a decade.

Silver in the City (3 books- meet the Silver crew you read about in Forged in the City) Available on AUDIO!

Forged in the City (3 books- a spin-off series from Silver in the City) Available on AUDIO

Find other books here - https://books2read.com/ap/RWrrNx/AD-Ellis

About the Author

A.D. Ellis is an Indiana girl, born and raised. She spends much of her time in central Indiana as an instructional coach/teacher in the inner city of Indianapolis, being a mom to two amazing older teenagers, and wondering how she and her husband of over two decades haven't driven each other insane yet. A lot of her time is also devoted to phone call avoidance and her hatred of cooking.

She loves chocolate, wine, pizza, and naps along with reading and writing romance. These loves don't leave much time for housework. Who would pick cleaning the house over a nap or a good book? She uses any extra time to increase her fluency in sarcasm.

A.D. uses she/they pronouns.

Sign up at http://www.subscribepage.com/ADEllisNewsMMRomance for a FREE book!

Website http://adellisauthor.com/

My direct buy site https://payhip.com/ADEllisAuthor

My merchandise site https://a-d-ellis-shop.fourthwall.com/

Find me EVERYWHERE at https://www.adellisauthor.com/mylinks/

Connect with A.D. Ellis

Follow my website http://www.adellisauthor.com or find me on Facebook

http://www.facebook.com/adellisauthor

If you want to get updates about releases, interviews, sales, giveaways, and more please sign up for my newsletter http://www.subscribepage.com/ADEllisNewsMMRomance

Find me on Spotify if you'd like to listen to the playlist for this book (mainly just the songs I listened to while writing). Just search for A.D. Ellis.

To make it easy, find me EVERYWHERE here- https://www.adellisauthor.com/mylinks/

Acknowledgments

It's always so hard to write this part because I'm worried I'll forget someone without meaning to.

To the readers who helped me pick songs for this story, thank you!

Readers- you are the reason I write. As long as you continue reading my stories, I'll continue writing them. Thank you for your support.

Bloggers & Influencers- your support, reviews, and promotion are very much appreciated. Thank you!

My author buddies- I don't know that I could keep doing this without our brainstorm sessions, Zoom writing, laughter, road trips, meals, wine, and friendship as my support.

Thank you to my alpha readers, betas, editors, proofreaders, and ARC readers! Your eyes and input are beyond important to me.

Brett and Gage- as usual, I doubt you even grasp how much your support, input, and friendship mean to me. This author journey has brought many wonderful things into my life, and you both are two of the BEST! I'm blessed to call you friends.

My family and friends- thank you for your love and support, always.

Cover Photo by Eric McKinney at 6:12 Photography

Cover Model: Bryan B.

Human Authored™, Reg #: 3674579, https://authorsguild.org/human

HUMAN AUTHORED™
AG THE Authors Guild
3674579

www.ingramcontent.com/pod-product-compliance
Lightning Source LLC
Chambersburg PA
CBHW031153050726
47495CB00019B/1684